NEITHER
DEATH
NOR
DISTANCE

Sabra Waldfogel

Neither Death Nor Distance by Sabra Waldfogel

Copyright © 2020 by Sabra Waldfogel. All rights reserved.

Cover Design: EbookLaunch
Author Photograph: Megan Dobratz

ISBN 978-1-953354-00-6—ebook
ISBN 978-1-953354-01-3—print

Sabra Waldfogel, Publisher
www.sabrawaldfogel.com

Published in Minneapolis, Minnesota

Table of Contents

Chapter 1

Dougherty County, Georgia
December 1860

ON HER WEDDING DAY, her stepfather said, "You look mighty pretty, Pen." He handed her the cloudy little mirror.

She tried to see herself in it, searching for special beauty in the coppery skin, the high cheekbones, and the full lips that she had inherited from her mother. Her late mother.

Pen's eyes filled with tears. Blinking them away, she said tartly, "Look like I always do. Just gussied up."

Worried, her younger sister, Cassie, asked, "Don't you like the way I fixed your hair, Pen?"

Pen touched the braids that circled her head like a crown. She squeezed her sister in a hug. "I do, sugar."

Then they were quiet in the cool air of December in Georgia. They remembered the woman who died a year ago of fever, too soon to see her daughter married. Pen thought of the father who had died long ago, when she was too young to know him, and her stepfather, Tobias, was the father she knew. His arm encircled Pen's shoulder. He said, "We best get going. Can't keep Jonas waiting."

She laughed. "He been waiting a long time. He can wait a little longer!"

Jonas had been her sweetheart for as far back as she could remember. They had been barefoot babies together and had started in the cotton fields at the same time. He had shown her how to reach for the bolls, and he had even risked punishment by putting cotton he'd picked into her sack. When they got older, they began to walk out together. They found their way into the woods one Sunday after church, and she slipped her hand into his. She had big hands for a girl, but he could enfold her hand in his own. The touch of that strong, cotton-scarred, calloused hand was the sweetest touch she had ever felt.

They kissed for the first time in the woods, too, and they confessed that they loved each other. He rested his hands on her hips, and she twined her hands behind his head. They looked into each other's eyes. He said, very softly, "Will you marry me, Pen?"

"Yes," she said, and they kissed again, sealing the promise.

Now she nodded at her stepfather, and the three of them left the cabin to take the path through the woods to the church.

When old Marse Thornton was alive, he was glad to see his slaves marry, and he asked the white minister to read the words of the ceremony. Missus gave the bride a dress and offered a frolic to all the people on the place. But his son, young Marse, was different. He held himself apart. He knew the names of the servants in the house, but neither he nor his wife, a girl from a haughty family in Savannah, bothered themselves with the hands who labored in the fields like the bride and groom.

They would be married in the slave church hidden in the woods, and the officiant would be the slave preacher from the neighboring plantation.

The church was full, every pew crowded, all two hundred of the Thornton slaves in attendance. The room smelled of sweat and pomade. At the altar, the preacher waited, as did Jonas, broad-shouldered and dignified in his go-to-meeting coat. As Pen walked down the aisle, her arm in her step-father's, Jonas turned to smile at her, making her heart soar.

They faced the preacher, the crowd hushing behind them. The preacher held the prayer book in his hands, but he looked up and spoke from memory. "All of you, dearly beloved, we come together before God to bless this union between Miss Penelope Smith and Mr. Jonas Mitchell. Husband and wife come together, heart, body, and mind, for their mutual joy and for help and comfort. And for children to raise up in the love of the Lord. Marriage ain't to be entered into lightly but with reverence."

"Amen," murmured the crowd.

The preacher turned to her. "Penelope, will you have this man to be your husband, to live together in the covenant of marriage? Will you love him, comfort him, honor and keep him? Will you forsake all others and be faithful to him as long as you both shall live?"

Penelope met Jonas's eyes and, as always, felt as though she would drown in their dark sweetness. "I will," she said.

The preacher turned to Jonas and repeated the words. "I will," Jonas said, his voice low and tender.

The preacher said, "Love is patient. Love is kind. Set it like a seal in your heart because love is as strong as death. Cleave to each other and become one flesh."

"Yes," the crowd murmured.

"Jonas, you take her hand, and repeat after me: 'In the name of the Lord, I take you to be my wife, to have and to hold from this day forward, for better and for worse, for richer and for poorer, in sickness and in health, to love and to cherish, until death or distance part us.'"

Penelope had been to a slave wedding before. In the midst of her joy, she heard the word *distance* like the sound of faraway thunder on a clear day. She pushed the thought aside, and with her hand in Jonas's, she repeated her vow to him.

The preacher smiled, and his voice rang out. "Now I say it, and all of you witness it, that Jonas and Penelope are husband and wife. God has joined them together. Let no one put them asunder!"

THEY HAD BEEN GIVEN a cabin of their own—the people on the place arranged it themselves, pleased to do it—and that night, after a day of feasting on chicken and roast pig and sweet potato and too many kinds of pie, they closed the door. Penelope felt suddenly shy. They had been sweethearts for years, and they had kissed, with a great deal of passion, when they were courting, but they had waited to come together until they were married.

Jonas caught her hand. "Don't tell me that you afraid."

She smiled. "Of you? Of us? Never."

"What do the women tell you?" He knew they had prepared her.

"Take it slow. It sweeter if you take it slow."

He laughed. "That what the men tell me, too." He

pulled her close and they kissed, even more passionate than ever, his hands tracing the bones of her shoulders. He had told her, "Just where you have wings, if you grow them." Now she laughed because it tickled in the best way. She caressed the back of his head. The nape of his neck. The strong muscles of his back. She let her hands fall lower. He laughed and said, "Why don't we get under that coverlet?"

"Not in our wedding clothes," she said.

"No. Like God made us. But in a hurry! Too cold to linger."

She hadn't expected the bliss of touching him everywhere. Under his shirt, a man's skin was as soft as a woman's. When he touched her, she thought of the words of the wedding, about coming together in joy. She felt him against her, against her belly, nothing between them. "Cleave to me," she whispered into his ear.

"Yes," he whispered back, and kissed her mouth.

A fleeting pain, then a fierce joy that spread through her whole body. To her heart. To her mind. To her soul. They cried out together.

He touched her face. "Hope I didn't hurt you, sugar."

"No. You didn't."

He smiled. "We do that every night, we have a baby soon."

"I like that," she said.

By February, when it was time to plow up the cotton fields to prepare them for planting, Pen was carrying. Jonas was solicitous of her, and her stepfather, who had been the driver on the place for years, was also careful with her. "You don't push a woman who carrying," he said.

The overseer didn't agree. Mr. Whitmore was a new arrival since young Marse Thornton had taken the reins of the place, and her stepfather had shaken his head after the first time Whitmore appeared in the field. The overseer's character and history were soon common knowledge. Her stepfather told Pen, "I see it before. A new massa tell the overseer to act harsh. And Mr. Whitmore the worst kind of overseer. He a planter who lose everything, and now he bitter and mean. He like to punish."

Today Mr. Whitmore watched Jonas tell Pen, "You take it slow, sugar."

Whitmore dismounted from his horse. He said to Jonas, "It ain't your business to tell her how slow to work."

Her stepfather stepped forward. "Mr. Whitmore, she expecting a baby, and it go better if she pace herself."

Whitmore snapped, "And it ain't your business, either, nigger!"

Her stepfather bowed his head, waiting for the storm to pass.

Whitmore raised the whip that he always carried. He used it on his horse, too. "All of you, get back to work. No loitering! No dawdling!"

"Yes, suh," her stepfather said.

When the day's work was done, Pen said, "Daddy, you be careful." She saw how weary he looked. Her mother's death had stricken him, and trying to keep Mr. Whitmore from hurting himself and the place was a bigger burden than usual.

He said, "Ain't just about careful."

"What do you mean?"

"He push us because young Marse push him. Young Marse in debt."

"Against the crop?"

"Oh, that, too. But young Marse marry that gal from Savannah. She extravagant. Spendthrift. July tell me all about the furniture she buy." July was the butler, and he was in a catbird seat to see how young Marse and Missus spent their money. Her stepfather went on. "The silver. The dresses. And he buy horses and two new carriages. That on top of the rest of the debt. July don't like it. It trouble him."

"Why?"

"If he get too deep into debt, he need to sell something," her stepfather said.

"What do he sell?" she asked, not wanting to hear the answer.

"Us," her stepfather said.

Pen didn't want to believe it. Old Marse Thornton, who knew the names of all his slaves, who knew their families, who had been as prudent as his son was profligate, had not been in the habit of selling his slaves. She knew how lucky she had been. All around Dougherty County, other planters felt differently. They sold slaves to buy their daughters' wedding dresses. They sold slaves to pay a gambling debt. They sold slaves because they didn't like their looks or their sass.

Death or distance. She put her hand on her rounding belly and shivered to think of it.

At the height of midsummer chopping season, when every field hand bent to the hoe, Mr. Whitmore came to the field with a stranger at his side. The stranger was short, with curly whiskers. He wore a top hat and an elegant suit that looked odd in a cotton field.

"Young bucks," the stranger said. "That's what we're looking for. Prime hands. They'll bring top dollar." He looked around. "How many did Mr. Thornton say?"

"About a dozen," Mr. Whitmore said.

"I ain't attached to any of them," the stranger said. "Let me choose."

Pen froze. *The man was a slave dealer.*

The two men began to walk the cotton rows, the way an experienced cotton grower would walk to gauge the future harvest. But these two were harvesting men, not cotton, and Pen watched them approach with a cold sensation in her belly.

The slaves put their heads down, as though refusing to look at him would spare them. The stranger stopped before Jonas and looked him up and down. "I like the looks of this one," he said to Whitmore. To Jonas, he said, "Open your mouth. Let me look at your teeth."

Jonas turned to the man. "I ain't a horse," he said. "You ask me how old I am, I tell you."

"Open your mouth, damn you, or I whip you."

Jonas stared at the stranger. Slowly, he laid his hoe on the ground.

The man said, "Hurry it up, nigger."

Jonas opened his mouth, and the man thrust his fingers inside, looking at his teeth. "Teeth are all right," he said, to no one in particular. "Jump around a little."

Jonas stared at the man as though he didn't understand.

"Move it," the man said. "I want to make sure you ain't

lame." He added, "If you sham me, pretend you're lame when you ain't, that's another reason for whipping."

Jonas walked a little way down the row and back. He said to the man, "You can see I ain't lame."

The man said to Whitmore, "This one will suit."

He would take Jonas away. Pen cried out, "If you take him, take me, too!"

The stranger glared at her. "I ain't taking any gals," he said. "They ain't worth enough." He saw the swell under her skirt. "No gals. Just bucks."

Pen began to scream. "No!"

The stranger said to Whitmore, "Shut her up, will you?"

Before Whitmore could reply, her stepfather grasped her arm. "Pen. Sugar. Hush."

Pen wept as she screamed. She struggled in her stepfather's grasp. "No! Not Jonas!"

Whitmore said, "Take her away. I'll deal with her later."

Her stepfather dragged her away as the man shackled Jonas. She screamed over and over, "No!"

Then she felt the cramp in her belly and the trickle down her leg. She cradled her belly and looked down. Blood pooled on her shoe. "The baby," she moaned, and she fainted.

WHEN SHE CAME TO, it was night, still hot. She was in her cabin, lying on the bed where she and Jonas had made the baby. She put out one hand to feel the empty spot where Jonas had always slept. The other hand went to her belly. It was sore, and it was flat.

Her sister sat beside the bed. Pen asked, "What happen to the baby?"

Cassie looked away.

"I lose it?"

A nod.

"Was it a boy or a girl?"

Cassie didn't reply.

"Tell me!"

Her sister put her hand to her face. Her voice came out as a croak. "Would have been a boy," she said.

"Where they take Jonas?"

"They take a dozen men. I hear to Mississippi."

Pen began to weep. Sold away. Carried away. Parted by distance, just as she had feared. Lost, forever.

Chapter 2

Yazoo County, Mississippi
June 1862

IT WAS COTTON-CHOPPING SEASON in Mississippi, but none of the slaves on the Newell place were chopping cotton. The blockade and the war had ruined the market for cotton, and none of the planters in Yazoo County had bothered to put in a crop this year. Instead, they grew corn and peas for the Confederate army. Corn and peas took much less labor than cotton, and slaves all over the county were idled.

Jonas, along with a gang of five others, had been set to the task of digging postholes for a new fence. He knew as well as anyone that the fence wasn't necessary. Every day, as he wielded his shovel, he felt more and more worried. He asked Hark, who was digging a hole a few feet away, "What do massa need us for, if he don't grow cotton?"

He and Hark shared a cabin, as did young, unmarried men, who were called bachelors in the plantation parlance. Hark was truly a bachelor, having never been married, but Jonas was not.

Hark grinned. He had a ready smile in a dark-brown face. He said, "Need us to dig more holes."

"He didn't buy us to dig no holes. What if he never need us again to grow cotton?"

Hark took off his cap and wiped away the sweat with his sleeve. "Now that ain't likely."

"I was sold away once," Jonas said. "For massa's debt."

"Who weren't?" Hark asked.

"What happen to you?"

"I was carried away from Alabama." His voice was matter-of-fact.

"I was sold for a debt," Jonas said.

Hark's pleasant expression suddenly slipped, and Jonas saw the grief beneath it. "Carried away from my mama, my brothers, and my sisters, and I never see them again."

Jonas struggled against the memory of Pen. He thought of the sunny flash of her smile, the piney scent of her skin, the lovely alto of her voice. The pleasure of her company and the joy of her body.

And the way she had screamed as she was taken away.

Jonas leaned on his shovel, overcome by the heat, which was so much denser and wetter than Georgia's. He tried to breathe deeply to steady himself, but it didn't help.

"Nigger, why ain't you working?" asked Mr. Evans. He was the overseer, a stocky, bowlegged white man whose florid face wore a perpetual expression of disappointment. He always carried a whip, although he rarely used it. Like the hands he oversaw, he worried about his own usefulness, and it made him sharper and meaner with the slaves.

"Just had to catch my breath, suh," Jonas said in a placating tone.

Mr. Evans's voice rose higher. "Don't think so," he said. "I believe that you're shirking."

Jonas straightened. "No, suh," he said softly. Since he had come to Mississippi, he had always spoken softly.

Enslaved Levi, the driver and foreman who kept his eye on Jonas and his gang even when the overseer wasn't around, hurried to them at the sound of Mr. Evans in a temper. Intervening, he asked, "Mr. Evans? What's the matter, suh?"

"This man ain't working," Mr. Evans said.

Levi glanced at Jonas and said to Mr. Evans, "I know this man. He a hard worker, never give me any trouble."

"Can't have any malingering. You know that."

Levi looked more closely at Jonas. He said, "Mr. Evans, let him set in the shade for a moment, drink a cup of water. Then he be all right and he go back to work."

"Mr. Newell won't like it."

"Marse Newell don't like it if anyone keel over," the driver reminded the overseer.

Mr. Evans looked disgusted. He growled, "All right."

Jonas said to both of them, "I'm grateful, suh." He walked back to the bucket of water and poured a dipperful into a tin cup. The water was warm and a gnat had fallen into the bucket, but he drank it, and afterward, he shambled toward the big live oak that grew at the edge of the cotton field. He sat heavily on the ground and wiped his forehead with his sleeve. Despite the heat, he felt cold, and shaky into the bargain.

As much as he tried to push them away, memories of Pen returned, and this time he succumbed to them. He thought of the way she smiled when she told him she was carrying and how she cupped her belly when she began to show, protecting and caressing the child in her womb. He thought of his last memory of her, how she had pleaded with the slave dealer to take her, too.

He believed that she was alive, as he believed in the Lord, without any proof that it was true. If he let himself think otherwise, he would fall into despair. He had seen men like that, broken by anger and grief. They had nothing to look forward to, not even Heaven, and he couldn't live like that.

He hoped that the baby was alive and that it comforted her.

He leaned against the broad trunk of the tree, feeling the bark scratch through his shirt, and closed his eyes.

"Jonas?"

He forced his eyes open. It was Levi, who had come to see how he fared. "How you do?"

Jonas nodded.

Levi said, "You look ashy."

"I'm all right," Jonas said.

"No, you ain't. Don't want you in the sun. Go back to your place and rest."

"Mr. Evans won't like it."

"Massa won't like it if you work until you take sick. I fix it with Mr. Evans."

Jonas rose. When Levi saw how unsteady he was, he said, "Hark walk back with you and make sure you're all right."

Hark held out his arm, but Jonas shook his head. They took the path around the cornfield that abutted the main road where the carriages ran. Despite all the disruptions of the war, white folks still visited back and forth, drinking coffee made from acorns and eating poor dinners of ham and cornbread.

As they walked, they heard the swift clip of hooves and the whir of wheels. It was a smart little buggy, bright yellow, new and gleaming, drawn by a pair of horses. The man who held the reins and encouraged the horses was hatless, and he was laughing. But Jonas had seen him before, and he knew it was Marse.

Jonas had never spoken to Marse Newell, and he doubted that Marse Newell could distinguish him among the hundred slaves he owned. He only knew Marse to see him from afar like this. He wondered how Marse could look so carefree. How he could laugh.

Hark said, "That's massa's new carriage. Spanking new. Team is new, too." Hark knew the groom, who kept him apprised of everything in the stables.

Jonas eyed the horses, a matched pair of bays, their reddish coats glowing in the sun, their legs flying. "Them horses are beauties."

Hark said, "Massa love his horses. Fuss over them. Dote on them. He take better care of his horses than he do of us."

Jonas watched as the carriage rolled down the road. Marse made sure that his slaves were well-fed and well-rested. But he did the same for his mules.

A man, even if he was a slave, was not a mule.

Hark stopped at the trees that divided the slave street from the fields. "You all right?"

Jonas said, "Don't fuss over me like I'm a woman carrying a baby. I can walk a few feet."

"Tetchy," Hark said, and he turned to walk back to the field.

The slave street was deserted at this hour. The hands who weren't in the fields were on the grounds of the big house, doing the wash or tending to the yard or looking after the children. Only one person stayed at the quarters during the day. Caleb wasn't old, but he was so badly crippled that he seemed to be.

In an unusually hushed voice, Hark had told him Caleb's story. As a young man, Caleb was rebellious, and he had run away more than once. The third time, Marse Newell sent the patrollers after him, accompanied by a pack of bloodhounds. The dogs had mauled him so badly that his leg was crippled, and the beating he got when they brought him back had hurt him even worse. He was never the same afterward. The punishment had driven him crazy.

Hark whispered further that massa rued what he had done, ruining a slave like that. But he couldn't sell someone in that condition. He left Caleb on the place as a reminder of what happened to a runaway.

Unable to work, Caleb spent his days sitting on the steps of his cabin. Most of the time, he stared into space, his face vacant. Sometimes, he livened up enough to shout at something no one else could discern.

Today, as he saw Jonas approach, he raised his head, and his dull eyes were momentarily alight. He shouted at Jonas, "Hey, you! You lazy good-for-nothing! Massa whup you for this!"

Jonas ignored him.

Caleb yelled, "I see what you want. You want to run away!"

WHEN THE FIDDLES PLAYED on Saturday night and the whiskey jug came out, Hark, truly a bachelor, would join in the dancing and the drinking and enjoyed both. The women liked him, too. He was strong and graceful, with a ready, gleaming smile for any woman who pleased him.

That Saturday night, when dusk began to fall, the slave street livened. A crowd gathered in the open space between the cabins. The fiddler took out his fiddle, and those who drank took out the whiskey jug.

Jonas sat on the steps of his cabin, setting himself apart. He listened, not to the music and the singing that accompanied it, but to the booming sound of the frogs that lived in the swamp beyond the plantation. The swamp beckoned him. Hark had told him that it was impassable: mud up to a man's knees, cypress trees too tangled to move through, and poisonous cottonmouths slithering everywhere.

Jonas had said, "Why you caution me?"

"I see a glint in your eye."

Jonas had replied, "I see old Caleb, too." Poisonous snakes were the least of God's dangers for a man who made his way into the swamp.

Tonight, Hark came out of the cabin wearing a clean shirt.

Jonas raised his head. He asked, "Ain't that your Sunday shirt?"

Hark grinned, his teeth white in the dusk. "Don't think the Lord mind that I wear it to gladden myself on a Saturday night." He said, "Come on. Join us. Give yourself a little joy."

"No, I'm all right," Jonas said, even though he was not.

Hark gripped his hand. Even though Jonas tried to shake it off, Hark's grasp was tight. He pulled Jonas to his feet. "Come on, man," Hark said.

Jonas said, "Let go my hand. I ain't a child to be dragged against my will."

Hark loosened his grip. "Then come of your own free will."

"Free will!" Jonas snorted.

"Just for a little while."

"Will you let me alone if I do?"

"Maybe you enjoy yourself," Hark said.

Jonas shook off Hark's hand. He rose. Hark grinned again, and Jonas followed him into the street and into the crowd.

At the sight of them both, a man who worked in their gang, a friend of Hark's, lifted a whiskey jug. "Hark!" he said. "Want a drop?"

"I do," Hark said, smiling.

"And Jonas? Do he want some?"

"I speak for myself just fine," Jonas said quietly. "No, I don't."

"He a spoiler," Hark said, but his tone was jocular. He accepted a cup of whiskey and downed it in one gulp. "That's good!" he exclaimed. "You sure you don't want any?"

Jonas nodded.

A woman approached him. When he had first seen her, after church, the sight of her had given him a start. She was tall and brown of skin, like Pen. But she was not Pen. Her name was May, and she had been friendly to him. She was widowed, and everyone knew that she was looking for another husband. She had asked him why he was so quiet. Exasperated, he said, "Why you ask me that? I never ask anyone, 'Why you so loud?'"

Now she said, "They good, them fiddlers. Don't you think so?"

He was ashamed that he'd been so rude to her before. He said, "They good indeed."

"Haven't seen you dance. Do you like to dance?"

He remembered dancing with Pen at their wedding, and a wave of longing washed over him. "Haven't felt much like dancing."

She met his eyes. Her expression was kind. "I hear you lose someone," she said. "We all lose someone. Can't grieve forever."

"Didn't lose her. Know just where she is." The sounds of the frogs, croaking and booming, were audible even over the fiddling. Pen was beyond that swamp. She was unreachable.

"She ain't here. I am." May held out her hand. "Dance with me?"

He stared at her hand, not at her face. Then he shook his head. He walked away, disregarding May's remark, "No call to be so ill-mannered!" Miffed, she said to no one in particular, "I find a man who want to dance with me!"

Jonas ignored her. He walked with purpose past the cabins, past the strip of trodden ground behind them, and into the grove that separated them from the fields. There were no frogs in the grove, but there were birds. He had cared about birds back in Georgia. Now, in Mississippi, he heard the low vibrating call of the nightjars and the haunting cry of the whippoorwills. Were there barred owls in Mississippi? He had never listened for them.

He rubbed his face with his hand. In the same low voice he used in church, he prayed to the Lord to keep Pen well and make their child a comfort to her. He didn't ask the Lord to bring them back together. Distance had torn them asunder, and he doubted God could help him with that.

He peered into the darkness as though he could see the way back to Georgia through the swamp.

"Why you in there?" It was Hark.

"Go away."

"You rude to May," Hark said.

"She get over it."

"She like you."

"Don't matter. I'm married. Still married."

Hark came closer. He smelled of the whiskey he'd been drinking. "You sold away. Your wife left behind. You never see her again."

Jonas turned to look at Hark. All he could see were the whites of his eyes. He said, "Always be married to her. Nothing change that."

ON THE FOLLOWING MONDAY, Jonas had halted for a moment to straighten his back when Levi, the driver, strode down the row. "Get to work!"

"I always at work. You say so."

"Massa coming. With Mister Evans. Look like you working hard."

"Massa? Why?" Jonas felt a prickle of fear.

"Do he tell me? Make a good report of yourself. Don't lean on that shovel. Use it."

Jonas raised the shovel and brought it down with force into the shallow posthole. "Like that?"

"Look like you happy. Sing, maybe."

Jonas snorted. "Can't promise that." He put his head down and plied the shovel with his usual rhythm.

He had perfected the slave's ability to see from the corners of his eyes, so he knew when Mr. Evans was next to him. But it wasn't the overseer who spoke. "He looks strong. Is he a good worker?"

Jonas stole a sidelong glance. It was massa, who laughed as he drove the beautiful bay horses.

Why is he here? Why would he be asking such a thing? In the heat, Jonas felt chilled to the bone.

Mr. Evans said, "Levi tells me that he works hard and never shirks."

Evidently he had been forgiven for being overcome with the heat.

"I think he'll suit," massa said.

Lord, help me, Jonas thought, sick with the memory of being sold.

Massa added, "And this one. He looks strong, too."

Hark. They would be shackled together.

Massa asked, "You're sure he's all right? He looks like he's seen a ghost." He pointed. "You. What's your name?"

Jonas couldn't speak.

21

Mr. Evans said roughly, "He asked you a question. Answer him."

"Jonas, sir," he croaked.

"Are you all right?"

If he plan to sell us, what do it matter? He found his voice. "You sell us, sir?"

Marse Newell laughed.

How could he laugh?

Marse Newell said, "Why would I sell a fine field hand like you? The Confederate army needs strong men. That's why I'm sending you to Yazoo City."

Hark was so surprised that he blurted out, "Us, soldiers?"

Massa laughed again. "No, but you'll be helping the soldiers out. They need men to build fortifications. Who better than you?"

After massa and Mr. Evans left, Jonas allowed himself to feel faint with relief. "I thought for sure he sell us."

Hark asked, "What's a fortification?"

"Don't know."

Levi, overhearing them, said, "Earthworks. Build them in the battlefield. Or along the river. Soldiers stand behind them to shoot."

"Earthworks?" Jonas asked. "How we make earthworks?"

Levi said, "Dig up the ground and mound it up. Use a shovel."

"Fight for the Confederate army with a shovel?" Hark asked.

"Don't fool yourself," Levi said sharply. "A nigger with

a shovel ain't a soldier." He leaned close enough to talk softly. "Trade one massa for another."

In Yazoo City, Jonas and Hark joined a group of slaves from all over Yazoo County. Some of them had been there since April. The man who led their gang, Gabriel, had been a carpenter and a mason on his plantation. He was muscular and dark, with a scar that ran from the edge of his lips to his chin. His eyes were bloodshot. Like Levi, the driver on the Newell place, he acted as a buffer with the sergeant who supervised them.

Sergeant Mackay was from the pine barrens of eastern Mississippi. He told them that his daddy never owned slaves, and he didn't care for big planters or their niggers. Gabriel placated him by telling him that he was used to handling slaves.

Sergeant Mackay glared at him and said, "You're a nigger, too, and don't you forget it."

After Mackay left, Gabriel said to his gang, "As though we ever forget."

It was no better than digging postholes. They dug up the earth and mounded it into breastworks. They stood in the open, in the heat and humidity of the Delta summer, and Gabriel's refrain, when Mackay wasn't watching, was to tell them to take it slow and to drink plenty of water. "I see men laid out from not drinking enough water," he said. "You thirsty, you stop, you drink."

When Jonas leaned on his shovel to rest, Gabriel said

kindly, "You all right, son?" He was of an age to be Jonas's father, and it didn't sound wrong coming from him.

Jonas thought, *I ain't*. But it was nothing that a driver could fix for him. "I ain't thirsty, if that's what you're asking."

Gabriel said, "I hear that we stop building earthworks."

Jonas said, "They send us away?"

"No," Gabriel said. "We help the army build a ship."

"Why we do that?" Hark asked.

"Got a warship in Memphis that ain't finished. Can't leave it there because the Federals come too close. They bring it here, and we finish it."

"Us?" Hark said. "How?"

Gabriel said, "Before you build a damn thing, you fell trees and haul lumber. That's what we do."

Jonas said softly, "You was a carpenter. I bet you could build a ship."

Gabriel's eyes gleamed. "I could build an ark for Noah, if he ask me. But no one ask me."

"When that ship done, what the army do with it?" Jonas asked softly.

Gabriel said, "They take it to tangle with the Federals up the river near Vicksburg."

"Federals that close?" Hark asked. Vicksburg was fifty miles away.

"Yes," Gabriel said. "That close."

GABRIEL WAS RIGHT. WITHIN a week, the earthworks were abandoned. It took a while to assemble a team of woodcutters since they would use axes and saws, tools that only the steadiest slave could be trusted with. Gabriel vouched for Jonas and Hark, and they joined the group that moved into the woods. They weren't shackled, but they were guarded as closely as prisoners.

The Confederate soldiers were boys, raw recruits, who didn't look old enough to hoist a gun, let alone fight a war.

The Confederate soldiers and the conscripted slaves walked half a day to find the forest, where the trees stood undisturbed by clearing. The group halted to stand in the midst of a grove with years of old growth and looked up to the canopy. Jonas, standing still, listened to the birds. They were familiar: the shriek of a jay, the trill of a chickadee, the whistle of a cardinal. High above, a woodpecker tapped.

One of the soldiers said, "Those are mighty big trees."

"You don't have to fell them," another soldier said.

The first soldier said to Gabriel, "You want to set these niggers up?"

"Yes, suh," Gabriel said. "You move out, stay clear, and I set the men up."

The soldiers backed away, willing to watch, and Gabriel glanced up. One of the soldiers said, "What are you waiting for?"

"Figuring," Gabriel said. "That tree fall wrong, it put someone in a world of hurt."

The two soldiers backed farther away.

Gabriel found a smaller tree. He set Hark and Jonas on either end of a cross-cut saw and explained how to use it. After their initial effort, they had barely scratched the trunk.

Hark stared at the tree. "They set us to fight. Have to fight this tree all the way through."

Jonas thought of the Union army, so close by, up the river in Vicksburg. He murmured, "We fighting, all right. But we in the wrong army."

Chapter 3

Dougherty County, Georgia
January 1863

WAR HAD BROKEN OUT, and Jonas had been gone for more than a year, but Pen showed no sign of recovering from her loss. The light had gone out of her. She worked in silence with her head down, whether it was chopping cotton or shucking corn. Nothing roused her, neither a midsummer frolic nor the promise of a rest at Christmas. Her sister, Cassie, fell in love, and she got married a year after the guns fired on Fort Sumter. Pen sat in the front pew in the church, wearing the dress she had worn to her own wedding, her face ashen, her hands clenched in her lap. She remained at the celebration afterward for a few minutes, no more, and when she excused herself, she fled into the woods where she could be alone, and she grieved for Jonas all over again.

In the first year of the war, once the cotton crop was in, a man warmed by his Christmas rum asked if she'd walk out with him when the weather got better.

She turned to him, her eyes dull, and she said, "How dare you. I ain't free to walk out with anyone. I'm married!"

He tried to reach for her arm, but she yanked it away. "Leave me alone!" she said, and strode toward her cabin, her whole body stiff with anger.

Her stepfather, Tobias, who knew her hiding place, followed her into the woods. She said, "Daddy, you leave me alone, too."

"Oh, sugar," he said, reaching for her, but she withdrew. "Pen, please, listen to me." When she didn't reply, he said, "It hurt me to see you like this."

She shook her head, not wanting to say: "It hurt me worse, and you know it."

"Pen, he ain't coming back. He's gone forever. Can't live like this, half alive. Got to get past it."

"No," she said.

"Someone else love you. Marry you. Give you a family. Give you joy."

She raised her eyes to her stepfather's face. Her breath caught in her throat. When had he aged so much? Had she given him that much to grieve for, as she grieved for Jonas? She said, "Daddy, don't mean to pain you."

"I know," he said, and when he reached for her hand, she let him take it. It hurt to feel a man's fingers, toughened and work-worn, curled tenderly around her own.

She brushed her eyes with her hand, pretending that she had something in her eye. She said, "Still love Jonas, and love him with all my heart. Always will. Still married to him, wherever he is. Can't think of marrying any other."

Throughout 1862, the war was far away. The people on the Thornton place heard about it through the human telegraph. Somewhere, someone was able to read a newspaper, and the tale of every battle in Virginia, Tennessee,

South Carolina, or Mississippi raised or dashed the hopes of those held in bondage. Everyone on the Thornton place revered the president. When they spoke of him—which they did, in low tones, far from the big house—they called him Marse Lincoln.

The Thorntons felt the war through those who were absent. Young Marse Thornton, full of fire for the South, had received a commission in a Georgia regiment just after the first shots were fired at Fort Sumter, and Mr. Whitmore, to everyone's relief, mustered in to the regiment as well. Both of them left for Virginia in the summer of 1861. Neither fared well. July knew, because he heard when Missus wept to her friends. Young Marse Thornton had been captured, and he was in a hellish Union prison, Camp Douglas, far away in Illinois. Young Marse also wrote to tell her that Mr. Whitmore had fallen in battle in Virginia, but no one on the Thornton place wept for him.

With the master and overseer gone, Missus installed one of her cousins, a man too sickly to fight, to take charge of the place. Without the effort of Pen's stepfather, who took on the overseer's tasks, the place would have been in total disarray. Pen wondered why he did it. "It ain't your place," she said, savoring the dual meaning—neither his plantation nor his obligation.

He said, "I know it ain't. But I take care of it all these years, and it hurt me to watch it go to rack and ruin."

A SURPRISING NUMBER OF the planters in Dougherty County, which had plantations with hundreds of acres and hundreds of slaves, took advantage of the planter's exemption. Any man with more than twenty slaves could return his place and sit out the war, and those who did felt no guilt about it.

Despite the shortages imposed by the blockade, Missus still gave dinners for the gentry who remained in Dougherty County. Pen and her stepfather heard about them from the butler, July, who served the food and stood against the wall, waiting for the pleasure of Missus and her guests. July told her stepfather, "They act like I ain't there. Like I'm deaf. Like I'm no different from a piece of furniture." He snorted. "I hear it, all right, and I tuck it away to tell you."

On New Year's Day of 1863, late in the afternoon, July found his way through the early darkness to her stepfather's cabin. Pen sat with him before the fire. The fire smelled of pitch and pine as it cast a pleasant, flickering light. July settled into a chair and stretched his hands toward the fire. He sighed. "On my feet for hours."

"No rest for you," her stepfather said.

"Missus have a big dinner for her neighbors today. They all come, everyone who ain't in the Confederate army, and all the womenfolks, too."

"You got something to tell us, July?" her stepfather asked.

"They all stirred up," he said. "Got news from Washington, and it don't make them happy." July rested his hands on his knees and licked his lips, the storyteller's gesture. "Marse Lincoln make a proclamation, and they call it the devil's work and say they never accept what it say. Rather die than let it stand, they say, even though the man who say it was mighty drunk, and I don't think he could fight a kitten even when he sober."

Pen rested her hands in her lap. July relished his role as the bearer of news. He would tell it slowly.

He said, "I get a fair notion of what this Proclamation say." He paused and let his gaze rest on her stepfather and then on her. He grinned. "It say that we slaves are free."

"Free?" Pen asked.

"All of us in the secesh states. By law, we free now. Free to work, free to fight. Lord, they was in a buzz, talking about what we do with our freedom! Talk like we free to murder them in their beds!"

Pen said slowly, "Free to marry?"

"No one mention it, but if you free, I reckon you free to marry, too."

"Free to find anyone who was carried away?"

Her stepfather's face clouded as July said, "I reckon that part of being free, too."

THAT NIGHT, PEN COULDN'T sleep. She rose quietly, pulled her coverlet over her shoulders, and went outside to sit on the steps in the January cold. In a dark, velvety sky, the new moon cast little light, and the stars glimmered through wispy clouds. From the trees behind the cabins, a horned owl called, and another answered. Jonas, who liked birds and knew their calls, had told her that horned owls behaved as though they were married and stayed faithful to one another.

For the first time in a long time, she allowed herself

to think of Jonas. To remember. The first smile. The first brush of hands. The first childish kiss and the first adult one. Their wedding, when his eyes alit with joy. Their wedding night and all the nights after it.

The sound of his laugh. The smell of his skin—a musky, earthy scent that she liked even after a long day in the sun and in the field. The touch of his fingers, long and tapering and beautiful, despite the scars from picking cotton. The feeling of them cleaving together, one flesh, with a joy that wasn't in the Bible verse.

Tears filled her eyes, and she made no effort to brush them away.

She let herself remember the worst of it, how he had been taken from her. She recalled the feeble winter sun on her neck and the smell of fresh-turned dirt in the newly hoed cotton row. Tonight, as then, her arms ached, recalling the weight and the rhythm of the hoe.

She closed her eyes as the tears trickled down her face. She didn't feel the cold that seeped through her thin, makeshift shawl. The humiliation of seeing him treated like a mule, put through his paces, his teeth checked. The horror of watching the shackles lock around his ankles. And the agony when she knew that the slave dealer would take him away forever.

She covered her face with her hands and wept.

She lifted her head at the sound of the door closing. The stairs creaked as her stepfather sat beside her. He didn't say a word, just put his arm around her shoulders. She laid her head on his shoulder, and he stroked her hair, as he had when she was a little girl. "Oh, Pen," he murmured.

Without moving, she said, "Couldn't sleep." She took a

breath, and it was still ragged with tears. "Thinking about July's news."

"Marse Lincoln's news."

She sat up. "That we free," she said, meeting his eyes.

He sighed. "Not yet, sugar."

"Oh, I know. Marse and Missus ain't made a proclamation. But it got me thinking."

"Free to marry," he said, echoing her words.

"Free to find Jonas," she said.

"Pen, sugar, how you do that?"

She wiped her face with her hand. "Go to Mississippi."

"All God's dangers in your way."

She sat up very straight. "What do the preacher say when we marry? He say that love stronger than death."

"Stronger than a patroller? Stronger than a slave catcher?" her stepfather said, his voice very quiet.

She asked, "Daddy, do you ever think about being free?"

The horned owl called again, and its mate answered.

He turned to look at her, and even in the darkness, she could see that his face was deeply sad. "All the time, sugar."

HER STEPFATHER WAS RIGHT about the dangers of stealing herself away, and they made her shudder. When she thought of them, she was so afraid that her gut clenched. And then she thought of Jonas, alive somewhere in Mississippi, missing her and loving her as she loved and missed him, and her longing overpowered her fear.

If she left, if she stole away, if she set out to find him, how would she do it?

33

She knew her way through Dougherty County, and she knew the path to neighboring Calhoun County, where she had friends and kin on the plantations nearer the county border. What lay beyond, she didn't know.

But the slaves on those places might know what lay just beyond.

Would they welcome her? Or would they betray her? That she couldn't know. She would have to find out. She wondered if they knew about the Proclamation. If they knew they were free.

She could tell them. Like her stepfather, they were likely to long for freedom as powerfully as she longed for Jonas. What did the song of praise say, that she knew so well from the church? That when she heard the good tidings from Heaven, it set her soul free? She could carry that news to Calhoun County and whatever lay beyond it.

She might be a fool to think that the Lord would help her. She would have to help herself, too.

She gathered a few things that no one would miss, small enough to fit into her pockets. A scarf to bind around her head, and a comb. A little wooden box with matches in it. And the only thing that she owned for herself, the penknife that had been a present from her stepfather. He was clever at whittling, and he had taught her and encouraged her. The little knife, with its bone handle, would help her along the way and remind her of him. Her eyes stung as she hefted it in her palm. She wondered if she would see her stepfather again if she left.

A week later, Pen asked her stepfather if they could speak privately after dinner. He said, "I know what this about, Pen."

"I'm going to Mississippi. I'm leaving tomorrow night."

He put his hand on her arm. "Pen, how can you?"

"What do we sing every Sunday? That when the Lord call us, we can't stay behind? That's the road I intend to take, Daddy."

He looked away.

She said softly, "You free, too. Remember that."

He shook his head.

"Help me," she said.

"Of course I help you."

"Lie for me. Missus's cousin, who try to run the place, he don't even know my name. Don't let him know that I've gone."

With a rueful smile, he said, "He won't ask, and I won't tell."

IT WAS HARDER TO tell Cassie that she was leaving. Cassie wept. "Don't go, Pen," she said. "It too dangerous. The patrollers with them dogs, they find you for sure."

Pen put her arms around her sister and wept with her. "Can't stay behind," she whispered.

"You crazy. What if he marry someone else? What if he dead?"

"He ain't dead. And he ain't married to anyone else."

Cassie wept afresh. "Can't bear to think that I never see you again."

Pen tightened her grip on her sister. "Don't know that."

Cassie stepped back and grasped Pen's hands so tight that it hurt. "You determined to go."

"I am."

The tears trickled down Cassie's face, and Pen watched her, willing herself to memorize her sister's face. Cassie might be right. They might never see each other again.

Cassie said, "Take my shawl."

The shawl had been their stepfather's gift to Cassie last Christmas. It was a paisley pattern that made Cassie's skin glow, and it was warm. "Not your shawl! To wear in the woods!"

"To keep you warm." She didn't need to add: *To remember me.* She said, "Won't take no for an answer."

"You crazy, too, Cassie, giving away your finest thing."

"Not as crazy as you," Cassie said, her eyes filling up again.

ON THE NIGHT SHE left, Pen wore all the clothes she owned. She hid Cassie's shawl under her dress and over her chemise. She put her extra stockings on her hands for makeshift gloves. She checked her pockets. She had johnnycake in addition to her penknife and some matches. And her comb for vanity.

She didn't know the road she would take, but she'd go west, through neighboring Calhoun County. After that, she didn't know how she'd go. She'd have to trust in God.

The moon was half full as she slipped through the familiar woods. She was at home here, but her feeling of safety was an illusion. The patrollers, who had joined the Confederate army and now thought of themselves as the militia, rode through these woods, looking for runaways. Every rustle in the trees gave her a start.

These were woods that she had walked with Jonas. She let the memory of him come to her so vividly that he seemed to walk with her. In the darkness, she whispered, "Are you all right? Are you alive? Where are you, sugar?"

But there was no answer, only the haunting cry of a great horned owl.

Chapter 4

Calhoun County, Georgia
January 1863

IT WAS ONLY SEVEN miles over the Dougherty County border to the Cullen place, a familiar journey. She had been to frolics and picnics and weddings there. She knew the cook, and before dawn broke, she was behind her cabin. Through the oilpaper that covered the window, she pitched her voice low. "Maggie?"

Someone stirred within and groaned. She called again. "Maggie?"

Someone rose, grumbling. "Who there at this hour?"

"Pen. Pen Mitchell."

The door opened just a little, and Maggie, dressed in the chemise and petticoat she slept in, her hair disheveled, said in a voice hoarse with sleep, "Pen? Why you here? Ain't no time for a visit."

"This ain't a visit." She whispered, "Jonas go to Mississippi. Now I follow."

Maggie woke, and her face registered her understanding. "You steal away."

Pen nodded.

Maggie opened the door, and Pen slipped in. Maggie's four children were still asleep. Maggie talked softly, not wanting to wake them. "You can't stay here."

"I know. I stay in the woods."

"You alone?"

"Yes."

"How you find your way?"

"I ask as I go."

Maggie considered this. "You go into the woods. Over there." She gestured. "I come to find you later. Bring you something to eat." She shook her head. "You crazy to do this. They find you and put you in chains, take you right back to the Thornton place."

One of the children stirred. Maggie whispered, "Go hide yourself."

Pen walked back into the woods. Cassie's shawl had bunched around her shoulders, and she felt the cold. She slipped her hand into her pocket and pulled out the johnnycake she'd brought with her, which had bent in her pocket and become rubbery in the cold. She sat down to eat it.

The ground, covered with pine needles and last year's oak leaves, felt cold and damp through her dress. She was suddenly overwhelmed with fatigue.

As the sun rose, her eyes dropped shut, and as the slaves in the nearby cabins woke, ate their meager breakfasts, and went to work, she slept.

The hand on her shoulder startled her awake, and her heart raced until she heard Maggie say, "It's me."

Pen sat up, blinking against the winter daylight. Her back ached, nearly as much as after a day of hoeing cotton.

Despite Cassie's shawl, she was chilled all the way through.

Maggie knelt and handed her a tin plate, warm to the touch, and a spoon. Pen cradled the dish in her hands, savoring its heat, and ate the peas and rice gratefully, letting the food revive her.

Maggie said, "I think about where you go next. My cousin live on the Alexander place. About ten mile from here."

"How do I get there?"

Maggie said, "The road run right to it."

"Open road? Where the patrollers ride?"

"Woods on either side."

She didn't like it. The dogs could run through the woods to find her. She swallowed and said, "All right." She handed Maggie the plate.

Maggie took the plate and asked her, "Ain't you afraid?"

Pen said, "Terrified."

EVEN THOUGH SHE SET out at night, it felt too treacherous to stay on the road. With every step, she imagined the sound of hoofbeats—the patrollers were always mounted—and the panting of dogs. She slipped into the woods, thinking that she might be able to walk alongside the road from the protection of the trees.

But the underbrush barred her way and forced her deeper into the woods until she could no longer see the road. She stopped, trying to get her bearings.

And heard something moving.

She stood still, listening. A rustling sound. A light step. A human step. But none of the sounds of a horse. He was on foot.

Did the patrollers do their work on foot in Calhoun County?

The steps came closer. She thought, *If I run, they know where I am.* She stood, unmoving, scarcely daring to breathe.

Then she saw them: two men with rifles slung over their shoulders. They came closer. Close enough for her to see their faces.

They were Black men.

She didn't move. They were armed. They were out at night, in defiance of their master. It was a different kind of danger than a patroller, but it was still a danger.

They came closer, soft of step. Closer.

Should I run?

"Daddy, do you see that?" It was a boy's voice.

"Yes, I do," he said. Before she could decide to bolt, they had both found her. The man stared at her. "Who are you?" he demanded.

She was shaking. "Who are you?"

"You live around here?"

"Do your massa know you're out hunting?" she asked.

"Do your massa know you roam at night?" he countered.

"Why you ask? You a patroller?"

At that the man chuckled. He lowered his rifle. "No. Don't want to meet a patroller any more than you do."

Her knees buckled with relief. "I'm bound for the Alexander place. I'd be obliged if you show me the way."

"Do better than that," the man said. "We live there. We take you there. Who you visiting?"

Maggie had given her a name to ask for. "Miss Janie," she said.

"She kin to you?"

"She kin to my friend Maggie, who live in the Cullen place."

He slung the rifle over his shoulder, a sign that hunting was over for the night. "Come on, son," he said. "We take this gal with us."

They threaded their way through the woods with ease. Of course they would, since they slipped out all the time. At the sight of the slave cabins, the man turned to her. He said, "I can tell you ain't here to visit anyone."

"Why would you think so?"

He chuckled again. "You steal away, don't you?"

She said, "Do you know that you free now?"

"Free?"

"We all free. Marse Lincoln say so." She added defiantly, "Make a proclamation to free us."

"My massa ain't heard yet," he said. "Your massa free you?"

"I go to Mississippi to find my husband, who was sold away before the war."

"Damnedest thing I ever hear."

The boy said, "Daddy, don't curse. Mama don't like it."

"Let me stay in the woods near your place," she said. "Send me on my way tomorrow, to the next place that will shelter me."

The boy looked at her, his eyes bright with interest. "Mama feed you."

THEY DID MORE THAN that, and their generosity shamed her. The nighttime hunter—his name was Jim—and his wife, Ella, hid her in their cabin and insisted on giving her a blanket they couldn't spare. Before dawn, Jim took her to their church, which was buried deep in the woods, telling her, "No one come here, and it ain't as cold as being outdoors." At dusk, both of them brought her food. It was leftover johnnycake, but she ate it with gratitude.

Jim said, "I been thinking. You don't know the countryside, and it ain't safe for you to wander about. I can show you the way to the next place. We go through the woods, the patrollers don't see us."

Pen had never expected such kindness from a stranger. "Thank you. Can't tell you how grateful I am."

"Wouldn't you do the same?" the woman asked softly. "For someone who steal away?"

Jim said, "We go in daylight. I shoe horses and mules, and I always have a reason to visit a neighboring place. Can even get a pass from my massa."

"What about me?" Pen asked.

"Oh, we make up a tale for you, if we have to," he said. "But I don't think we have to."

When they left, Pen stretched out on one of the pews. She made a pillow of her sister's shawl and drew the blanket over her. Oblivious to the daylight, oblivious to how hard her bed felt, she slept.

That afternoon, Jim returned. He pulled a slip of paper from his pocket and grinned. The pass. "Come with me."

Even though the nights were cool, the days were warm enough that she didn't really need her shawl. Jim threaded his way into the woods. Then he paused. He said, "I can tell you ain't used to slipping through the woods."

"I know the woods around my own place," Pen said, stung.

"Of course you do. You at ease, you know the way, you ain't afraid. Not like that when the woods ain't familiar." Before she could retort, he said, "I can show you how a hunter walk through the woods. How to listen, how to hide."

How a runaway should walk through the woods, he was saying.

She nodded.

"First, you listen. What do you hear?"

She cocked her head. "Birds."

"Hush and listen."

She did. "Critters in the trees," she said. "Squirrels."

"Hush," he said, concentrating. "Do you hear that? Slithering sound in the brush?"

Now she did. "Snake."

"That's how quiet you need to be."

She nodded again.

"Follow me," he said. "We walk quiet, too."

"I can be quiet."

He laughed. "Last night, Jackie and I hear you from half a mile away," he said. "Watch me."

He showed her how to step gently, and even though

she couldn't match his noiseless step, she was quieter. She said, "If you still, you hear the woods better."

He grinned, and she followed him, walking as lightly as she could, listening. He halted, and she was immediately worried. "No, it's all right," he said. "You doing fine. Walk alongside me. I have another lesson for you."

"What?"

"Patroller or militia man, he make a racket. Warn you from far off. He on horseback, and the horse don't step lightly, either. If they two men together, they don't try to be quiet. Give you time to slip between the trees. Stand in the shadows. Don't move."

"What about the dogs?" she asked.

"Water," he said. "Find water. They lose you if you wade in the water."

"What if I can't find water?"

"Can you climb a tree?"

"If I have to," she said.

"You might."

AT THE NEXT PLACE, he left her in the woods. In the shelter of a little grove, she sank to the ground, her back against the rough bark of a pine tree. Now alone, she thought of the patrollers and the bloodhounds that accompanied them, and all the ease she felt with Jim deserted her. Fear shot through her. A bloodhound could tear a person up something terrible. That fear crowded out the other fears, like being re-enslaved or violated in a way that didn't show but that hurt worse than being whipped.

She buried her head in her hands. She felt terrified again, and she had so far to go. How could she manage?

"Miss Pen."

It was Jim, and with him was a woman in an apron and a kerchief. She said, "Jim tell me about you. That you intend to walk to Mississippi. Is that true?"

"I hope so," Pen said, her voice shaky.

"Well, we can't get you all the way there, but we help you get through Calhoun County and into the next county over, Clay. Guide you through the woods, hide you, feed you. One place at a time."

"Thank you," she said.

The woman regarded her with sharp eyes. "Ain't you afraid? A woman alone in them woods?"

"Of course," Pen said.

"What possess you to do this?"

"Marse Lincoln tell us we free," she said. "Did you hear that?"

She shook her head. "No freer than I was yesterday."

Pen said defiantly, "No. It different from yesterday. Free mean free to find someone sold away. That's why I do it."

"It crazy," she said.

Pen looked at Jim. He grinned and said, "What she do, journey to Mississippi to find her man, it the craziest thing I ever hear. But you know what? My spirit soar to know that she do it."

AS THE DAYS GREW warmer, Pen fell into a rhythm. She was borne from plantation to plantation in secret, and when she arrived, she was welcomed, fed, and offered an escort to the next place. If she could travel like this all the way to Mississippi, her journey would be easy. She doubted that she would be so lucky.

Her message of freedom was met with skepticism. Over and over, she heard her hosts say, "It a fine thing that Marse Lincoln say we free. My massa haven't said so yet."

Today, in a hiding place behind the slave cabins, she leaned against a pine tree, a blanket around her shoulders and an empty tin plate at her side. She allowed herself to feel how weary she was. A night's sleep on the forest floor was never restful. Even lying on the floor of her familiar cabin in Dougherty County had been easier. Suddenly she missed home. She thought of her stepfather whittling in the flickering light of the fireplace and of her sister, her mending in her lap. She shook her head and tried to replace that scene with a memory of Jonas. It hurt too much. She brushed away a tear.

The sound of footsteps broke her reverie, and she rose to peer through the trees. She heard the swish of a skirt. Not a patroller, then, or the cook who had brought her food. This woman's face was light brown beneath a white headscarf.

The stranger stepped into Pen's hiding place. She allowed herself a small smile and said, "So you're the runaway."

House servant, Pen thought, hearing her talk. *And high-rumped about it.* "Got a name," she said. "Penelope Mitchell."

She inclined her head. "I'm called Dido," she said. "Dido Prescott."

"You want something from me, or you come to gawk?"

Pen asked. She was immediately ashamed of how rude she sounded.

"Yes, I came to see you," Dido said. "I hear that you've been spreading the news of the Proclamation."

"I have," Pen said.

"How did you hear of it?"

"The butler on our place overhear Missus talking about it. He tell us about it."

"You didn't hear it read?"

"No," Pen said. "How could I?"

Dido reached into her pocket and, with a flourish, took out a scrap of newsprint.

"What's that?" Pen asked.

"The Proclamation. From the *New York Herald.*"

"How do you come by that?"

Dido's eyes gleamed. "My missus has a friend in New York who writes to her," she said. "This came in a letter."

"How you get it?"

"I know where Missus keeps her letters. I borrowed it."

"She don't whup you for taking it?"

"No, since I'm her maid and have been since we were girls together," Dido said. "She taught me to read, even though it's against the law."

Pen felt a powerful surge of envy for this light-skinned, well-dressed, well-spoken house servant who could read. She said, disliking the sulky tone in her voice, "Well, that fine for you."

Dido brandished the paper in her hand. "I can read you the Proclamation, if you'd like to hear it."

"You want to read it or tease me about it?"

Dido smiled and smoothed the paper. She began,

"'That on the first day of January, in the year of our Lord one thousand eight hundred and sixty-three, all persons held as slaves within any state or designated part of a state, the people whereof shall then be in rebellion against the United States, shall be then, thenceforward, and forever free—'"

Pen interrupted, "Forever free? Do it really say that?"

"Yes."

Dido continued to read, but Pen continued to hear "forever free," a refrain that wouldn't stop. In Georgia, in Alabama, and in Mississippi, those held in bondage were now free. Forever free.

Dido paused. "Are you listening?"

"Yes," Pen said. "Every word."

Still holding the paper, Dido asked, "Are you really going to journey all the way to Mississippi?"

"Yes, I am. A free woman in search of her husband, who's free, too." Pen met Dido's eyes. They were gray, the sign of white ancestry. She asked, "You read this paper, and you understand it better than I do. Why don't you go? Set yourself free?"

Dido regarded the paper in her hand. Then she met Pen's eyes and smiled. "Not yet. The Union army isn't here yet. When they get close enough, that's when I go."

Several hours later, Dido returned. She pulled another paper from her pocket. Pen said, "Don't tell me you find another Proclamation to read to me."

"No," Dido said. "Something even better." She handed the paper to Pen.

Pen didn't need to read it to know what it was. "Is this a pass?"

"Yes," Dido said. "It says that my missus gives you leave to travel through Clay County."

Pen stared at Dido. "Do your missus write this?"

"No. I did."

"What if they figure out—"

Dido snorted. "Some of those militia men can barely read."

"Why would you do this for me?"

"Don't you think that I want to be free, too?" She paused, and Pen saw her composure falter. She recovered and said, "Let me tell you how to travel."

She explained that there were two routes to take, a path through the woods and the road. Pen stared at Dido as though the house servant had lost her senses. "Walk on the road?" she said. "Let any patroller see me and stop me?"

"The pass," Dido reminded her.

"It a pass. Ain't a bloodhound. Ain't a rifle. What if they disbelieve me? What if they tear it up?"

"Then they answer to Miz Prescott," Dido said.

Pen turned to face her. "And then what happen when they drag me to meet her, who supposed to be my missus?"

Dido's face remained unruffled. "They won't. Stay on the road. It should take you westward to Alabama. Twenty miles. A couple of days."

ONE OF THE LESSER servants, the field hand who had first greeted her when she arrived, walked with her into the woods on the path. He said regretfully, "I can't linger to take you to the next place. But if you stay on the path, you stay hidden."

"Did you hear that Miss Dido get me a pass?"

He smothered a laugh. "She sign it in Missus's name, didn't she?"

"Who is she? Act like she Missus herself."

He laughed again. "You ain't seen Missus, have you?"

"No, why would I?"

"Tall. Haughty. Got a low voice. Gray eyes." At Pen's puzzled look, he said, "They sisters."

Pen didn't reply.

He pointed. "That way. Stay on it, follow it, and it take you to the next place." And then he was gone.

Alone for the first time in weeks, Pen felt her unease return. She was too far from the road to hear anyone who passed, and even though it was unlikely that anyone would crash through the woods on horseback, she started at every sound. The scrabble of claws nearly sent her out of her skin. She looked up to the flash of a plumy gray tail.

Squirrel. Spooked by a squirrel.

She reached into her pocket and fingered the pass. The paper was thick and substantial. She took it out and stared at the writing on it. She wondered what it would be like to be able to read.

Read! She was alone in the woods of Clay County, Georgia. She was a runaway, and not even her stepfather's best efforts would hide that she had left all these weeks after the fact. Young Marse would know that she had gone. She couldn't read, but if she saw a newspaper, she could tell if it had a notice for a runaway. For a man, it showed a trousered figure with a bindle over his shoulder, and for a woman, a figure in a dress and turban with a bag in her hand.

She put the pass back into her pocket.

The trees, young, spindly pines, enclosed her, but she didn't feel safe. It wasn't hot, but she began to sweat. She might meet anyone or anything in these woods. She thought of all the tales she'd heard back in Dougherty County, tales of bloodhounds and bears, equal perils. In full daylight, she had to pause because her heart hammered as though she'd been running.

A snake coiled across the path close enough for her to see its brown scales glint in the sun. It slithered away quickly, as though it were afraid of her. She had heard that snakes were shy, that they wouldn't bother you if you didn't bother them. Most snakes were harmless. But she waited until she was sure that the creature was far away.

Stop it, she told herself. *Broad daylight. Nothing to fear here.*

She fingered the pass again and forced herself to walk. She told herself to keep calm and stay steady. If she followed this path, she would find Black folks to shelter her.

Then she heard the hoofbeats.

She took a deep breath. Could be anyone, just going about his business. Not every man on horseback was a slave catcher.

Someone called, "Hey, stop! There's something in the trees!" A white man's voice.

Someone else said, "Last time you shouted out to me, it was a stray pig."

"There's a path back there. Between the Prescott place and the Burwell place. Niggers take it."

An exasperated sigh. "On errands for their masters and mistresses, no doubt. Why would you bother them?"

"Got to be vigilant."

"All right. Go look."

Should she run? Or would that raise his suspicion? She grasped for the pass.

The horse came through the trees. The rider, a slight man who sat crooked on his horse, cried out, "Hey! I was right! It's a nigger gal!"

The second horseman followed at a more leisurely pace. He was older, grizzled, with long gray hair under his hat and a carefully trimmed gray beard. He glanced at Pen. "So it is."

One crippled, one old: neither man was fit for war duty. Militia men or patrollers, it didn't matter. Both were on the lookout for runaway slaves.

She pulled the pass from her pocket. "I have this, suh."

He read it. "Prescott, is it?"

"Yes, suh. From the Prescott place." Which was God's own truth.

"Never saw you before," the younger man said.

"I'm new, suh," Pen said, directing her words to her accuser without lifting her eyes.

"Are you?"

The older man said to the younger, "Are you acquainted with every field hand on the Prescott place?"

"Let me see that pass."

The older man handed it to him. The younger man scanned it and stared at Pen.

The older man said, "I know Miss Prescott. She's liberal-minded. Allows her slaves to go back and forth."

The younger man tore the pass in two and let it fall to the ground.

"No call for that," said the older man.

The younger man asked Pen, "What's your missus's name?"

Dido had coached her. "Miz Eliza," she said.

"How long you been on the place?"

"Not long. A few weeks."

"Where you from?"

Pen thought of the little illustration in the paper of the runaway slave woman. Her mouth was so dry that she had to force the lie out. "Calhoun County."

"Who sold you?"

Exasperated, the older man said, "You saw the pass. She belongs to Miss Prescott. Do you think she carries her bill of sale around?"

"Pass be damned," the younger man said. "I think she's a runaway."

"Whoever she belongs to, her master won't take kindly to your interfering with her," the older man said.

At the word *interfering*, the younger man sat up, as much as he could with a crooked back. "I know what would satisfy me," he said, touching his belt buckle. To Pen, he said, "I'll take you into the woods."

In disgust, the older man said, "And you a good Christian man who just got married."

The younger man grinned. "I ain't that good a Christian."

Shaking, Pen gathered her wits. She faced the younger man and dared to look him in the face. "Suh, I ain't clean. I got a disease."

He stared at her. "How do you know?"

At his surprised expression, she added, "Believe me, suh, I know. A bad disease."

The older man said, "Your wife won't be glad to get it."

The younger man snarled at Pen, "Damn you for sass-ing me like that."

The older man leaned over and put a firm hand on the younger man's twisted shoulder. The younger man winced in pain. The older man tightened his grip. "If you know what's good for you, you'll let it go." He looked at Pen. "Let her go."

"Get your hand off me," the younger man snarled, and as soon as he was free, he turned his horse and urged it to gallop away, toward the road.

Without a word, the older man followed him.

Pen stood still, listening to the sounds of the birds that Jonas would know, if he were here. The sun was high in the sky. Shaking, she tried to figure which way might be west-ward. She smoothed her skirt with her sweaty hands, and she set out. She hoped it was westward, toward Mississippi.

Chapter 5

Henry County, Alabama
March 1863

AT THE EDGE OF Georgia, for the first time since Pen had left Dougherty County, the slaves had nowhere to direct her. "Don't know anyone over in Alabama," said the woman who brought her a plate of food, as though Alabama was a foreign country instead of the next county to the west.

She decided to risk traveling by day. If there were plantations in Alabama with slaves to greet her and hide her, she wanted to be able to see them.

She didn't know exactly when she crossed the border into Alabama, but she knew when the forest changed. Georgia's groves had been small and tame, the pine intermingled with live oak and pin oak. The first thing that struck her was the smell of the Alabama woods: a thick, oily odor reminiscent of turpentine. The trees were all pine, with tall, slender trunks and branches far overhead. Their canopy filtered the sun, turning the light a grayish green. It was cooler in this forest than in Georgia's clearings, but it was more eerie, too.

She leaned against the nearest trunk, feeling the rough

bark through her dress, and tried to get her bearings. She remembered Jim, the hunter who found her wandering in the woods in Georgia, and she was quiet. There were so many birdsongs that she couldn't distinguish one from the other. *Jonas would know*, she thought, and she blinked away the tears that rose to her eyes. She reminded herself to stay vigilant. That had been part of Jim's lesson, too. From somewhere above came a tapping sound. She couldn't see the bird, but she was oddly reassured. Woodpeckers lived in Georgia, too.

It was early morning, and the sun was still in the east. She took a deep breath of the turpentine-scented air and set out, turning west, keeping the sun behind her.

As the morning wore on, the light, grayish green like the trees themselves, brightened a little. The air warmed. The birdsong became a cacophony, with the tap-tap-tap of the woodpeckers as its refrain.

The woods stretched unbroken, with no sign of human habitation: not a path, not a clearing, not a house. Were there no plantations in this part of Alabama? Were there no slaves? Perhaps there were no patrollers, either.

Be still enough to hear, Jim had said. *Be aware enough to watch.*

As she stepped through the trees, trying to be noiseless on the dead pine needles that carpeted the ground, she looked around. The grass grew in clumps where the trees thinned a little, letting the sun through, stronger and brighter. The shrubs took their opportunity in the sunshine. Mostly magnolia, just blossomed, its white stars bigger than her handspan and fragrant even through the smell of the pines.

Small animals scratched and rootled—squirrels mostly. She saw the flash of a rabbit's tail. A snake crossed her path, and she waited until it was gone. She would never care for snakes, no matter how benign they were.

She had a johnnycake in her pocket, the last gesture of help and hospitality from Georgia, but she was thirsty. As she stepped carefully through the woods, she listened and was rewarded by a rushing, musical sound. She sank to her knees to drink from the rivulet. The water was cool and sweet. She washed her face, delighting in the feeling of water on her skin. She sat back on her heels to rest.

A fallen log lay in the water, and on it sat a big box turtle that blinked at her with hooded eyes. She laughed softly and blinked back. Damselflies, their bodies a jeweled blue, their wings green and lacy, danced over the water. A hapless bee entered a plant with a cup-like flower, and to her astonishment, the cup closed. She waited, but the bee never emerged.

She could not forget that there was menace in this forest, but there was beauty, too. She had never looked at the familiar groves of Dougherty County, the tame live oaks and pines, to see the splendor of the natural world. In the unfamiliar woods of Alabama, she saw it, and she saw God's hand in it.

"Lord, keep me safe," she whispered, and hoped that God would heed her.

SHE WALKED ALL DAY, stopping only to eat her johnny-cake, and when dusk fell, she kept moving. She wanted to be near water but not just to slake her thirst. Even though she hadn't seen a human soul or caught the clop of hooves or heard dogs panting, she wanted to be able to hide her scent. To wade in the water.

The woods were different at night. The canopy of the pines blocked the moonlight, and she moved in darkness. She felt for a path with her feet, and because she couldn't get her bearings, she bumped into trees and tripped over exposed roots. She stubbed her toe and stifled a curse. The smell of resin and oil was so strong that it overpowered the daytime perfume of magnolia. The air was thick with the miasma of pine. It wasn't an odor but a presence.

She stopped in the darkness, trying to let the forest in. The birds were quieter and fewer at night. The owls were out, with their haunting, hooting cry. Owls were a comfort, a reminder of Jonas and Georgia.

Unlike the birds, the animals were louder at night. Not just scrabbling but rustling. She froze at the sudden sound of a heavy, plodding gait. Then she saw the culprits: a band of raccoons making their way through the forest. Their eyes glinted through their mask-like markings, and their ringed tails flickered as they lumbered away.

She let herself feel her fear, and her imagination started to run wild. Were there bears in these woods? Wild pigs? Patrollers, with their dogs? Fear overwhelmed her. She hated herself for being so afraid. Thinking of Jim, she forced herself to calm down, breathe slowly, and quiet herself enough to hear what was truly in these woods and not just in her imagination.

Then she heard it.

A mewing, purring sound like a cat's, but deep and loud, as if a cat weighed as much as a human being.

Don't move, she told herself. *If it see me, if it run after me...* She was as still as a stone. She waited until she no longer heard that sound. Until it was gone. Whatever it was.

The nighttime forest was a landscape of fear and danger. The sound of a rattler's tail. The grunt of a wild pig. The purr of the giant cat. Those were God's dangers. Then there were human beings to fear, patrollers on horseback, their dogs in a pack, snuffling as they scented something, baying as they ran toward it.

She leaned against a tree. She tried to think of Jonas, but her terror crowded out every other thought. *I'll die here*, she thought.

She would die if she couldn't find water. Still afraid, still trembling, she pushed against the tree, propelling herself back into the darkness. She walked on, listening for the sound of running water.

THE NEXT DAY, SHE found another creek. No longer thirsty but beginning to feel the pangs of hunger, she decided to find someplace to ask for food. She couldn't imagine a place where no Black folks lived. But as she progressed, hoping that she was bearing westward, she saw no clearing in the trees.

Did no one live here? Was it a wilderness?

She could sleep on the ground. She could manage to find water. But she needed food and shelter, and she yearned for the sight of a Black face and the sound of a Black voice.

The hunger was a prickle at first, then an itch, and

three days into her sojourn in the pinewoods, it became a persistent ache. On the Dougherty place, there had been an old woman who gathered roots in the woods. She knew the plants, too, and she had come back from her rambling with mushrooms or greens in her basket. Pen had never learned what the old woman knew, and she stared at the plants, just beginning to furl, with an angry ignorance. Clumps of mushrooms grew here, but she remembered very well what the old woman told her. "Some mushrooms is good to eat, and some is poisonous enough to kill you. Don't pick some and find out the hard way."

There were rabbits and squirrels in these woods. But she had no way to hunt. There might be plenty in these woods, but she was unable to find it or catch it.

Somewhere, someone must live here.

And that day, around midday—the sun was high in the sky, and the light was as bright as it would ever be— she saw the cleared land just beyond the trees. Then she saw the house. A little log house.

On the steps sat a man, taking his ease by smoking a pipe. On the little wraparound porch, two women sat in rush chairs, sewing. In the dirt yard beyond the steps, two children played, surrounded by dogs, shoats, and chickens.

They were white.

They might be the kindest people on God's earth, good Christians who would help any hungry traveler. And they might be people who would be glad to summon the militia to shackle her and drag her back to Georgia.

She couldn't take the risk to find out. She took a deep breath and tried to ignore the ache in her belly. She turned to go back into the woods and got her bearings again, hoping that she was right about going westward.

TOO WEARY TO GO on, she fell asleep. She dreamed. Jonas appeared, not as she last saw him but smiling, as he did on their wedding day. "Don't worry, sugar."

In her dream, she cried out, "Where are you?"

He smiled so sweetly that she started to cry. "I'm all right," he said.

She reached for him, but he disappeared. She woke to find tears streaking her face.

Still half asleep, she thought, *He's alive. He's somewhere in Mississippi.* But she was in Alabama, lost and afraid. She was hungry and thirsty. She heard an eerie sound that had become familiar, a growl combined with a purr.

Was the dream a lie? Was Jonas lost, too? Was he in trouble? Was he dead? She buried her face in her hands, feeling despair.

A few days ago, she had let her fear talk to her to whisper, *I'll die here.* Now her good sense talked instead, and it was loud enough to make her ears ring. *I could die here. I see just how.*

Whoever roamed these woods after her would find the scrap of her shawl and a heap of her bones.

She heard the growling purr again. Louder. Whatever it was, it was closer. She didn't have the strength to run. Would it come for her?

She raised her head to see the flash of eyes somewhere in the trees, yellow and luminescent, like a cat's. It growled again. And then it turned and padded away. And she saw its shape in the moonlight. It was bigger than the biggest dog she had ever seen.

If she was going to die in the woods, she would have to get up and do it elsewhere. She didn't want to find out what had eyes like a cat and a purr like a cat and was the size of a bloodhound.

She rose. She was afraid, but it helped her. Her fear drove out her hunger and her weakness. She didn't bother to try to figure out which direction was west. She was going in the opposite direction of that growling sound.

SHE WAS WANDERING, LOST. She didn't know if she had gone in a straight line or in a circle. The landscape never varied. Trees, endless trees, without any landmark to distinguish them.

Water. She had to find water.

Then she heard it.

A snuffling sound. She drew in her breath. She knew that sound very well.

It was a dog. A tracker. A bloodhound? She froze, waiting, trying to see through the trees. The snuffling sound came closer. The dog whined. Had it scented her? If she ran, would it pursue her?

She hoped that fear would make her fleet, when she ran. But she waited for a moment.

Then it emerged from the trees.

It was a dog with a reddish-brown coat, about her knee height, the kind of hunting dog that Blacks and whites alike called a redbone hound.

When it saw her, it stopped. It cocked its head to the

side. It waited. When it moved, it sidled closer to her and looked at her again. She waited, too, thinking that the dog might have an owner close by. Not a patroller. She had never known a patroller to run a redbone hound through the woods.

But as woman and dog regarded each other, no human being emerged from the trees.

She released her breath. "What you doing out at night?" she asked the dog.

At the sound of her voice, the dog lowered itself to the ground. Put out its paws. Panted. And waited.

No bloodhound would sit like that.

She took a step forward and dared to extend her hand. The dog rose slowly, whining softly, to approach her. She held out her hand, even though it trembled. And she was rewarded by a lick from a wet, soft tongue. Sighing in relief, she reached out to scratch the dog between its ears. It whined again, very softly, as though it had missed a human touch.

It was someone's dog, and she didn't want that someone to come looking for the dog and find her. Even as she rubbed the dog's rough, hard head, she said, "You go on home."

The dog didn't move.

"No, you go on," she said. She straightened up and turned to walk away. The dog didn't move. She took a deep breath and plunged back into the forest, ignoring the plaintive whine.

She hadn't taken three steps when the dog came and stood by her side. When she tried to shake it, it followed.

She stopped again. "You can't come with me," she said. But when she moved along, it trotted beside her.

She reached down to scratch the dog's ears, and it panted with pleasure. She said, "Are you lost?" The dog regarded her again. "Are you a runaway?" Even in the dark, she could see that it had a sweet, plaintive gaze. Like a man trying to sweeten her.

She looked down to check. It was a boy dog, all right.

"I guess you come with me," she said.

He wagged his tail.

He followed her until she began to falter. All the fear and emotion wore off, and she was bone weary again. And hungry. And thirsty. She sank to the ground, telling the dog, "Got to rest a moment."

She laid her head on her knees. She had never felt so tired, not even at the height of cotton season when she picked two hundred pounds of cotton a day from dawn to dusk, from can't see to can't see. She remembered feeling so tired that she wanted to die on those awful nights in September back in Georgia. She had been such a fool to think that hard work was as bad as being lost in the wilds of Alabama.

The dog nosed her arm. When she didn't respond, he nosed her harder. She raised her head. She met the dog's eyes. They were a deep, liquid brown, like a Black man's. The dog nosed her leg this time, with enough force to make her move. "Quit that," she said, trying to push away the determined muzzle. He nudged her again.

"I guess you pester me until I stand up." She stood.

This time, he didn't wait for her. He trotted ahead, and

when she lagged, he waited for her to catch up. He didn't seem playful. He was leading her somewhere.

She stumbled after him, too tired to think that he might be returning to the master who had let him loose.

Suddenly he bounded away, barking. What had startled him?

She stopped to listen. But the woods were still. No man, no horse, no bear. No great cat, either.

She followed his lead. When she lagged too far behind, he ran back, as though he were making sure that she was all right. "All right, all right," she said. "I come with you."

She heard it before she saw it. The trickle of water. She hastened her pace.

The dog stood next to a stream. He raised his head as if to say, "Look what I found for you!" Then he bent to lap from it.

She sank to her knees. It was a tiny creek, only a few feet across, but the water ran deep. She put her hand into the water, startled by its chill. She scooped it up and drank from her cupped hands until her thirst was slaked and her belly was full. Then she collapsed onto the ground, not knowing whether she felt creek water on her face or tears.

She fell asleep like that, and in the night, when she woke for a moment, she felt a hard spine curled against her belly. Startled, she reached out and touched the wiry fur. He woke and sniffed her hand. Then he licked that, too.

IN THE MORNING, SHE woke to the sound of a low whine. It tore her from sleep, and she sat up with terror in her heart.

It was the yellow hound. He sat on his haunches, with the carcass of a swamp rabbit between his paws. She stared at the rabbit, then at the dog. The rabbit's neck had been broken, a clean break, but the body was undamaged, save for a few toothmarks around the rabbit's scruff. "You bring me this?" she asked, as though he could tell her.

The dog waited. She touched the rabbit and felt the fat under the fur. A big 'un. A good meal.

She said, "You bring us our breakfast." He came close, nosing her hand, looking for approval. "Look at you, trying to butter me up." He licked her fingers. She smiled. "All right. I guess you earn your keep."

She skinned and butchered the rabbit with her penknife and dared to light a fire with one of the matches in her pocket. The smell of roasting meat was better than any barbecue she'd ever attended. When the meat was cooked, she divided it, and woman and dog both ate until they were satisfied.

"Have to call you something. Since you stay with me." He cocked his head, as though he could understand what she was saying. She spoke as though he could. "Call you Toby."

She stood. She got her bearings and reckoned which way was west. She set out with Toby trotting beside her.

Chapter 6

Dale County, Alabama
March 1863

PEN WAS GLAD FOR Toby's ears and his nose, which were keen enough to know what she didn't. She was still jumpy.

Tonight, they had a half-moon to light their way, a faint, silvery light through the canopy of the pines. The owls were out, their calls low and haunting.

Toby ran ahead and halted, waiting for her. When she caught up to him, his ears were pricked at something she couldn't hear. She said, "We ain't going hunting at this hour." But he didn't bolt, as he would after game. He stood still and began to growl, a low, threatening note she had not yet heard from him.

She rested her hand on his neck, feeling the growl vibrate through his body. She went still, too, listening for what he could hear and she could not.

Footsteps. Careful and quiet.

A hunter's or a militia man's?

Toby growled louder, but he remained obedient under the pressure of her hand.

Someone glided between the trees into her sight. A white boy dressed in faded, tattered clothes, with boots so badly worn they were wrapped with rags. But he carried a rifle.

He halted a good distance away, hearing that Toby still growled, and regarded both woman and dog with surprise.

Behind him, another white man appeared. He was a little older and a little taller than the boy, and he was similarly ragged and ill-shod. He was also armed. "What's this?" he asked the boy.

The boy said, "It's a nigger gal." And to her astonishment, he looked at Toby, who was poised to defend her, with longing. He said, "Jasper, she has a dog that looks just like Buck, back home."

The man asked Pen, "Who are you?"

Restraining Toby, she said, "Who are you?"

"Soldiers," he said, and she saw that the rags had once been gray.

Fear sparked through her. "Are you militia men?"

He shook his head. He was barely grown, weather-beaten from the sun but thin as a spavined mule. He looked haggard as well as hungry.

"Are there more soldiers here?"

"Not here," he said. "Just us."

"Where are the rest of them?"

The boy said, "They're back in Tennessee."

"You run off from the army?"

The young man gave her a long, searching look. "You're one to talk. Where are you from?"

That stopped her short. She had no pass, no destination, and no excuse.

The young man said, "I reckon you run off, too."

Toby growled. She grabbed him by the scruff. "You two call the militia on me?"

The young man said, "We don't want to meet the militia any more than you do."

She said, "I go on my way, and you go on yours."

The boy said, "Jasper, if that dog's like Buck, he's a good hunter."

"You touch my dog, you try to take him from me, I sic him on both of you," Pen said, trembling.

The boy cast an imploring look at the young man. Then at Pen. Then at Toby. "Wouldn't do such a thing."

The young man said, "Lucas, let's leave her alone."

Lucas asked, "Where are you bound?"

"Why do you care?" Pen said.

"We're going west," he said. "Dale County."

Jasper said, "As though it's her business! Maybe she'll turn us over to the militia!"

Pen wanted to laugh. It was fear, she knew. She said, "A nigger gal? A slave? A runaway? Over my dead body."

Lucas said, "See, Jasper? We stay away from the militia, all three of us." He glanced at Toby. "All four of us."

Jasper said, "That's a damn fool notion."

Toby growled again. Pen said, "Is it? Common cause. Stay away from the militia. Go west."

Jasper said, "Let's find a spot to set, and we'll talk it over."

"What's your dog's name?" Lucas asked.

Pen released her grip on Toby's nape. "You quiet," she

said. "It all right." She looked at Lucas. *Lord, he's just a boy.* She couldn't believe he was old enough to fight. "Toby," she said.

THE TWO CONFEDERATE DESERTERS knew their way through the woods. They wound their way through the trees as though they were at home in the pines. Jasper found them a stream, and they all stopped to drink. Then he said, "Don't want to be far from water," and he found them a clearing nearby. The two men unslung their guns and sat wearily on the ground.

"Wish we had something to eat," Lucas said.

"Tomorrow," Jasper told him.

"You want a fire?" Pen asked. "I have matches."

Jasper said, "Save them."

Pen sat, and Toby curled against her leg. Toby wasn't sure of Lucas and Jasper yet. Pen wasn't, either. She felt wary. She heard the sound that had been bothering her since she crossed into Alabama, the growl and the purr together. She started. "What's that?"

"Painter," Jasper said. At her surprised look, he added, "Catamount. Mountain lion. Big cat."

Pen said, "I saw how big."

"Close up?" he asked, interested. "They're shy of people."

"In the trees. That was close enough," Pen said.

He asked, "Don't they have painters where you're from?"

She shook her head. "No."

"Where is that? That you never saw a painter?"

She ignored the question. Somehow, Toby's presence made her bold enough to be rude to a white man. She had heard them call each other by name, but she wanted a proper introduction. "Who are you?" she asked.

He gave her a long look. He heard the rudeness, too. But he said, "Jasper Wilkinson, and that's my brother, Lucas. We hail from around here. Dale County, Alabama. And you? What are you called?"

"Pen." She added, "Short for Penelope."

Lucas said, "Never met a nigger gal named Penelope."

"Don't they have Black folks in Dale County?" Pen asked.

"Not many," Lucas said.

"But they do where you're from," Jasper said, fishing again.

"Told you. Rather not say," she said. She rested her hand on Toby's nape, and it continued to give her the courage to defy a white man. He was still a white man, even if he was a ragged runaway.

"Don't trust us yet, do you?" Jasper asked, his face even more haggard in the darkness.

She ruffled Toby's fur. "I do not."

IN THE MORNING, AS he had promised, Jasper told Pen that he and Lucas would find them some breakfast. Pen asked, "What is there to find?"

"You'd be surprised," Jasper said. He seemed in a better temper. He looked better, too.

Lucas gazed at Toby, who leaned against Pen's leg. He pleaded, "Can we take him with us?"

Without waiting for Jasper, Pen said, "No."

"I can handle a dog," Lucas said, wheedling.

She rested her hand on Toby's head. "He only answer to me."

Jasper said, "We'll all go. You too, Pen. And your dog."

Pen asked, "Did you command anyone in the army?"

Jasper snorted. "I commanded my brother."

"He did not," Lucas said. "He was a private, just like me."

"Do you want breakfast or not?" Jasper asked his brother. "Come on."

The Wilkinson brothers stepped quietly through the trees, as the slave Jim had. It was clear that they had been hunters before they were soldiers.

Toby pricked up his ears, and Lucas said, "Jasper? You hear that?"

"Rabbits," Jasper said.

Lucas said to Pen, "Your dog. You run him after rabbits?"

"Run him?"

"Send him off to catch rabbits."

Pen said, "He run himself."

Toby took off through the trees, and Lucas watched as the dog disappeared. They all heard the scuffle and the triumphant bark, and soon Toby came loping back with something in his jaws. He dropped it at Pen's feet. Lucas bent to examine it. Toby growled. Pen said, "It all right, Toby," and he quieted.

Lucas said, "Someone trained that dog to be a fine hunter. Barely a mark on this rabbit." He rose. "Where did you find him?"

"He find me," Pen said. "In the woods east of here. Don't know exactly where."

"Can I run him?"

"You saw. He don't need no encouragement."

Lucas bent and addressed himself to Toby. "Run, boy! Get us a rabbit! Run!"

At the sound of Lucas's voice, Toby streaked back into the woods. Lucas grinned. "Yes, someone teach him, just like I taught my dog."

How had this boy ever managed to be a soldier? Pen said, "What did you say your dog's name was? Buck?"

Lucas nodded.

Teasing, Jasper said, "When he left to fight, I swear he missed that dog more than he missed Ma and Pa."

"As much as I missed Ma and Pa," Lucas said, teasing back.

Toby returned with another carcass, and this time, he dropped it at Lucas's feet. Lucas bent to rub Toby's ears, saying, "Good dog! Good boy!" Toby didn't mind it. He nosed Lucas's arm, snuffling and whining softly. "You like me a little, don't you, Toby?" Lucas crooned.

Pen said, "Toby! Come here and stay with me."

Lucas glanced at Pen and straightened up. He gave Toby a pat on the head. "You go on," he said. "Go to Pen."

Toby returned to Pen's side. In forgiveness, he nosed her hand until she stroked the side of his head. "Still mine, ain't you?"

Jasper said to Lucas, "You take the rabbits. I want to look for something."

He led them to the nearby stream and bent down in the midst of a patch of what looked like low-growing weeds. He picked a sprig and tasted it. He broke into a smile. "Thought I'd find it."

"What is it?"

"Cress. Don't they have cress where you come from?"

"No," she said. "We have mustard greens we grow in the garden."

He nodded and picked another sprig to hand to Pen. "Try it. It won't poison you."

She took it tentatively. She tasted it. It was sweet and pungent. "It ain't bad," she said. "How do you know to find it?"

"My ma taught me about cress," he said. "We've been picking it in the woods since we were boys." He began to harvest it. When he had several handfuls, he said, "Can you carry it in your skirt?"

Surprised, Pen said, "I guess so."

He rose, smiling. "Now we have breakfast."

ONCE THE FIRE WAS lit and the rabbits were on a make-shift spit, Lucas said, "I'm wore out." He stretched on the ground and was immediately asleep. Toby, liking the heat of the fire and the smell of the meat, stretched out near him.

Pen said, "How old is he? Your brother?"

"Just eighteen." Jasper sighed. "He lied about his age when he mustered in."

"Why did you join up? Either of you?"

"Couldn't say no," he said. "Every man in Dale County signed up to fight. The Colonel—we called him that because he fought in the Mexican War—he raised the regiment, and God help you if you refused."

"Where did you fight?"

"Virginia, at first. Bad'uns. We had a bellyful of fighting. Then they sent us toward Tennessee, and that's when we ran." He looked at Pen with curiosity. "Why would a nigger know about the war?"

"We hear about it," Pen said. "We ain't fools." She wondered if he knew about the Proclamation. She doubted it, and she wouldn't be the one to enlighten him.

"Never knew any niggers in Dale County."

"Don't you have plantations there?"

"Couldn't call the Colonel's place a plantation. My daddy's a farmer, and so was I, before I mustered in."

"Cotton?"

He snorted. "No. Corn. A hundred acres. Never owned a slave and never wanted to." He gave Pen a fierce look. "My daddy and I, we never cared for the Colonel or the niggers who made him rich."

Pen said, "Don't get mad at me. I never had a say-so about being a slave." She thought of the oddity of being bound, if only temporarily, to a Confederate deserter with no love for Black folks. She wouldn't tell him that in Dougherty County, a white man with no slaves, less than a hundred acres, and a crop of hog and hominy was considered little better than a slave.

He asked, "Why did you run away?"

"Why did you?"

"Couldn't bear it anymore."

"Neither could I."

He looked away, as though he knew he'd been thought-less. That was a surprise to her. No white man had ever bothered to feel ashamed of himself in her presence.

She said, "Well, you ain't in the army anymore. And I ain't a slave anymore. So I guess we're even. Deserters and runaways together."

He said, "I never talked to a nigger like this before."

"And I never talked to a white man like this, either," she said, surprising herself.

OVER THE NEXT FEW days, they made their way through the woods, deserters and fugitive, runaways together. Pen was grateful for the Wilkinson brothers' familiarity with the terrain and their skill as hunters and foragers. This morning, as they had every morning since they banded together, Jasper took Pen to find some cress. She told her-self that cress wasn't so bad, if you didn't allow yourself to think of mustard greens cooked in bacon grease.

As they approached the stream, they heard the purr of a painter. "Do it follow us?" Pen asked.

"No," Jasper told her. "These woods are full of painters."

"That don't cheer me."

He didn't reply. He listened, his ears almost as keen as Toby's. "Hear that?"

Yes. The sound of hooves on dirt. "Militia men?" she whispered.

"We don't linger to find out. Follow me."

As she followed in his footsteps, she wondered if he knew about wading in the water. The sound of the hooves grew fainter and fainter. He halted and put his finger to his lips to tell her to hush.

They waited.

He said, "I think we're all right. Let's go."

She hurried to keep up with him. "If the militia men catch you, what happen?"

"They arrest us and send us back to fight," he said. "What happens to you?"

"They put me in chains and send me back to slavery."

He said, "I'd rather die first."

She said, "I'd rather not."

THAT EVENING, AS LUCAS slept and she and Jasper sat together in the darkness, she asked him, "Where's your place?"

"North of here. I've got my own place, next to Pa's. Lucas still lives on Pa's place."

"Bet you'll be glad to see it again."

He looked away. "It's gone to rack and ruin."

"No one to tend it?"

"I left my wife to tend it."

"She couldn't manage it?"

"She caught the fever. Died last winter. The baby, too. Little Tom." She heard the catch in his throat. "That's when I decided to quit the army. When I knew I lost everything dear to me."

Why did his confession bring the tears to her eyes? He was a stranger, and in a few days, they'd part company, and she'd never see him again.

"I'm sorry," she said, and to her surprise, she meant it.

"Pen? When you run off, who did you leave behind?"

She thought, *Don't be kind to me. I won't be able to bear it.* She forced herself to sound hard. "Didn't happen that way."

"You all alone in the world?"

She hesitated because if she spoke, she would start to cry. She took in a deep breath and was appalled that it sounded ragged. Anyone could hear the tears in it.

"Pen?" Jasper asked, his voice soft. "Something bothering you?"

"No," she said.

"That's a lie," he said, but his voice was still soft. "I know when a woman's about to cry. Who did you leave behind?"

She took another deep breath. He knew she was upset enough for tears. Not having to hide it made it easier. She said, "My husband was sold away from me. I was carrying our baby. After they took him away, I lost the baby, too."

"Oh, Pen," he said, heartbroken man to heartbroken woman.

"No," she said. "Don't you start with me."

"Just sorry for you, that's all."

"My husband ain't dead," she said, her voice low and fierce. "He alive. He in Mississippi. That where I'm bound, to find him. I'm married in my heart and my soul. Always will be."

Jasper's voice was still soft. "What's his name?"

"You care about a strange nigger's name?" She wanted to sound harsh because she was uncomfortably sorry for him, too.

"My wife's name was Jane. We called her Janie. I believe I'll miss her until I die."

Oh, she understood that, too. She whispered, "Jonas. Jonas Mitchell."

IN THE MORNING, JASPER took her aside, out of Lucas's earshot. He said, "I talked out of turn last night."

Pen said, "It ain't wrong to miss your wife."

"Didn't mean to trouble you."

Pen didn't reply.

Jasper took a deep breath. "Haven't talked to anyone like that since I left for the war. Used to talk to my wife like that. Forgot myself."

"So did I," Pen said.

He smiled. "I reckon we're even." He held out his hand.

"Can't shake your hand. Haven't got that far."

He said, "I never talked to a nigger like that before. Like a friend."

She raised her eyes to his. She had never looked into blue eyes before. She said, "*Nigger* a mean word. Don't care to be called that."

"It is? Never thought of that before. What should I say instead?"

"Colored. That's kinder."

When they returned, Lucas asked, "Where did you go?"

Exasperated, Jasper said, "Can't a man do something private without being bothered?"

"You and Pen? What do you do that's private?"

Jasper tried to look severe. "I relieved myself, and I didn't ask what she needed to do."

But Lucas didn't respond with a tease or a smile. "I hear something. Do you?" He glanced at Toby, who had pricked up his ears.

They fell silent, and they all heard it: the muffled sound of hooves on dirt and a snuffling sound.

Pen's throat went dry. Mounted men and their dogs. She whispered, "Militia men."

"Wait," Jasper whispered back. "If we go, we do it quiet. And we make sure to go in the other direction."

They waited until the hoofbeats and snuffling sounds abated.

Jasper said, "We go northward."

"Pa's place?" Lucas asked.

"No. Mine. It's deserted. No one to be bothered about Pen."

Pen asked, "Is there water on the way?"

"There will be," Jasper said.

"We walk through it. Wade in the water. Throw them dogs off our scent."

Lucas and Jasper exchanged a look. "We know that," Lucas said.

"Yes, because you hunt," Pen said. "But you never been hunted before."

They crept through the forest, listening for hoofbeats, voices, and the sound of dogs. Despite the presence of the Wilkinsons, Pen's fear returned. The smell of the pines was oppressive today, like being forced to breathe over a bucket of turpentine. The birdsong was a loud distraction that masked other sounds that she dreaded to hear. She didn't mind her feet and stumbled over a tree root.

"Quiet!" Jasper hissed.

She straightened herself, feeling tears rise to her eyes. She hated that she might cry for fear. "Doing my best!" she hissed back.

By the time the sun was high in the sky, they came to a stream that was a few feet wide. "Water," Lucas murmured.

Jasper said, "Not enough to drown our scent."

"Better than nothing," Pen said.

"I'll be the judge of that," Jasper said.

So fear make him sharp, Pen thought.

He said, "We go a little farther, and then we lie low. After this, we travel at night."

THAT NIGHT, THE MOON lit their way. They had waded through more than one creek to get here, and they had drunk their fill. Despite Toby's protective presence, despite the rifles the Wilkinsons carried, Pen felt as afraid as she had when she first blundered into the pinewoods. Every sound made her start.

Jasper said, "Quiet yourself, or we'll be in trouble."

"Ain't you afraid?" she whispered.

"Would I say so if I was?"

"There's no water here. If they come with them dogs, should we climb up a tree?"

He looked up, even though there was nothing to see but the canopy of the pines, black in the moonlight. "Painters live up in the trees."

They fell into a rhythm. Creep, halt, listen. Toby kept close to Pen, and he was unusually quiet. As they stopped to listen, Pen heard the now-familiar sound, the growling purr. "Painter," she whispered to no one in particular.

"If you don't bother it, it won't bother you," Jasper whispered back. "Painter's not our worry tonight."

Creep, halt, listen. They heard the nighttime sounds of the woods, the owl's call, the skitter of possums, the slither of snakes. And the painter's sound again.

They all heard the unfamiliar voice and froze.

"Saw something in the woods," the voice said.

"Painter?" the second man asked.

"Not a painter."

Men on foot. Hunters? Pen held her breath.

Then the snuffling sound. A dog. Toby growled, and the dog bayed. It was a bloodhound. Another dog bayed in response. Two dogs. Maybe more.

They were hunting, but they were hunting for human beings.

"Dogs found something, all right," the first voice said.

The dogs bayed as they came closer, and the men, not bothering to be quiet, ran after them.

Toby growled, and Lucas grabbed him by the nape. "Stay," he growled back at the dog, and even though Toby's tail thrashed, he obeyed.

Jasper unslung his rifle and aimed it toward the baying sound. He fired. As the dogs howled, he fired again. The dogs followed their noses into the woods. Jasper aimed carefully. He shot, and one of the dogs dropped to the ground. The other shrieked in pain, and when Jasper shot again, the second dog dropped, too. The baying stopped.

Jasper whispered to Lucas, "They're coming. Let them get closer." To Pen, he said, "Get back."

Before she could move, the shots began. One of them whistled by her, and she cried out in surprise. She didn't know if it was wiser to stand still or to run. A bullet lodged in a tree that she could reach out to touch, and that shocked her into movement. She turned, and the next bullet caught her in the shoulder. She screamed.

Jasper shouted, "Run, damn you! You and Toby! Run!"

"Can't leave you," she panted.

"Get the hell out!"

She backed away, praying that no one would aim at her. When she was ten feet away, she heard Jasper scream. And then Lucas.

Holding her shoulder, Pen ran, and Toby ran with her. Together, they crashed through the trees, making headway as fast as they could.

There were footsteps behind her. Pen was too frightened to pray. She put her head down and ran harder. The sound of footsteps grew louder.

And a voice: "Hey! Don't shoot! It's a gal! A nigger gal!"

It was over. She would go back to Georgia with a chain around her neck.

Then she heard a familiar sound: the growl. And then there was a new sound, an unearthly scream, like a woman in peril, and her heart hammered so hard in her chest that it was hard to run and breathe at the same time. She didn't dare turn to see what it was that fought and growled and screamed.

Then it was quiet, except for the sound of purring and the flash of a long tawny tail.

She slowed, gasping, and pain shot through her shoulder. She let go of her shoulder, and her hand came away soaked with blood. She bent over, feeling the pain, feeling her weakness.

Toby nosed her hard, and she straightened up and forced herself to run again. He kept pace with her. She didn't know where she was. She didn't know where she went. But she ran until the pain and shock overcame her, and she sank to the ground.

She held her bleeding shoulder and thought, *I'll die here.* She closed her eyes. She wondered if Jasper and Lucas were dead. She would never know.

She sat heavily on the ground. The rough dirt, full of scratchy pine needles, felt as soft as a feather bed.

Toby whined. He nosed her hand. She didn't move. She couldn't. "Leave me be." He nipped at her hand. "No," she groaned.

He took her skirt in his teeth and tugged hard. When she didn't get up, he nudged her wounded arm. Pain shot all the way through her. "Damn you!" she said, and raised herself.

He ran ahead of her and waited, as he had when he first found her. She struggled to her feet. He yelped. It was agony to walk, but she caught up with him. He ran ahead again.

She thought of the night that he had led her to water. Did he know where he was going? Did he know where he was leading her?

Water, she thought. *He'll find us water.*

Now that she was walking, however painfully, he matched his pace to hers. When she stopped, crying out, he stopped, too. He nosed her good hand and licked it, as though apologizing for hurting her before, and waited for her.

Suddenly he picked up his pace. He trotted ahead, and when she saw where he waited, she made her way there.

It was a clearing, and a path ran through it. It looked just like the paths worn through the Georgia woods that slaves took between one place and another.

Was there a place here? Might there be shelter?

She made her way down the path, and suddenly a man was on the path before her.

In the moonlight, she saw that he was armed and that he was Black. He was tall and muscular, his hair closely cropped, and in the silvery light he looked like an apparition.

He asked, "You run away?"

Before she could answer, he said, "Oh Lord, it don't matter. You hurt!"

It hurt to talk. "Yes," she said, answering both questions.

"We all runaways here. Come with me." He caught her, and the last thing she remembered before she fainted was feeling his strong arms around her.

Chapter 7

Yazoo County and Vicksburg, Mississippi
1862 to 1863

AFTER FINISHING THE CSS *Arkansas*, Jonas and Hark, like the rest of the slaves, were returned to their plantations. They went back to the Newell place before what would have been cotton-picking season, if there had been any cotton to pick.

After the first of the new year, Marse Newell decided to put in a crop, and Jonas and Hark resumed their usual tasks, plowing up the dead cotton stalks and readying the land for planting. Nothing had changed on the Newell place. Levi still drove them and protected them from Mr. Evans, the overseer, who kept a sharp eye for malingering. And Caleb still sat idle on the deserted slave street, raising his voice at something—or someone—only he could see.

Early in January, as Jonas and Hark returned from a day in the fields, they found Caleb standing on the steps before his cabin, rubbing his hands together and tearing them through his hair, which was wild and long since he now refused to let anyone touch his head to cut it. He stared at Jonas and shouted, "President Lincoln free the slaves!"

Hark said, "He crazier than usual."

"Proclaim it up in Washington! We all free now!"

Hark rolled his eyes.

A few weeks later, a visitor drove past the cotton field in a dilapidated buggy drawn by a tired horse. He wore a gray uniform, the worse for wear. Jonas said to Hark, "See that braid on his shoulder? He a lieutenant in the army."

"Why he visit Marse Newell?"

Jonas shrugged. "Who know? Friend, maybe. Or relation."

"Might he have army business?" Hark asked.

"What you mean?"

"Need another gang to build more of them fortifications?"

Jonas shook his head. "Hope not."

Later that morning, as Jonas and Hark rested by the water bucket, Levi stopped and knelt down. He spoke in a low voice. "You right about that man who come here. He in the army," he said.

Jonas said, "Thought so."

"Marse Newell so unhappy to see him that he don't even invite him inside. They talk on the steps. I stand in the yard, and I hear the whole thing."

"Tell us," Jonas said, impatient.

"He tell Marse Newell that the army want more men. Negroes, he call us. He tell Marse Newell that he have to give up half his good hands—just men, no women—and their drivers and Mr. Evans, too. Need us at Vicksburg to build more of them earthworks."

"What do Marse Newell say to that?" Jonas asked.

"He start to shout. He say that he already give up a gang for that fool navy yard in Yazoo City and that he done his duty by the Confederacy. And he also say that he don't appreciate that the army treat his slaves, his valuable property, worse than mules. He say no."

"So we don't go?" Hark asked, hopeful.

Levi dropped his voice even more. "The army man tell Marse Newell that if he don't give us up of his own free will, the army impress us. Seize us, shackle us, and take us off to Vicksburg, whether he like it or not."

Jonas's eyes gleamed. "They shackle up Mr. Evans, too?"

"Don't be a fool," Levi said. "The army man tell Marse Newell that they ain't done with him, and then he go off on his rattletrap buggy. That's a mighty ragged army, them men in gray."

"You think he come back to seize us?" Jonas asked, alarm rising in him.

"Can't say," Levi whispered. Slaves said this when they meant *Yes, but I shouldn't say so*.

THE NEXT DAY, THREE carts rumbled down the road that ran past the cotton field, each drawn by a team of mules. The carters wore shabby gray uniforms, and all of them were as burly as they were seedy. Each man carried a whip. They clambered down from the carts, holding the whips in their fists, and stared at the cotton field.

Jonas, who was plowing a row, stopped his mule. He

stared at the men in gray. They were here to harvest men. *Not again.*

He dropped the reins and turned to run. But he was caught roughly before he could take a step. Not by Mr. Evans, but by Levi, who said, "Do you want a whipping before they shackle you up?"

"No!" Jonas shouted, and he tried to shake free. Levi grabbed him to hold him fast. "Damn you, nigger. Do you want all of us to get a whipping?"

Jonas struggled to get his arms loose. He wanted to knock Levi down and bolt into the woods. "Marse Newell say no! It ain't running away!"

Mr. Evans hurried down the row. "What the hell is this?"

With difficulty, Levi said, "I try to calm this man down. Don't want trouble."

Mr. Evans said, "No, we don't." To Jonas, he said, "If you don't calm down, I'll whip you myself."

Jonas shouted, "They take you, too? They impress you along with us?"

Mr. Evans hit him over the head with the butt of the whip, and Jonas fell to the ground, insensate.

When Jonas came to, he ached all over. He was propped upright in the bed of a wagon, and the press of bodies around him kept him from flopping over. His head hurt. He tried to touch it, but his hands had been manacled together. He moved his leg and felt the shackles on his ankles. As in his worst nightmare, he was shackled to Hark.

Hark said bitterly, "Because of you, they treat us like runaways and criminals and shackle all of us."

Jonas turned his head. Levi's gang filled the wagon,

ten men shackled so tightly that they could barely move. One of them, a man who had offered Jonas whiskey on Saturday nights and who had greeted him pleasantly in church, now said angrily, "Nigger, this all your fault."

Levi spoke, able to make his voice carry even in a low tone. "You all damn fools. They come here with those shackles. They know we don't go willingly. They ready to treat us all like criminals. All you niggers, you shut up."

They rode painfully in the carts to Yazoo City, where they were loaded onto a steamboat, still shackled, to sit on the lower level, which usually carried cargo. Jonas's head still hurt. When a soldier brought food, another undid the manacles on their hands so they could eat their luke-warm peas and dry cornbread. Jonas pushed his away, too miserable to eat. He couldn't lie down. He couldn't move without discomfort. Hark stared at him in disgust, even after Jonas said, "Take my portion. Can't even look at it."

He could look out at the river, and he watched it go by, the water too murky to sparkle in the sun. He'd been told that the Yazoo was called after an Indian word that meant "river of death." He stared at the opaque brown river, his ears aching with the roar of the engines, his eyes burning with coal smoke. He wished he could sleep. He closed his eyes, and Hark shoved him. "Don't you fall asleep and sprawl on me!"

Jonas opened his eyes and watched as the steamboat roiled the water, making it even muddier.

WHEN THEY ARRIVED IN Vicksburg, they were un-loaded like cargo, their hands shackled again, and they were loaded into another cart driven by a soldier. Levi asked him softly, "Suh, where we go?"

"There's a camp next to the earthworks for you niggers."

Jonas slumped, as much as he could without making Hark angrier with him, and Vicksburg passed by in a blur.

Still in the cart, they jolted down the road eastward until they came to the embankments. The cart followed the curve of the fortifications that had already been dug and stopped at a large expanse of trammeled dirt. On it milled a crowd of ill-clad Black men who greeted the new-comers with derision.

"You all shackled up!" one of them catcalled. "What you do to be shackled up?"

Soldiers stood at the edge of the crowd, rifles over their shoulders, watching.

The cart stopped, and the carter pulled them out with some difficulty since they were still shackled together. Jonas stood uncomfortably close to Hark, who regarded him with disgust. He shivered despite the coat he'd been wearing when he was taken from the field in Yazoo County. His wrists ached, and his hands were stiff with cold.

One of the soldiers, a sergeant by the stripes on his sleeve, strode toward the new arrivals. He glanced at the shackles. "They give you trouble?" the sergeant asked.

"Not after I chain them up," the carter said. "They're all yours now."

The sergeant beckoned one of the soldiers, and the soldier unlocked the shackles. Hark jerked away from Jo-nas, still mad, as Jonas rubbed his wrists, which had been chafed raw. As the men were unshackled, the soldiers moved in, their hands resting on their rifle straps.

The sergeant said, "If anyone gives me any trouble, those shackles can go back on." He had a weather-beaten face, hair of no particular color, and eyes that were a pale blue. He looked as though he'd been an overseer before the war, the kind who hated his work and loathed the men he supervised. "I'm Sergeant Peyton, and you'll address me as sir." He glared at them and said, "What do you say to me?"

They murmured, "Sergeant, suh."

"Can't hear you."

Jonas shouted with the rest of them. "Sergeant, suh!"

Peyton turned to the nearest soldier. "Get these men settled. They'll be assigned to a gang tomorrow."

Levi said timidly, "Sergeant, suh. Who drive us?"

"Did I speak to you?"

"No, suh."

"I'll tell you what to do, and you'll do it. Now shut up, all of you."

The soldiers herded them away, and Jonas glanced at the impassive white faces above the gray uniforms. His eyes lingered on the rifles. *Would these men shoot an unruly man? Would they destroy a massa's property like that?* Jonas wondered.

They were frog-marched to a cluster of makeshift little huts. Jonas had seen henhouses better built. One of the soldiers said, "You'll sleep here. Four men inside."

Jonas, Hark, Levi, and Pompey, who had once offered Jonas whiskey in amity, entered the hut. It was windowless and dark inside. The floor was bare dirt. There were no bedrolls and no blankets. Still timid, Levi asked the soldier who stood in the door, "Do we get bedding, suh?"

"You? No. Make do." And he left them there.

Hark asked, "How we sleep in here? Can barely fit all of us to stand."

Levi said weakly, "I guess we make do."

Dinner that night was scant. The dish of peas and dry cornbread on the boat had been a harbinger of their rations here. Hark stared at the meager portion on the tin plate and asked, "How we work with only this to eat?" He glared at Levi. "Don't say make do."

Levi was silent.

That night, they arranged themselves on the dirt floor. They were packed close enough to catch each other's breath and body odor. Hark, who seemed eager to complain, said, "Any man fart in here, he rue it."

Pompey, whose good cheer had melted away, said irritably to Hark, "Why don't you shut up?"

Jonas stretched out on the dirt. The ground felt cold and hard. He was uncomfortably close to Hark, but whenever he tried to roll away, Hark said, "Quit that. You wake me up every time you move."

Jonas lay as still as he could. His head still ached. He never thought that he would recall his cabin on the Yazoo County plantation with longing, but he let himself grieve for the loss of a straw mattress, a wool blanket, and Hark's voice wishing him a good night.

Breakfast was no better than supper had been: the same small ration of peas and pone. They ate outside surrounded by the strangers who had jeered at them the day before. The sky was overcast, and it was unseasonably cold for winter in Mississippi. The strangers were clad only in their shirts. One of the strangers asked them, "Why you have your coats?"

Hark said, "We wear them when we taken away."

The stranger stared at their shoes. "Decent shoes, too." He stretched out his feet, and they saw how his shoes were worn through in the sole and bound with a rag.

Jonas thought of Christmas Day in Yazoo County, when massa had handed out the new shoes as a gift.

Hark asked, "They don't give you shoes? Or a coat?"

The stranger laughed, an ugly sound. "They don't give us nothing," he said. He laughed again. "No, I wrong about that. They give us all a shovel."

After breakfast, Sergeant Peyton returned. With him was a young man in a coat with gold braid on his sleeves. Under his cap, his hair glinted gold, too, as did the hilt of the sword at his side. He regarded the new arrivals. "Are they in order, Sergeant?"

"Yes, sir."

Jonas relished hearing the sergeant say "sir."

The officer faced the men and said, "I'm Captain Frederick Grenville, and I'm in charge of the effort to build the fortifications. You are my men, and I expect a good report of you."

Jonas thought, *You ain't my massa. And I ain't a soldier. Good report! Got them soldiers fire a report from them rifles.* But he kept his face impassive. He recognized the officer as he had recognized the sergeant. Young massa, who grew up on a big plantation but who had never walked the field or talked to a driver. He let the overseer do his work for him, whether it was the good, clean work of hoeing or picking cotton or the dirty work of jailing and whipping.

They each received a shovel, and Sergeant Peyton showed them where to dig. He watched them long enough to make sure they knew what they were doing, and he left behind an armed soldier to make sure they kept up their effort and pace.

At the midday break, Jonas, still sore from the blow to his head and the journey in the wagon, whispered to Levi, "Feel like we in jail."

"Hush," Levi said, too cowed to speak above a whisper.

THEY WORKED ALL DAY Saturday, and dinner that night was no better than any other. Hark stared at his plate and said, "Wish to God I had a spot of whiskey."

The man with the ruined shoes said, "You think they let us have whiskey?"

"They let us go to church?"

"No," the man said.

"Can't get damned or saved," Hark said.

The man shook his head.

Jonas, who had become quiet again, suddenly felt too much emotion to stay silent. He began to hum. Levi hummed, too. Hark caught the melody and began to sing softly. Pompey added his harmony, and they raised their voices together, as they had in their church back in Yazoo County. The stranger began to sing, and more men drifted over, drawn by the singing. They added their voices as well, and soon the refrain of "Roll, Jordan, Roll" sounded through the group.

When the song ended, another refrain rose: "Lonesome Valley."

Jonas sang and thought his heart might break. He was

in the lonesome valley, and he had no idea if he would ever emerge from it.

The singing drew a crowd of soldiers. It drew Sergeant Peyton. And it drew Captain Grenville, who put his hand on Peyton's shoulder to restrain him when he started forward. The captain listened to the singing with a wistful look on his face. He said to Peyton, "The people on my place sang like that."

Jonas wished that he had drowned on the river of death and had never come here.

Awake, he didn't let himself think of Pen. It was too hard to remember the man he had been: able to court his sweetheart, able to cleave to his beloved in the middle of the night. Now he was driven like a mule and treated worse than a mule. It was hard to feel like a man.

Cold, hungry, sore, and weary, he lay on the ground to sleep. To his surprise, he dreamed of Pen. She didn't speak. She appeared before him in a cloud of light, her shape shimmering. "Is you alive?" he said in his dream. "Is you all right?" She didn't reply. She faded away, until he found himself staring at thin air.

He woke weeping, and Levi said irritably, "Shut that up. We trying to sleep."

DAY TO DAY, THE captain, a softhearted young massa, was far away. Sergeant Peyton was their daily cross to bear. Hark muttered. Levi whispered. Jonas put his head down and tried to endure.

On the plantation, the rhythm of the crops, cotton and corn, marked the passing of time and gave it shape.

Here, the days and weeks ran into each other. How long had he been here? He didn't know.

More slaves arrived at the camp, and all the sergeants who acted as overseers, including Peyton, were stretched too thin. Jonas was glad to see how Peyton ran himself ragged, trying to supervise five gangs at once. He muttered to Levi, "If he had a grain of sense, he'd find a driver."

Levi, who was still sore at being demoted to a hand with a shovel, said, "He too damn stupid to allow it."

But someone wasn't, because Captain Grenville intervened. On a chilly day in February, before they began their work, Captain Grenville arrived with a Black man in tow. He said, "Sergeant Peyton, you can't oversee so many men. I've assigned you have a driver to work this gang."

Peyton said stiffly, "Yes, sir."

At the sight of the new driver, Jonas raised his head in surprise. It was Gabriel, the driver from Yazoo City, who had boasted about being a good enough carpenter to build an ark. Gabriel regarded his gang and took in their condition and their misery. "All of you, tell me your names and where you hail from."

When it was Jonas's turn, Gabriel said, "I know this man and the man next to him. Jonas, ain't it, and Hark? I work with them in Yazoo City. We build the ship *Arkansas* together. Dig many a hole and fell many a tree."

It was the first moment of warmth that Jonas had felt since he came to Vicksburg. He said, "You drive us?"

Gabriel shook his head, taking in the threadbare, dirty clothes and the look of hunger. "I do my best to take care of you."

Gabriel, who had been managing his master for years, did his best to soften the rough edges of their army overseer. With a quiet voice and a manner that let Sergeant Peyton believe he had thought of it, Gabriel asked for a little more food. And got it. It was still peas and cornbread but in bigger portions. He asked for blankets. They got horse blankets, which smelled so bad that everyone suspected they'd been taken off dead horses, but they were better than shivering at night. Gabriel also encouraged Sergeant Peyton to allow the men more frequent breaks, and as the weather warmed, more water.

Jonas watched Gabriel with surprise. He hadn't believed that anyone could sway the sergeant. After the day's work was done, Jonas lingered, and Gabriel walked with him to their hut.

Jonas asked Gabriel, "How you do that?"

"What?"

"Make the sergeant do your bidding, and all the time he think it were his idea."

"Get round a white man? Been doing that all my life."

"Don't it make you mad?"

"It work, don't it?"

Jonas considered this.

Gabriel said, "You still down in the mouth, son?"

"Farther down than that," Jonas said.

"Always reason for hope," Gabriel said.

"I know about them gunboats on the river," Jonas said. "They still far away."

Gabriel dropped his voice. "You don't hear about the Proclamation?"

Dimly, he recalled Caleb's crazy talk. "What Proclamation?"

"That we free."

Jonas snorted. "We as free as a mule yoked to another mule, and both of them harnessed to an army cart."

Gabriel dropped his voice still lower. "From Washington. From the president himself. On New Year's Day, he say that we slaves are free."

"You crazy."

"Crazy to hope, maybe. But not crazy to know."

Jonas gestured toward the embankments. "If you let them know what you know, they put the hurt to you."

Gabriel smiled. Such a subtle smile for such a rough-looking man. "I know what to say to a white man and what not to."

Jonas let himself smile a little, too.

Gabriel said quietly, "Let me know if I can help you."

Jonas nearly said, "Send me back to the Newell place," but he did not. He let himself think that Gabriel might be able to help him. He asked, "You ever leave anyone behind?"

"Yes," Gabriel said, and not more.

He was reluctant to remember, but Jonas pressed him. "What happen?"

"Twice. Sold away from my mama and daddy when I was a boy and sold away from my wife and children when I was a man. Who you leave behind?"

He let himself feel it, a rush of love and pain. "My wife. Pen. Penelope. She carry our baby when they took me." He looked away, then said in a throaty voice, "Do it ever go away?"

Gabriel didn't move. For a long moment, he didn't speak. Finally he said, "No, son. It do not."

GABRIEL'S SUCCESS IN IMPROVING their material lot affected Hark, too. One evening, he sidled up to Gabriel to ask, "Might a man make a request of you?"

"You can request all you like. Whether you get what you want, that a different matter."

"Might we get some whiskey, like the soldiers do?"

"You thirsty?"

Hark's eyes gleamed. "For more than whiskey," he said. "Is it true that the army employ laundresses from the town? That they come here every week to do the officers' wash?"

Gabriel laughed. "You want a gal to wash them rags of yours?"

Hark stretched out his arms and looked at the rips in his sleeves. "No," he said. "I want a gal to talk to. To see if she want to get friendly."

Gabriel roared with laughter. "Man, even the soldiers have to be content with each other," he said. "You want me to smuggle in a gal for you?"

"I know where they bring the wash," Hark said. "Just want to stop by. Find a reason. You clever that way."

"Clever enough to know that the sergeant would have my hide for it, along with yours," Gabriel said. "And don't try to sneak and creep to do it."

Hark went away, downcast. Jonas, who had been listening to this exchange, said, "Why don't you help him?"

"What, you want to see a gal too?"

"No," Jonas said. "Don't want any gal besides my wife."

"Wife? The one you never see again?"

"We still married, Pen and I," Jonas said. "Nothing change that."

"How you figure that, son?"

Jonas said, "A man might seek his family, if he can."

Gabriel looked at him in surprise.

"If he free," Jonas said, very softly.

A few days later, when Sergeant Peyton came by to tell them to quit for the day, Gabriel leaned on his shovel and bent his head in deference. He said, "Sergeant, suh, I have a notion. Might help the men work better."

"What is it?"

Overhearing, Jonas marveled at Gabriel's delivery. He should be in a theatrical, like the ones the soldiers put on when they were bored. "Well, suh, I see how the soldiers have a spot of whiskey of a Saturday night. See how it cheer them after a week of soldiering. These men"—he nodded in the direction of his gang—"they work hard all week. Don't have much to cheer them. Suh, might you consider, in the kindness of your heart, to allow them a spot of whiskey, too?"

The sergeant stared at Gabriel. He said, "Stop toadying me, you damn oily nigger. Give these men strong drink? I won't hear of it. Do you want me to tell the captain? He'll be glad to punish the lot of you."

Gabriel bent his head. "Didn't mean to give offense. Sorry, Sergeant, suh."

"Whiskey for a bunch of niggers who want to run off.

Who think about caving our heads in with them shovels. Spot of whiskey!"

Jonas thought, *Why didn't I think to cave his head in with the shovel?* He snorted at his own thought. *Because someone would shoot me dead and laugh at my massa when he ask for recompense.*

The sergeant said to Jonas, "Hey. You. What are you sniggering about?"

Jonas thought, *I can play Br'er Rabbit, too.* "Laughing at the notion of us niggers drinking whiskey," he said, in as mild a tone as he could manage.

"I don't trust you either," the sergeant said. He raised his voice and looked over the gang, who were all leaning on their shovels and listening to this exchange with their eyes down. "Whiskey! Shut up, all of you."

THAT SATURDAY NIGHT, AFTER their meager dinner, Gabriel's gang sat on the ground near their huts. Jonas felt too tired to talk, but one of the men began to hum. All of them knew that song. It called on Gabriel to blow his trumpet so the sound could bring them home to Jerusalem. Every man knew the message beneath the hymn. Hark joined in the singing, although Gabriel himself did not. When the song ended, Hark nodded to Gabriel and rose.

"Where you go?" Gabriel asked.

Hark said, "Find Jerusalem," and he walked into the darkness.

Jonas asked, "You go after him?"

"No. No need. He won't get far."

But he hadn't returned by the time the men wearied of singing and retired into their huts to wrap themselves in their malodorous blankets. Jonas stretched out on the hard ground. He fell into a light, uncomfortable sleep.

The commotion woke him immediately. Hark was outside, yelling and obviously drunk. "Can't a man have a spot of whiskey?"

Jonas ran outside to see Sergeant Peyton holding Hark by the arm, saying, "What did I say about whiskey, nigger?"

Gabriel sidled up to the sergeant. "Suh," he said.

"This ain't your worry," the sergeant said.

"He's just a fool nigger from the country. Couldn't help himself."

"Of course he could," the sergeant growled. "Damn deceitful lying bastard. What did I tell all of you about whiskey?"

"Suh, I know he ain't a soldier, but if he was, what would you do to him?"

"He ain't a soldier. He's a damn nigger."

"Suh. Don't whup him. You can whup me. Since he in my gang."

"I might. After I deal with him. He's going into the stockade tonight, and tomorrow we'll punish him."

HARK SPENT THE NIGHT locked up, and in the morning, Gabriel went in search of Captain Grenville, who appreciated the sound of Black voices raised in song. Gabriel wasn't gone long. He returned trailing behind the captain, who looked furious and was saying, "Where's Sergeant Peyton?"

"Here, sir."

Captain Grenville didn't stand on ceremony. He walked up to Peyton and spoke in an icy voice that carried so that every Black man in the vicinity could hear it. "What is this? You locked up a negro man because he took a nip of whiskey?"

"After I forbade it, sir."

"Clearly you've never managed a negro in your life. If a negro wants to drink a little on a Saturday night, let him. And for God's sake, don't treat him with a heavy hand. The rest of them will take notice, believe me. They'll malinger. They'll shirk. They'll never take an order from you again."

Peyton blushed a deep red, like a turkey cock's comb. "I was following your orders, sir."

"I ordered you to supervise these men to work. Not to treat them like criminals for acting like negroes do."

"What do you want me to do, sir?"

The captain glared at his subordinate. "Let the man out of the stockade," he said. "Forget this ever happened. And if a negro man wants a spot of whiskey of a Saturday night, let him have it."

"Yes, sir," Peyton said, so red that he looked like he might have apoplexy.

After that, Peyton watched Hark all the time. Hark said to Jonas, "He don't bother me. But he have his eyes on me, and it feel wrong."

Jonas was surprised that Hark would confide in him. He said, "The captain humiliate him over you, and he don't forget it."

"I should keep my head down. Like you do."

Jonas thought of the Saturday nights on the Newell place, when Hark preened and beamed and danced with every woman who would take his hand. He shook his head.

Hark said, "Like this." He hung his head, dropped his eyes, and let his tongue loll out, as though he were a panting dog.

"Not like that," Jonas said.

Hark recovered. He said, "You forgive me for what I say to you when we taken away?"

"I forgive you for the way you acted since," Jonas said.

But that day, when Hark took the second break of the afternoon, Peyton walked up to him and said, "Are you malingering, nigger?"

"No, suh," Hark said. "Just thirsty. Gabriel, he tell us to drink water when we thirsty."

"He ain't over you. I am."

Gabriel, who had the driver's sixth sense for knowing when to intervene, said, "Sergeant, suh, please let the man have a cup of water."

"Get back to work," the sergeant said.

Hark raised the cup to his lips. The sergeant dashed it away. Hark said, "I wasn't too happy when you tell me not to drink whiskey. But can't work if you tell me not to drink water."

The sergeant raised his hand and slapped Hark across the face. Hark stood still for a moment. Then he turned his back on Sergeant Peyton.

"Hey! Don't you disrespect me like that!"

Hark didn't turn around. He walked away.

Peyton didn't run after him. He shouted, "I ain't finished with you!"

HARK DISAPPEARED THAT AFTERNOON. He never returned to the hut. The next morning, he was still gone. Jonas was sick to his stomach. He asked Gabriel, "Where is he?"

Gabriel looked as though he'd been kicked by a mule. He said, "Could have fallen into the river. Could have been the victim of foul play. Could have run off. Don't know."

That day, Captain Grenville ordered a group of scouts to look for Hark. He said to them, "Don't harm him. If he's run away, bring him back in one piece."

They looked all day and through the night.

The next morning, they found Hark's body in a hole next to an abandoned embankment. The soldiers brought him back to the slave laborers' quarters. They had carried him in a horse blanket and dumped it on the ground. The slave laborers stood back, afraid to look. Jonas pushed through the crowd. One of the soldiers asked, "Nigger, what are you doing?"

Gabriel was at his elbow, holding on to it. He pressed forward and said, "This man were in my gang."

"What do you know about it?"

"Not a thing," Gabriel said. Jonas struggled in Gabriel's grasp.

"Who's that?" the soldier asked.

"He work with the man. Come from the same place."

"Does he know anything?"

"No," Gabriel said.

"Let me see him," Jonas said softly.

The soldier shrugged.

He had been badly beaten. His face was bruised and bloody, his eyes puffed shut, his cheeks split, his hair matted with blood. His shirt was a bloody rag.

Jonas raised appalled eyes to Gabriel's, and Gabriel understood. They both knew who had killed Hark.

Captain Grenville came to the building site and pulled Sergeant Peyton aside. "Do you know anything about the man who died?"

"No," the sergeant said.

Jonas leaned on his shovel and wished he had the courage to use it to cave Sergeant Peyton's head in.

Captain Grenville was in a rage. "Do you know what a slave like that is worth?"

The sergeant spat. "What a dead nigger is worth?"

"I don't know about you," the captain said, "but I mustered in to defend slavery."

"I didn't," the sergeant said.

"Now I have to write to the man's master and tell him that we injured his valuable property—damaged his valuable property." He raised his voice and leaned so close that he could spit on the sergeant's face. "Murdered his valuable property."

But the matter ended there. No one questioned Sergeant Peyton, and no one thought to relieve him of his duties as an overseer. Peyton himself ordered the gang to bury Hark. Hark was buried on the fort's grounds but not in its cemetery. The men who had dug fortifications with him also dug his grave. Peyton watched as they dug, as they did day after day, and he continued to watch as they buried Hark, still wrapped in the horse blanket, without ceremony.

Afterward, Jonas seethed to Gabriel, "We bury him just like you'd bury a mule." Full of bitterness, Jonas said, "If I die here, will I be buried like that? Like a dead mule?"

"We sing at your funeral," Gabriel said. "What you want?"

Jonas said, "Sing 'Steal Away to Jesus' over me. Sing it loud for Captain Grenville."

Gabriel said, "The Federals just down the river at Natchez. They been holding it for a year."

"They ain't here," Jonas said bitterly.

Gabriel said, "Why do you think we build them fortifications? Who they shoot at when they stand behind them?"

Jonas raised his eyes to Gabriel's face. "The Federals."

"How long before they come up the river for Vicksburg?"

Jonas was still bitter. "How long, oh Lord? How long?"

"We bide our time. Just bide our time."

Chapter 8

PEN DREAMED. IT WAS dusk, and she stood on the bank of the river. The grass was cool and muddy under her bare feet. She gazed at the silty water, the greatest expanse of water she had ever seen. The opposite bank was so far away that she could distinguish the trees as only a gray-green blur. Mist rose from the water. Damselflies danced in it, their bodies a jeweled blue even in the low light, their lacy wings a glittering green. The air smelled of longleaf pine, as pungent as turpentine.

As the sun set, the mist turned into fog, the slightest rain on her bare arms. She shivered in the sudden chill. The fog became so dense that she could no longer see the water.

She heard a splashing sound coming closer and closer. She strained to see, but the boat remained invisible until it pulled up to the bank. Well-made but not very big, it was a raft, and on it stood a Black man, his hair long and twisted into locks. He had a seamed, pitted face, and he wore the dress of a field hand: an osnaburg shirt, unusually white and clean, and nankeen trousers. In his hands he wielded a pole that he used to pull the raft to the edge of the bank and moor it.

"You come with me," he said, and this close, she realized how much he looked like her stepfather. For a long moment, she missed him sorely.

She asked, "Where do we go?"

He gestured with his chin. "Across the river."

She clambered onto the raft and stood beside him as he navigated through the fog. "How do you know where to go?"

"I know."

The river was still, without any current. The water was too murky to see if there were fish in the depths. A pair of froglike eyes emerged from the water, then a pebbled snout. "What's that?" Pen asked.

The raftman smiled. "Gator," he said. "Gator can take a man down, if he want."

"Will he bother us?" Pen asked, as the scaly body emerged too, then the long tail.

"No," the raftman said.

Pen raised her eyes. Now they were close enough to see the trunks of the trees on the shore. Tall pines, like the ones in the Alabama forest. She asked, "Where do you take me?"

He smiled again. "The other shore."

"Why?"

He didn't reply. They continued in silence until the bank was in sight. He pulled the raft onto a sandy spit. "You here," he said. "You go."

"Alone?" Pen asked.

"Only way to go."

Reluctantly, she stepped from the raft onto the sand. It shifted under her feet, making it hard to take a step. She turned to say to the raftman, "Wait for me!"

But he was already pulling away. "Don't wait for anyone."

She peered beyond the spit into the trees. The sight was familiar. It was the piney woods again, the one she had wandered through before Toby found her.

As she hesitated, she heard the call of a horned owl: the bird that Jonas had taught her to recognize and that he loved because the birds were faithful unto death.

She walked into the woods.

She tried to find a way through the trees that grew so close together. She strained to squeeze through them. She struggled until she came to a clearing, where a woman sat.

She wore her gray hair in a neat braid around her head, and her calico dress was spotless. She turned, and Pen cried out, "Mama!"

Her mother rose and held out her arms. "Pen, sugar, so good to see you!"

"Mama, what are you doing here?"

"Waiting for you," her mother said, smiling, and she enfolded Pen in her embrace.

Pen breathed in the familiar smell of woodsmoke and her mother's only extravagance in life, lavender soap. "I've missed you so."

"I know," her mother said, stroking her hair.

"Can I stay here with you?"

Her mother let her go. "Not yet," she said. "Your journey ain't over yet." She smiled again, and walked away, into the woods, disappearing in the dark.

"Mama!" Pen cried, and the grief hit her all over again, as painful as the day her mother died. Pen wept, the sobs tearing at her chest.

Then she heard a child's laughter. She turned her head.

Just outside the clearing, at the base of a tall pine tree, a little boy played. He was bathed in moonlight; she could see the fine wiry curls on his head, the dimples in his hands, and the sweep of his cheekbone, which had just lost its baby fat. He rose. He was old enough to toddle, and he toddled toward her.

Her hand went to her mouth. If her son had lived, he would be just this age.

The little boy came closer, and she saw how much he looked like Jonas. The beautiful brown skin, soft on a child's body. The dark, understanding eyes, too old for such a little boy. The smile, sweet despite all the world's pain.

She knelt and reached out her arms for him. She couldn't call him by name; he had never had a name. But he was her son.

He stopped short. He didn't speak. She didn't move. And as she stared at him, he turned away, as her mother had.

"Don't go," she pleaded, but he didn't heed her, any more than her mother had, and he disappeared into the woods.

WHEN PEN WOKE, SHE was in a real bed with a mattress. Her head lay on a feather pillow that smelled of lavender. Her hands rested on a quilt, the cotton soft under her fingers. The room, which had glass windows, was filled with light, and through the open windows came the scent of magnolia.

At her bedside sat a woman with brown skin light enough to show a spray of freckles over her nose. She wore a pretty calico dress, and she was smiling. "You wake up," she said.

"Where am I?" Pen asked.

"We shelter runaways here. You safe with us."

"How long I been here?"

"A while. You give us a fright. You mighty sick. How you feel?"

Pen tried to sit up, and her shoulder protested. She winced and touched it, feeling the bandage beneath her nightdress. "Not sure yet."

"What's your name? It bother us, all of us, not to be able to call you by name when you had the fever."

"Pen," she said. "Penelope Mitchell. Who are you?"

"My name Kate Garnett," she said. "Don't try to get up. You ain't ready for it."

It began to come back to her. She cried out, "Where's my dog?"

"Right here. He sleep at your feet." She touched Toby's head. He woke and shook himself. At the sight of Pen being awake, he picked his way across the covers, as though he were afraid to hurt her.

Kate said, "Wouldn't leave you, not for a moment."

Pen raised her hand to rub Toby's head, and he licked her hand in relief. She had never felt anything so welcome.

"What your dog called?" Kate asked. "Felt bad about not knowing that, too."

"Toby," she said, cradling him with her good arm.

Kate let her rest, then brought her a bowl of broth. Pen said, "You kill that chicken for me?"

"That chicken die of old age," Kate said. "But we put it to good use, feeding you."

Pen sat up, wincing at the pain in her shoulder. She asked Kate, "How bad was I hurt?"

"More nasty than bad," Kate said. "But it tore you up."

"Will I be all right?"

"Sore and stiff for a while. But I believe you heal all right." Kate asked, "You need any help with the bowl?"

"Think I can manage." Pen lifted the spoon with her good arm. She closed her eyes with the pleasure of eating. "That's good." Toby, always interested in food, nosed her leg.

Laughing, Kate patted Toby on the back. "No, that ain't for you," she said. To Pen, she said, "I feed him just now. He's funning you."

Pen let the spoon rest in the bowl. "He save my life more than once," she said, her voice shaking.

Kate said, "You eat and rest up some more before you tell your story. This ain't the time to remember something that trouble you."

When Pen was finished, she asked Kate, "Who live in this house?"

"I do," Kate said. "This my house that my daddy build for us, when he was with us."

"Gone now?"

"Lived a good life," Kate said. "My mama did, too. Now I stay here."

"What is this place? Who live here?"

"Runaways, like I tell you before, and other people who don't fit anywhere else. Most of the folks here were in slavery, and they run away. My mama was a slave, but my daddy was a white man. No, not like you think. He love my mama; he want to live with her, husband and wife. So he come here, and they welcome him. He belong here, as much as anyone."

Pen said, "I met some runaways before I came here."

"Slaves?"

"Deserters." She tried to keep her voice level, but at the memory of Jasper and Lucas, her eyes filled. "We travel together, help each other."

Kate said, "You call out for Jasper in your fever."

"He was one of them."

Kate laid her hand on Pen's good arm. Pen remembered her mother's embrace from her dream. Her eyes filled again at the kindness of Kate's touch. Kate said, "You ain't all right. Still all shook up. You rest and get better, and then you confess all you want."

PEN RESTED, AND KATE brought her food, progressing from the invalid's broth to the meat of the unfortunate chicken with a slice of white bread beside it. Pen asked, "How do you come by white wheaten bread?"

"We grow a little wheat," Kate said. "Grow everything we need. Wheat, corn, vegetables. Keep chickens and pigs. Have a creek nearby, Rushing Water Creek. Full of fish."

"You grow any cotton?"

"Why would we? We can sell corn and hog meat if we need to."

"How you buy anything if you secret in the woods like this?"

"Have friends who can go into town for us," she said, smiling.

"Do they hate slavery?"

"Don't care for it. Not many do, in this part of the world." She smiled again. "Besides, some of those folks is my relations. Blood do tell."

Toby, who was also recuperating by sleeping on the bed next to Pen, opened his eyes and flicked his ears. She touched him, reassuring herself that they were both all right.

"When your dog feel like it, I take him out," Kate said. "We have a passel of dogs here. He can frisk with them."

Pen crooned to Toby, "Would you like that? Do you want to play with other dogs?" Toby licked her hand. "We both stay here for a bit before we frisk."

Kate said, "Would you like me to stay with you?"

"Don't have to."

"I did, when you so sick with the fever."

"That's kind of you. But you don't have to stay with me unless you want to."

"I set quiet. You sleep, if you want to."

Pen lay back on the pillow. She felt pleasantly drowsy, but sleep wouldn't come. Kate sat in the chair by the bed. She glanced at Pen, then pulled a book from her pocket and began to read.

Pen asked, "What you read?"

Kate held up the book. It was small enough to fit into the palm of her hand. "A book of poems by Mr. Walt Whitman."

"You can read," Pen said, in awe.

"We all can," Kate said. "Man, woman, and child. You can't read?"

"No," Pen said. Longing swept through her. "But I would dearly love to."

Kate laughed. "When you feel better, I can teach you."

"To read them poems?"

"Start with something easier. Have a picture book we use for the children. Teach you from that."

Pen shook her head. "What kind of a place is this?"

"Special place," Kate said, her eyes gleaming.

WHEN PEN COULD MANAGE to stay awake for several hours running, Kate deemed her well enough for visitors. Pen asked, "Who visit me here? I'm a stranger."

"You see," Kate said.

As soon as he came into the room, she remembered him. She blurted out, "You rescue me!" In daylight, he was strikingly handsome, with high cheekbones and keen eyes so dark that they looked black. He had a nose as proud as an eagle's beak, and he bore himself with the princely posture that she had seen even in her haze of pain and fear.

He said, "So you're Penelope."

She was suddenly embarrassed to talk to him lying down and wearing nothing but her nightdress. She tried to sit up and pull the quilt over her. It was a painful effort.

"No, don't trouble yourself. Kate tell me that you ain't all right yet." He said, "My name Denmark Avery."

Kate said, "Denmark the closest we got to a mayor here."

Pen was too surprised to take in the thought of a Black

man as a mayor of a town. She said, "Denmark? Never heard that for a name before."

He sat in the bedside chair and smiled. His teeth were a dazzling white. "My mama was from South Carolina," he said. "She name me for Denmark Vesey, who lead a slave rebellion in Charleston. He a hero to the slaves in Carolina."

Pen felt light-headed and lost her manners. She asked the first thing that came into her mouth. "Did he free them?"

"No," Denmark said. "But he put the fear of God into the massas, and he help the slaves stand tall and proud. That's why we remember him, to this day."

Pen couldn't bear to lie flat in the presence of a handsome man who was trying to charm her. She forced herself to sit up and remembered to pull the quilt to her chin. "We all free now."

His eyes gleamed. "You hear?"

"President Lincoln proclaim it." And she was overcome with the emotion of it and of everything she couldn't yet speak of. She lay back on the pillow and closed her eyes.

"Denmark, you tire her," Kate said.

"Kate, you like a mother hen," he said. He rose, smiling. "When you feel better, Miss Penelope, we talk again."

THAT AFTERNOON, AS PEN dozed, she started awake, thinking of Denmark Avery. *Shame on you*, she told herself. *Married to Jonas and thinking of Mr. Avery, just because he handsome and smile at you.* She remembered the feeling of his arms around her when he rescued her, and she felt the heat that meant a blush, even if it didn't show on her skin.

That evening, when Kate brought her dinner, Pen was fully awake. For the first time since she had recovered from her fever, she was restless. She asked Kate, "What you bring me tonight?"

"Ham and black-eyed peas," Kate said.

"What happen to the wheaten bread?"

Kate laughed. "You ain't an invalid anymore. Good, plain heavy food all right for you now."

Pen let Kate settle the tray on her lap. She said, "I never ate so much meat before."

"Thought so," Kate said. "Peas and cornbread, weren't it?"

Pen had to finish chewing before she could talk. The ham was succulent, flavored with acorns and pinecones. The pigs must roam in the woods. "Yes," she said. "And a little bit of barbecue a few times a year."

"Where do you hail from?"

"Georgia. Dougherty County, not too far from the Alabama border."

"What bring you across the border?"

She thought of Jonas, and she remembered the child in the dream with Jonas's face. She winced.

Kate said, "Shouldn't press you. Eat your dinner."

Pen ate. When she was finished, she said, "You mighty easy with Mr. Denmark."

"I know him all my life," Kate said.

She was light-headed again. "Were you ever sweet on him? Or him on you?"

"Lord, no," Kate said. "He like a brother to me."

"Are you married?"

"No, hasn't been my fate in life."

That an odd way to put it, Pen thought. "Why don't you ask me the same?"

"Because if you run away, you leave someone behind. A world of hurt in that." Kate's eyes, a light brown flecked with copper, gleamed in her ivory-skinned face.

"I am married," Pen said. "Don't matter where he is now. Still married. Always married."

"You feel strong enough to confess?" Kate asked, her voice soft.

"Yes," Pen said, and she told Kate why she had left Georgia.

Kate listened quietly. Then she said, "If you intend to walk to Mississippi, you stay here long enough to build up your strength."

WITHIN A FEW DAYS, Pen was recovered enough, and impatient enough, to get up. She wobbled a little as she swung her legs over the edge of the bed. She wasn't dirty, to her surprise. She blushed, realizing that Kate had likely bathed her when she was feverish. But her skin itched, as though it yearned for soap and water, and her hair felt so dry that she wanted to put her head under a pump. She stood. She had to steady herself by grasping the chair. She waited until her head cleared. She let go of the chair back and took a tentative step.

Kate came into the room and smiled. "You up. You feel all right?"

"Light-headed."

"Take it slow."

"I want to look around," Pen said.

Kate took her arm. "We go for a little walk around the house." She led Pen into the front room, Toby following them, and settled her into the rocking chair before the hearth. "You need a blanket?" Kate asked.

"Thought I was done being an invalid," Pen said.

Toby tucked himself around Pen's feet. Kate laughed. "You got a footwarmer," she said. Toby sighed as he settled.

"Has he been a trouble to you?" Pen asked.

"Not at all. He a good dog. It make me glad to see how much he care for you."

Pen looked around the room. She had never known a Black person to live in a house with four rooms, and glass windows in every one. The rocking chair faced the hearth, where no fire burned in the warmth of spring, and across from it was a wing chair. Pen wondered if the wing chair had belonged to Kate's father and the rocking chair to her mother. She could see them together, the chairs arranged so that they could look up and smile at each other.

Before the hearth lay a rag rug, beaten clean, its colors bright.

Pen turned her head, taking in the dining room table with four chairs around it, and in the corner, saw the shelf full of books. "All them books!" Pen said. "You read all them books yourself?"

"I do."

The door was ajar, and beyond it was the porch. Pen thought of the log cabin she had seen in the piney woods, with the wraparound porch where the woman sat at her sewing. The air that wafted through the open door was warm and fragrant. Magnolia and something else fragrant but unfamiliar. She sat still for a moment and listened to the chirps and calls and trills of birds. It was a luxury to listen without vigilance. For the first time in a very long time, she felt a spark of something besides fear and sadness.

THE NEXT MORNING, SHE got out of bed. She told Kate, "I sit at the table with you if I wash first." When Kate brought her a pitcher of water and a bar of soap, Pen added, "I get dressed too, if you bring me my dress."

Kate said, "Your dress was torn and dirty. Blood all over. I burn it. No matter. I bring you something to wear."

After Pen scoured her skin clean and poured the water over her hair, Kate brought her a chemise, a petticoat, and a calico dress. Everything was fresh and whole, and the calico was stiff with last week's starch. Pen stammered, "Are these your things? I can't take them."

"Of course you take them, unless you want to greet strangers in your nightdress," Kate said, smiling.

Pen sat down on the bed, undone. "Why you so kind to me?"

Kate sat next to her. "You a runaway. That all we need to know. We take you in, and we help you."

Pen was suddenly overcome. All the weariness of her journey welled up in her, and she slumped forward.

Kate put her arm around Pen and drew her close. She stroked Pen's hair, as Pen's mother had done in her dream. She said, "Let us take care of you. All of us."

That evening, Pen sat on the porch in a cane-bottomed chair, letting the sweet, cool air of late spring flow over her. Toby, well fed by Kate, lounged at her feet, drowsy and content. Pen bent down to rub his head. With affection, she said, "You get fat and lazy, living like this."

Kate had neighbors. The houses in this place were arranged in a neat row along a wide and well-raked street, even if it was unpaved packed dirt. Children played in the street, engrossed in a game of marbles. Dogs wandered among the children, as did hens and shoats. Pigs and dogs were similarly small and dark of coat.

Along the street strolled Denmark Avery, stopping at the game of marbles and bending down to take a turn. He rose to pat a dog and to gently discourage a shoat from investigating his shoes. When he saw Pen, he waved and quickened his pace to bound up the steps. He smiled. "Kate tell me that you better."

"I am." She gestured to the empty chair. "Sit with me?"

"Gladly." He sat. "How do your shoulder feel?"

She tried to raise it. "Sore."

"You use it, it get less sore and less stiff."

"You been wounded?"

He laughed. "You want to see the scars?"

"Depends on where they are," she said, surprising herself.

"Then you won't."

She laughed, too. "Because they private?"

"Now that depend on how close you get," he said, leaning toward her. He had a good smell, a man's musk and the sweet odor of cedar.

Kate came through the door to stand on the porch.

"I hear all that, Denmark," she said, her eyes crinkling in laughter. "You watch it. You make sure Miss Penelope strong enough before you flirt with her."

"She seem to be all right," Denmark said. "Ain't you, Miss Pen?"

Was it disloyal to Jonas to take pleasure in a man's attention? She didn't mean to do more than tease. She felt light and easy in her body. She thought, *Is this what it like to feel happy?* "I am," she said.

SHE LINGERED WITH THE runaways, letting Kate persuade her that she wasn't fit to travel yet. Kate kept her word. From her shelf of books, she pulled a small blue-covered book and opened it to show Pen a picture of a cat. The cat sat on a mat, and it stalked the rat, and soon, Pen knew the alphabet. The letters arranged themselves into words, and Pen flew through the little blue book. She learned to write her name, gripping the pencil with effort. She stared at the letters she had shaped and felt pride suffuse through her. She touched the signature with the tips of her fingers. "Penelope Mitchell," she murmured, as though the writing had a life of its own. A power of its own.

"You mighty quick," Kate said.

"Can I read them poems of yours?"

"Soon," Kate said. "Just a little longer with the cat and the rat."

HER SHOULDER WAS BETTER, but it was still stiff and sore. Kate encouraged her to use the healing left arm, even

though it pained her. She gave Pen a salve made of com-
frey leaves. "Takes away pain," Kate said.

Everything in this place took away pain. The plentiful
food. The kindness. The reading lessons. Even Toby felt at
home here. He joined the pack of dogs in the street and
spent his days playing and pretending to tussle with them.
He was only fooling; they were smaller than he was.

Rushing Water Creek ran so close to the settlement
that Pen could hear it as she sat on Kate's front porch. On
a warm spring morning, Pen felt strong enough to walk
down to the creek. The sight took her breath away. Unlike the pinewoods, a profusion of trees grew along this
bank: oaks and birches familiar from Georgia. Their canopy filtered the light but not the eerie gray-green of the
pines. This was a green suffused with brilliant sunlight.
She made her way along the bank, Toby at her heels, looking for a spot where she could sit and dangle her feet in
the water.

She halted under a birch that bent its branches toward
the water. The ground beneath it was dry and sandy. She
found a spot to sit, and she unlaced her boots and took off
her stockings. She dipped her toes into the water. Satisfied
that it was warm enough, she submerged up to her ankles.
She breathed in the scent of flowers. Near the magnolia,
which had blossoms as wide across as her hand, grew the
fiery red and fiercely fragrant bush that Kate told her was
azalea. She watched the bugs fly over the water. Midges
swarmed and damselflies danced, as in her dream, their
bodies a brilliant blue, their wings a jeweled green. She let
all her muscles ease. She felt as though she had forgotten

how to take a deep breath and had now remembered. Toby, catching her mood, rested his muzzle on her leg. As she stroked his head, he sighed and closed his eyes. He was glad to catch his breath, too.

"Toby, should we stay here?" she asked him.

He opened his eyes at the sound of her voice and closed them again, snuffling a little as he fell asleep.

So peaceful here, she thought. *No slavery here. Everyone free. Everyone know how to read. Everyone so kind to me.* To her surprise, she let herself admit it. *Feel happy here.*

KATE NOTICED HER EASE, and with an eerie accuracy, she answered the question that was uppermost in Pen's mind. "You could stay with us," she said.

"I should go once I get better."

She looked at Pen with her light-colored eyes. Thoughtfully, she said, "If you determined to walk through the countryside, you should learn how to shoot."

Startled, she said, "How would I learn how to shoot?"

"Someone might teach you."

"Could you?"

Kate smiled. "I know how to shoot," she said. "But I know a better teacher."

Denmark had visited often. He continued to tease her, and she teased back. His smile was one of the many things that gave her joy in this place.

On the day he appeared with a rifle slung over his shoulder, she said, "Are you going hunting?"

"No," he said. "Have something else in mind."

"What?" She knew, but it was a pleasure to toy with him a little.

"Someone tell me you want to learn how to handle a rifle," he said.

"Do I?"

He regarded her with those dark, melting eyes, and said, "If you bound and determined to walk through the woods again, I wouldn't want any harm to come to you."

He had readied for her. He had set up a paper target in an open space. "You ain't a danger to anyone here. No matter how bad you shoot."

He showed her how to hold the rifle, then handed it to her.

She said, "Even I can tell that this is a fine new rifle. Where do you get it?"

"We have our ways," Denmark said. "Hold it like I show you."

It wasn't hard to hold the stock in her right hand, but raising her shoulder to rest her left hand on the trigger sent an agony of pain through her shoulder. She bit her lip against it, but she couldn't force her way through it. She dropped her left hand and let the rifle dangle in her right. She gasped, "Can't lift my arm high enough."

"Don't press it."

"How do I get better, if I don't press myself?"

"We take it slow," Denmark said. "We do it day after day, and it get easier." He smiled with too much sweetness for a man talking about target practice. He took the rifle from her.

"Is that a promise?" she asked, with too much warmth for a woman talking about learning to shoot.

"Yes," he said.

DESPITE THE PAIN IN her arm, the shooting lessons were a pleasure, including the pleasure of Denmark's attention. As he had promised her, using her arm and shoulder loosened the mending muscles and diminished the pain.

"Denmark like you," Kate said.

"I know," Pen said. Along with the pleasure, she felt a wash of guilt. She had loved Jonas through so much pain and trouble. How could she let go of his memory, just because she felt good for the first time in a long time?

She said to Kate, "I'm married."

"I know. You already tell me that."

She reminded herself by saying, "Carried away to Mississippi. I go there to find him."

"Well, he ain't here," Kate said, with a gleam in her eye. "And Denmark is. Think about that."

She did, and her awakening bothered her.

HER ARM FELT BETTER, but it still troubled her. After a few tries, she had to lay the rifle on the ground. "It still hurt."

Denmark moved close and gently touched her arm. "Here? Do it hurt here?"

She nodded, and he massaged her upper arm, moving

to her shoulder and then to her back. He asked, "Do that help?"

"Yes. It take the hurt away."

Smiling, he touched her back as though they were dancing. She didn't pull away. He looked into her eyes, smiling, and he leaned forward. He kissed her. His lips tasted sweet. She didn't resist, and as the pleasure of his hands and his mouth suffused through her, she thought of the last time a man touched her like this.

Jonas, the night before he was sold away.

She raised her good arm and laid her hand on his chest. She was gentle, but her meaning was clear: to push him away.

He stepped back, searching her face.

She said, "I wish it could be. But it can't."

"Why not?"

She met his eyes. "Don't Kate tell you I'm married?"

"I thought your man was sold away."

"He was. But I still married."

He let her go. She took a deep breath. "I tell you the story." She told him about Jonas, and the telling made him real again.

Denmark was silent.

She said, "That's why I can't say yes." As soon as she spoke, she realized that she was refusing more than Denmark's seductive sweetness. She was refusing to stay with the runaways, by their rushing creek, in this place that was a refuge from slavery and war.

She had to resume her journey.

She laid her hand on Denmark's cheek to diminish the

sadness she felt. "I bound for Mississippi," she said. "I have to go."

BEFORE SHE LEFT, KATE altered two of her dresses and gave them to Pen. She insisted that Pen keep the chemise and the petticoat, too. She also found her a straw hat with a broad brim. "Keep the sun off your face."

Denmark gave her a stout leather bag with a strap that she could sling over her good shoulder. It was heavy. He said, "Put a few things in there for you."

She reached into the bag. She pulled out a knotted handkerchief. By the feel of it, it was full of coins.

"Ten silver dollars," he said. "You can sew them into your dress, if you want to. Keep them safer."

"I can't take this."

"If you love me, you can," he said. "That bag ain't empty yet. Keep looking."

She pulled out a piece of paper, folded small. "What is this?"

"Unfold it."

It was a map, showing her how to chart her path through Alabama. "Them places that are marked with an X. What are they?"

"Places where we have friends. They can shelter you."

Her eyes brimmed with tears. "Don't know how to thank you."

"Keep looking. You might get a notion."

Something small and round. Metal, cool to the touch.

"A compass," Denmark said. "So you always know where you are."

She turned it in her hands and watched with surprise as the needle pointed north.

"You ain't finished yet."

The heaviest thing had settled on the bottom of the bag. She knew what it was without seeing it. She curled her fingers around the handle and drew it out. It was a pistol.

"Wish we could give a rifle, but this safer. Protect you from anyone who get too close. And you can hide it in your pocket."

Tears trickled down her face. "Can't believe you so kind to me." She looked up. "When I say no to you."

He smiled. "That's nothing," he said. "Already forgot about it." He moved closer and put his arm around her shoulders, as her stepfather used to. "We take care of everyone who come to us. Some of them stay, and some of them go. We help them all."

On the morning of her departure, Kate made up a packet of food. "You take this. A long way to Mississippi. Two hundred mile, Denmark tell me. Ten days if you hurry and longer if you don't."

She hugged Kate, and the tears came afresh.

Kate said, "Don't you weep."

"I never see you again."

"Who know that? You find your husband, you remember us. We still here."

Pen nodded.

Kate said, "You still got room in that bag, I know. One more thing to give you." She pulled a book from her pocket. A book small enough to fit in her palm. "This for you."

Pen cradled the book in her hands and spelled out the words on the cover. "It say, *Leaves of Grass*," she said. "Your book of poems."

"Yours now," Kate said.

"I read them someday."

Kate smiled. "Of course you will."

Chapter 9

Vicksburg, Mississippi
May and June 1863

As WINTER GAVE WAY to spring, the masters of many of the impressed men reclaimed them, and the slave labor force of a thousand dwindled to a few hundred. Jonas's master did not recall him, and neither did Gabriel's. Gabriel said, "Maybe my massa forget about me." His eyes glinted.

"Maybe he don't care about you," Jonas said.

"Man, you bitter. You still grieving for your friend?"

Jonas turned away. He had not recovered from the loss of Hark, nor from the contempt shown by his burial. Every Sunday, he visited the spot where Hark lay and left a few stones on Hark's grave in remembrance.

The work on the fortifications continued in a desultory way. Jonas and Gabriel were set to digging shallow holes in the ground at ten-foot intervals, connecting the earthworks they had already built. It was easier than constructing batteries for guns. Jonas wondered what these holes would be used for, but he had learned not to ask the why of a task. He always got a curt reply: "Don't matter to you, nigger. Just dig."

As he worked, the sergeant who acted as overseer watched. He took his ease, and he didn't snap to attention when one of the engineers, a lieutenant who outranked him, approached him. "How does it go, Sergeant?" the engineer asked.

"All right," the sergeant said.

"Don't let these men slow down," the engineer said. "Grant is on the move again. He's come down the western bank of the river, and he's crossed at Bruinsburg."

"Won't do him any good to come up the eastern bank," the sergeant said.

"Oh, he can't," the engineer replied. "The only way to approach is by the roads we've blocked with our fortifications. I don't know how he thinks he'll get his men through eight solid miles of fortifications around Vicksburg. We don't know how he'll approach, just that he will."

Jonas glanced at Gabriel, who was listening as intently as he was. Jonas pushed his spade into the earth, looking as though he were working, and strained to overhear.

"So we'll have a dustup with the blue-bellies," the sergeant said. "Do we know when?"

"Whenever they come, we need to be ready," the engineer said.

The Union army was on the march, and it was coming for Vicksburg. Jonas leaned on the handle of his spade and thought that he might need to be ready, too.

WITHIN A FEW DAYS, Jonas and Gabriel were pulled from their duties. Jonas wondered if they might be sent back to their plantations and their masters now, but he was wrong. They joined a gang of fifty laborers, slaves like themselves, just hired—or impressed—from neighboring plantations. All of them had been assigned to a company of engineers with a new commander: Major Blakely, an engineer as well as an officer. Under him were several lieutenants, also engineers, and sergeants to supervise the Black laborers. A group of white soldiers, in the sorry uniforms of Confederate privates, were also attached to the company.

The Black men assigned to Major Blakely had always known that a white man's character determined the conditions of their lives, and they soon learned what they could about him. Jonas discovered that Edward Blakely hailed from Virginia, like General Lee, which explained the courtly tone in his voice. More recently, he had married a cotton heiress in Alabama, and just before the war, he had been helping his father-in-law run a hundred-hand plantation. He was an accomplished engineer. He had the cachet of having attended West Point. One of the laborers said with pride, "All the best officers go there, and he one of the smartest in his class."

Jonas didn't need a report to know that Major Blakely was at ease with slaves. When he assumed command, he walked among the men, asking how they did, and he remembered the names of the laborers, even if he called them by their first names or nicknames rather than their surnames, as soldiers were addressed. He had brought his manservant to war with him. Gabriel told him, "I meet that manservant. He bright and quick, and he serve Marse Edward for years. They friendly toward each other."

"What come over you? You like him because he don't whup his valet?"

"No," Gabriel said. "He all right. Better than that popinjay Grenville or that bully Peyton. That count for something."

Jonas said, "Don't matter that he talk sweet to us. We ain't soldiers."

Gabriel grinned. "Listen to what he agree to, for me."

"He free you?"

Gabriel shook that off. "You know we short-staffed. Only have eight of them mechanics. Could use a carpenter for them platforms and them embrasures. So I tell him I can carpenter and ask him if I can help out."

Jonas said sarcastically, "You tell him about that ark you plan to build?"

Gabriel ignored him. "Well, at first he say, 'I wish you could help us, but the mechanics won't allow it.' White men, touchy. So I explain, 'I don't ask to work alongside them like I one of them. I help them, as they order me.' He know what I mean."

"You do a carpenter's work, but you act a nigger and a slave," Jonas said.

"No. I playact a little, and I use the skill God gave me. Who know, maybe I save someone's life doing it. Maybe yours."

THE ENGINEERING COMPANY WAS divided into smaller groups, each with a lieutenant to command and a sergeant to carry out his commands. Jonas was part of a gang of ten laborers, all newcomers who had never been beyond a cotton field. Building fortifications was a mystery to them. They soon realized that Jonas knew what he was doing. They began to treat him as their driver and expected him to act as their buffer with their sergeant, whom they correctly identified as their overseer, and their lieutenant, who stood in for Major Blakely, their massa.

Lieutenant Johnston, like Blakely, was an engineer, but he was also an officer, and that complicated matters.

Sergeant Gallagher's role was easier to understand. Gallagher had worked for a big planter in Claiborne County before the war, and he was enormously proud to have managed to buy a slave of his own. When he met his laborers, he boasted to Lieutenant Johnston, "I own a nigger, and I get a full day's work out of him!"

The lieutenant, a planter's son, followed the paternal example of Major Blakely. Johnston said sharply, "Watch your tongue around these men. We need them to work hard for us."

Ever since he had come to Vicksburg, Jonas had worked during the day, but on May 17, the whole crew, white and Black, soldier and civilian, free and enslaved, was told to gather at night. As they marched, Jonas and his ten laborers were accompanied by several white soldiers who also carried shovels.

The sky was clear enough to show the stars, and the air was still warm. Nothing grew here, since the laborers had long ago dug up the earth for fieldworks and destroyed every living thing in it, but it was the time of year for fragrant blossoms like magnolia and azalea elsewhere.

Jonas knew better than to ask what they were doing. Now he carried a shovel over his shoulder and realized that if he had a rifle, he'd carry it the same way. *Rifle! Might as well wish I could fly.*

The laborer next to him asked, "Anyone tell you what we do tonight?"

"No," Jonas said curtly.

To Jonas's surprise, one of the soldiers with a shovel, who wore a private's uniform and cap, fell in alongside them. He said, "I hear that we take a look at the fieldworks and make sure they're in good repair before Grant gets here."

Jonas said, "They got you digging, too?"

The private said, "I'm a sapper."

"What's that?"

He grinned. He had a boyish face despite the shadows under his eyes. "Fancy word for a soldier who uses a shovel." He asked, "What's your name?"

"Jonas." Something about the soldier's demeanor made him risk his full name. "Jonas Mitchell."

"Elias Huntoon," the soldier replied.

"You under Sergeant Gallagher?"

Huntoon grinned. "I'm a private," he said. "Bottom of the heap. I'm under everybody. What about you?"

Jonas said, "You don't know? I ain't a soldier. Laborer. We lower even than you."

After they finished their task near dawn, Huntoon caught up with Jonas. His pale skin was smeared with dirt. "Long night."

Jonas nodded.

"You look beat," Huntoon said.

Wearily, Jonas said, "Yes, sir, I am."

"You're a good man. You been working on the fortifications long?"

"Since January."

"I never planned to be a sapper," Huntoon said. "But when the army found out I could carpenter, they made me a pontonier. Building bridges. Now they've got me sapping." He flexed his arms, which looked too fragile for a man who had to wield a shovel. "Digging holes, just like you."

Jonas didn't reply. Whatever Huntoon did at the Confederate army's behest, he was a soldier. He got rations, however poor, and he got paid, even if it was in Confederate scrip. Jonas got neither. Too weary to say more, he replied, "Yes, suh, Private Huntoon."

Because they had been out all night, the laborers were allowed to bunk down to sleep during the day. The soldiers lived in canvas tents and were given bedrolls, threadbare as they might be, but Jonas and his gang stayed in an abandoned building that had likely been a shed. They slept on the floor.

Despite his fatigue, Jonas fell into an uneasy sleep. A few hours later, in broad daylight, he woke to an unfamiliar din: a roaring sound, then a whistle, then an explosion, and all the while, a screaming sound. He jumped up and ran outside to see the smoke rising over the city of Vicksburg. As his fellows woke and rushed to join him, they bunched together in astonishment.

"What happen?" someone exclaimed, his eyes bleary with sleep.

Jonas said, "I guess Grant get here, and the battle start."

That night, Lieutenant Johnston, accompanied by Sergeant Gallagher, rounded up the crew and told them, "We're going out tonight to repair the damage from the bombardment today."

During the day—he had given up trying to sleep—Jonas had learned to decipher the sounds of bombardment. The roar of the mortars. The whistle, and just after, the explosion of the shells. The scream of rifle fire.

Jonas looked up at the night sky. The bombardment hadn't stopped at nightfall. As the mortars flung their shells into the city, the explosions lit up the heavens. If they hadn't been so deadly, they would have been a spectacle like fireworks.

The new men clustered around Jonas, their faces lined with fear. One of them nudged Jonas, reminding him to say something on their behalf.

Jonas, who had watched Gabriel do this many times, hung his head a little and addressed Lieutenant Johnston. "Lieutenant, sir, I ain't a soldier, so I don't know how to say this. But if I can, I ask you. We go out to work in this?"

Lieutenant Johnston looked at him as though he were mad. "Yes, by Major Blakely's orders."

A soldier would know to shut up, but Jonas played on Johnston's feelings as a massa. "What if they fire at us?"

Lieutenant Johnston began to say, "Soldier—" and cut himself short. He realized that he was talking to frightened slaves. His voice softened and took on the paternal tone that he must have used with field hands, assuming they had the understanding of children. "You'll be all right. They won't be firing at us. They're bombarding Vicksburg."

Jonas looked uneasily at the shell-brilliant sky. "But if they fire at us, what do we do?"

Johnston took in his frightened, noncombatant laborers. "We have a way of saying it in the army. 'Stand from under.'"

"Sir, tell us. What do that mean?"

Jonas hadn't seen Huntoon in their detail, but he piped up, "That's how military men say get the hell out of the way."

Lieutenant Johnston said, "That's enough out of you, soldier." He was curt with Huntoon.

"Yes, sir," Huntoon said, but the tone didn't match the words. Jonas recognized that note of sly insolence.

All that night, as they repaired the damaged fortifications, armed only with the pick and the shovel, they worked to the Union army's deadly song. The roar of the mortars. The whistle of the shells. The scream of bullets. The flash of explosion and the smell of gunpowder and smoke. Despite Johnston's reassurance, Jonas couldn't shake the fear of being hit.

Huntoon wasn't bothered. He wielded his shovel as though he were spading up a cornfield. He paused to watch the explosions. "Those mortars ain't far away."

"How do you know?"

"This ain't the first time I've worked under fire."

"How far away, do you judge?"

"About a mile." He added, "Coehorn mortar can throw a shell farther than that."

"So the army a mile away, too."

Huntoon leaned on his shovel, showing his own fatigue. "That's damn close," he said. "Too damn close for me."

Jonas listened to the sound of bombardment. *The Union army only a mile away. A shell could fly a mile. And a man could walk a mile. So close, and so far.* The mortars, the shells, and the bullets sang the alluring sound of the Siren's song. It could mean death, or it could mean freedom.

A WEEK AFTER THE battle began, Jonas lay down to the sound of mortar fire. He slept well into the day and woke to a silence so profound that his ears rang. Beside him, exhausted men still lay, sleeping. He crept from the shed to find out what had happened to the battle.

At the closest earthworks, he saw the white flag stuck in the dirt. He asked the nearest soldier, "What happen?"

"Flag of truce," the soldier said.

"What's that?"

"We stop shooting."

"Why? Someone win?"

The soldier snorted. "No. The Union has so many dead out there that they stink to high heaven. We're letting them clear them off and bury them."

"Just stop the war like that?"

The soldier said, "This ain't a brawl. There are rules of war, both for us and for them. Flag of truce goes up, the shooting stops." He said, "If you want a better view, you can put your head above the parapet. It's safe today."

Since the shooting began, the sharpshooters on both sides had hidden behind the fortifications and had tried to pick off anyone foolhardy enough to put his head above the parapets. Coming back from night duty, Jonas had watched the soldiers amuse themselves by putting a hat on a stick to draw Union fire. The hat was immediately riddled with bullets. If it had been a man, he would have died at once.

Jonas watched as the men in blue walked without fear to retrieve the dead, wrap them in blankets, and lay them gently in wagons. Men in gray, also unafraid, mingled with the enemy. A Confederate officer moved through the crowd, and to Jonas's surprise, he took the hand of an officer in a Union coat. The two men embraced. Today they were old friends. Tomorrow they would be enemies again.

Jonas stared at the area between the Confederate and Union fortifications. Tomorrow, when the sharpshooters returned to their posts, it would again be a deadly gauntlet. That narrow strip of land would again be a vast distance, filled with the smoke and the fire of bombardment.

AFTER THE SHOOTING RESUMED, Lieutenant Johnston's group had a new task. Johnston had learned to explain what they were doing, even though Sergeant Gallagher complained that he coddled the niggers and there was no reason to tell them anything. Laborers and sapper alike would start to dig a trench—with a stern look at Huntoon, Johnston explained, "That's what we army men call a sap"—toward the Union lines. They would start at the big fortification called the Third Louisiana Redan, named after the regiment that currently defended it. Jonas had known it as the Jackson Road Redan when he built it earlier this year to protect the road that led into Vicksburg proper. Anyone who breached it could march into Vicksburg. Jonas didn't see how digging a trench would stop that.

He didn't bother to ask the lieutenant why they were digging the sap. He asked Huntoon.

Huntoon said, "We want to get closer to the Union lines."

"Thought you were afraid they were too close already."

"They are. Forty yards."

The words "forty yards" went through Jonas like a gut pain. He had chopped shorter cotton rows. "Where are them mortars? The ones that fire a shell over a mile?"

"They ain't planning on using a mortar."

"What do you mean?"

"They're digging a sap, too. They want to get close enough to dig a mine. A mine goes underground. It's just what it sounds like, a shaft and a hole underground, the same as for mining coal. But there's no coal down there. They put powder in it and blow it up—blow a hole in our fortifications and try to get through."

"And we in the way."

"Not if we sap and dig a mine to stop them first."

JONAS HAD GOTTEN USED to the sound of the mortars. He had learned to keep his worry at bay by believing that Lieutenant Johnston was right: the mortar fire was for Vicksburg. Tonight, he didn't pay much attention to the familiar whistle, assuming it would land far beyond him. But as it came nearer and nearer, he realized that it wouldn't continue its path above his head and over the fortifications. It was headed for the men on the fatigue detail. He and his fellows were the target.

As the shell began to descend, Jonas froze, afraid that moving would put him in even more danger. The shell hit the ground a few feet away, throwing dirt into his face with a force that rent his skin. It exploded downward into the earth, making a crater and throwing up more dirt.

After the shell exploded, Lieutenant Johnston was at his elbow. "Are you all right?"

Jonas touched his stinging face. "Just scraped a bit."

Huntoon said, "You're the luckiest man here tonight."

Then they heard the whistle of the next shell.

Johnston didn't have to call "Stand from under!" They all ran. Sappers and laborers alike retreated to safer ground, and as the shells continued to hit their fortifications, Johnston had to call a halt to work for the night.

Jonas walked back to his quarters on shaky legs, listening to Union bombardment and recalling the sound of the shell that had nearly killed him. Now he felt the terror. He was no soldier, but he could die, just as surely as a soldier might. He thought of Pen. It was unbearable to think that he might never see her until they met in Heaven. So close to the Union lines, and yet so close to death.

FOR THE LABORERS, THE rations had always been short, but now the soldiers felt it, too. Huntoon said, "We're eating ground-up peas and cornmeal. Call it cush-cush." He looked at Jonas. "You men hungry?"

Jonas said, "What do you think?"

The night after they were bombed out, Huntoon

caught up with him on the way to the redan. "You won't believe what I ate for dinner tonight."

Jonas shook his head.

"Ate a rat." At Jonas's disgusted expression, he said, "Wasn't as bad as I thought it would be."

"You funning me."

"I ain't." He reached into his pocket and pulled out something wrapped in a handkerchief. "Brought you something, too."

"Is it a rat?"

"No. Corn cake."

Jonas took the handkerchief, looking dubious, and unwrapped it on the spot. It was corn cake.

Huntoon said, "Come with me. I have something to show you." He clambered up the earthwork, which was low-slung, and put his head above it.

No shot rent the air.

Huntoon waved to their pickets below, and one of them called out, "How are you, soldier?"

"I'm all right!" he called back. Still looking down at the picket line, he said to Jonas, "It's safe. They don't shoot at each other at night."

"Them sharpshooters? They quit at night?"

"Watch."

The Union army was closer than he'd ever seen: ten yards away. One of the Union men called out, "Johnny Reb, did you bring us that tobacco you promised?"

A Confederate picket called back, "If you brought us that coffee you promised!"

"We keep our promises! We'll see you in Vicksburg!"

"So do we! You won't!"

But the tone was in the best of humor. A man in gray detached from the picket line, and so did a man in blue. They crossed the open ground to meet in the middle. Incredulous, Jonas watched as the Confederate handed over the tobacco and the Union man returned the favor with coffee. They shook hands afterward. They were as amiable as two men meeting after church.

Jonas dropped behind the earthwork. He asked Huntoon, "Why they do that?"

"Sick of fighting," Huntoon said. "Who ain't?"

"They do that every night?"

"As far as I know."

So close. Ten yards apart. But Jonas could see no possibility of crossing those ten yards without incident, even if the pickets observed the civility of holding fire.

MAJOR BLAKELY'S MEN NOW went underground. Jonas worked to dig out a shaft under the direction of a man who had been a miner before the war. They dug and dug, and as Jonas stood at the bottom of the shaft, he heard voices.

They were not voices he knew.

Yankees, talking as they worked. And responding to them, in lower tones, the voices of Black men, with the accents of Mississippi and Alabama.

He leaned on his shovel as it struck him: these men were contrabands working for the Union army. Close by, so close he could distinguish what they said. They were men who had escaped slavery and now were digging a shaft for a Union mine.

Underground, the sound of war was very faint. Underground, the Siren began to sing a new song: "Contraband."

It was no secret that Sergeant Gallagher disliked and distrusted the Black laborers who did the lion's share of the sapping work. He assumed that the tired, hungry, dispirited men he oversaw were lazy. He liked to say, "Wish I could give them a whipping. That would smarten them up!"

Jonas loathed the sight of Gallagher. When he heard the shells whistle by, he wished that one would make its way to Gallagher and blow him to pieces. He liked to think that there wouldn't be enough of him left to bury.

As Jonas ate his meager dinner—a piece of cornbread supplemented with a bit of bacon—he overheard Gallagher blustering to Johnston: "Did you hear about that skirmish we had up at Milliken's Bend?"

"No," Johnston said. He looked hollow-eyed. He had enough to worry about right here, right now, at Vicksburg.

"I hear we whupped them blue-bellies. Sent them running!"

"That's good," Johnston said, no doubt thinking about how to keep a fatigue detail of men with shovels alive during a Union bombardment.

"Did you know they fought a bunch of niggers?"

Jonas was suddenly taut with the effort to overhear.

"The Union is using negroes for soldiers? How is that?"

"Nigger soldiers. Think of that. The Federals are trying to make soldiers out of niggers!"

Jonas's hands shook so much that he had to set his tin plate on the ground. Black men, fighting for the Union. So the Union army had other uses for contraband than to put picks and shovels in their hands.

GABRIEL HAD BEEN FAR away, working with the mechanics on the railroad line, and Jonas hadn't spoken to him since the siege began. Early one morning, before he had the chance to try to sleep, a stranger approached his shed to hail him. "We ain't acquainted, but I work with Gabriel. I know you his friend."

Jonas was instantly worried. "What happen?"

"Came to tell you he hit by a shell last night."

"How is he?"

"He gone." At the stricken look on Jonas's face, the man said, "Happened in a moment. He didn't feel a thing."

"Where is he?"

"Brought him back to our encampment. We bury him proper."

"Let me help you."

"We all be obliged," the stranger said.

Jonas joined the ten men of Gabriel's fatigue detail on a grassy spot behind the lines. All of them worked together in a silent, reverential rhythm to dig the grave. Gabriel's fellows had wrapped him carefully in a blanket, as the Confederate dead were shrouded, and together, all of them laid him gently in the grave. They worked together to cover him, as they had to dig. When they were finished, Jonas leaned on his shovel. "Heaven is my home," he sang, very softly, and the rest of the men joined him, singing to a man who had been a stranger here and who was now going home to eternal peace.

They left a rough wooden cross on the grave, as for the soldiers, to mark his resting place.

JONAS HAD WATCHED AND schemed and tried to plan as the Union line drew closer, but two days after Gabriel was laid to rest, God gave him his chance.

The night was warm and overcast, obscuring the moon and the stars, and the darkness was velvety and deep. If the birds hadn't been shocked out of their trees by the shelling, this would be a time for birdcalls.

Instead, he heard the sounds of confusion among the pickets. He raised himself up to look over the embankment and saw not two orderly lines but pickets from both sides intermingling in a confused throng. It didn't seem to be friendliness, as it was the other night. Just a muddle. But no one was shooting, and Jonas saw his chance. In a moment, he slipped over a low point in the fortification and melted into the crowd, walking deliberately as though he belonged there. Despite his fear, no one challenged him.

He made his way through the crowd to find the Union picket who stood the farthest back. "Contraband," he whispered. "Come from the Rebs. Been working on them fortifications and know all about them. Glad to tell everything I know."

The soldier was older than most privates, and he had a lean, intelligent face. "Follow me," he said, and he led

Jonas through a low point in the Union fortifications. On the other side, he was met by a sergeant who asked, "What's the password?"

"Ithaca," the soldier said. "And you know who I am."

"I've got to ask. Who do you have with you?"

"Contraband. Knows the Confederate fortifications, he says."

Jonas said, "Worked on them since January. Been working on the mine on the Jackson Road."

The sergeant said, "Fortifications? Jackson Road?" He asked Jonas, "What regiment?"

"Under Major Blakely. Chief engineer. Sappers and miners."

"Engineer? Our chief engineer will be interested in this." He nodded at Jonas. "I'll escort him to see Major Leverett."

"Wake up Major Leverett?"

"Major Leverett never seems to sleep."

Jonas followed the sergeant to the Union encampment. This part of the line was quiet at night. The sound of the mortars echoed from farther away, and the sky lit up in the display that these men, from their safe spot behind the lines, could admire as though they were a show of fireworks.

The encampment was quiet, too. The men were sleeping. Jonas envied them. He hadn't slept at night since the siege began.

They stopped before a tent bigger than the others, where a bearded man sat at a table piled with papers. Even from a few feet away, Jonas could see that they were maps.

The major looked up. He had dark circles under his

eyes, as though he hadn't slept much at night since the siege began. Even though he was tired and a little disheveled, he had the same air of competence that radiated from Major Blakely: he would get things done. "Yes, Sergeant?" he asked.

"Brought you a contraband who just came to us. He's worked on the Reb fortifications, sir. He says he has information for us."

"Has he?" The major's eyes gleamed. "What's his name?"

Jonas spoke. "Jonas Mitchell, sir."

Major Leverett took in Jonas's condition: his rags, thin frame, and haggard face. "Let's get this man a plate of food. Then we'll hear what he has to say."

Jonas sat at the major's worktable, and when the food came, the major pushed aside his maps to make room. Jonas leaned over the plate, taking in the fresh beef and the wheat bread. With it came a cup of coffee. He fell on the food, too hungry for manners. As he took a swig of the coffee, with its ambrosial smell, the major watched him. "I hear you men are on short rations."

Jonas set down the cup. "We eat whatever we can get, sir."

"Who did you work for? What did you do?"

Jonas explained. "Fatigue detail. Work with a shovel and a pick. But I work alongside the sappers and the engineers, and I listen to what they say, and I remember." He took a deep breath. "Been digging the sap and the mine from the redan on Jackson Road. Near your men."

Major Leverett asked more questions and took notes as Jonas answered. Then the major asked, "Can you draw?"

"No, sir, but I can tell you what I see, and if someone else draw it"—he gestured toward a map—"I can say if it's what I see or not."

The major found a fresh piece of paper and a pencil. "Tell me what you saw," he said, and as Jonas spoke, the major drew.

When Jonas had finished speaking and the major had finished drawing, the major said, "You've done us a great service, Mr. Jonas Mitchell." His businesslike expression softened a little. "Would you like to work for us?"

Jonas, who had leaned back in his chair with exhaustion, sat up and said in surprise, "You ask me? I can say yes or no?"

"Of course," the major said.

Jonas was suddenly overwhelmed. "No white man ever ask me what I prefer, not once in my life!"

A shadow passed over the major's face. "We do," he said. "Mr. Mitchell, what do you prefer?"

Shaking, Jonas said, "Don't want to pick up a shovel, not ever again." He dared to look the major in the eye. "Want to join the Union army as a soldier. Want to muster in to that Black regiment that just fight a battle up at Milliken's Bend."

Chapter 10

Western Alabama
June 1863

AS PEN TRAVELED THROUGH western Alabama, the spell of the runaways' paradise lingered. In Coffee and Covington Counties, as in Georgia, she was welcomed, fed, and sheltered. These were small cotton plantations, with ten to twenty slaves, but the slaves knew how to keep a secret. When she told them about the Proclamation, they smiled and said, "We know."

Farther westward, she was in the piney woods again. With no plantations to stop at, Toby hunted and she foraged. She looked for cress again. And she ate it, even though it made her think of Jasper, and her eyes misted with tears. She and Toby roamed through the woods without incident. She was surprised that a day's journey could be uneventful enough to bore her.

They had found plenty of creeks on their journey, but now they were stopped by a river too wide and too deep to cross. The water was sluggish and silty as in her dream. She shivered, even though the sun warmed the air beneath the pines. She said to Toby, "We look for a better place to cross."

She walked downriver, hugging the bank. She kept going, hoping to find a better crossing point. No luck.

She was so intent on the water that Toby's muffled bark startled her. "What is it?" And then she heard it. The sound of hooves striking the dirt and the bay of a bloodhound.

Wade in the water. She stared at the river, where the muddy water seemed to mock her. She had never learned how to swim, and she didn't even like the thought of dipping her foot in that liquid silt. The dogs came closer. She scrambled down the bank. Toby jumped into the water, paddling with his front paws, keeping his head above the muck.

Her hand went to the strap on her shoulder to touch her bag with all the precious things in it, none of which could get wet. She glanced at the water, listening for a moment to the dogs. Then she unslung the bag and dropped it on the shore. Either she would retrieve it later, or she would never need it again.

She hiked her dress up to her knees and slipped into the river.

The water was shallow near the shore, only up to her waist. It felt unpleasantly warm and smelled of fish and rotting vegetation. Midges swarmed around her head, and she swatted them away, feeling for the bottom as she waded farther out. She stepped on something sharp and prayed that she hadn't cut her foot. Toby paddled nearby.

The sound of the bloodhounds snuffling and baying

was terrifyingly close. She didn't know if standing so near the bank would be enough to foil the dogs or not.

The snuffling sound became louder.

An arm's length away, the water roiled, and a scaly snout began to surface. Then the eyes. Then the head.

If she reached out her hand, she could touch the gator. She was suddenly in a sweat of fear for Toby, not knowing if a gator might eat a dog.

The dogs on the shore. The gator at her elbow.

Pen felt the brush of a scaly tail and submerged herself in the water. Underwater, she couldn't tell how close the dogs were. She held her breath until she thought she might die. Wherever the dogs were, she had to breathe. She broke the surface.

The gator raised its head and opened its mouth, showing its pink maw and all its teeth. If she hadn't been so frightened, she would have thought it was grinning at her. And it closed the maw and slowly, too slowly, submerged, jaws first, then its eyes, and finally the flat top of its head. It thrashed its tail in the water, letting her know that it was too close for comfort, and swam away.

Her heart pounding, she listened for the dogs. But the baying was now faint. The dogs and patrollers must have gone up the river. She waited in the muddy water until the sound of dogs and horses and men had faded away.

Toby paddled to the shore and leaped onto dry land. He was so dirty that his yellow coat had turned grayish brown. He shook himself, and muddy water flew everywhere. He barked at her.

"Is it all right, Toby?" she whispered.

He sat on the shore, his tongue out, panting and waiting for her.

She dragged herself onto the shore. Then she collapsed next to Toby since her legs were too weak to carry her.

Toby nosed her. "Yes, I get up," she said, hoarse. She stood. Toby ran back the way they'd come. She wondered why and realized that he was smarter than she was. It would confuse the bloodhounds if they came back here.

She retrieved the bag—everything in it was dry and safe—and they were on their way.

As they retraced their steps, Pen tried to look down the river. All she could see were the graceful birches arching over the water. Tired and discouraged, she kept going, glancing at the river, still hoping for it to narrow. She thought that she might have found a spit. She went to investigate. It was an outcropping of rock, but it was clear of trees. Just up the river, beyond it, she could see clear enough to what looked like a landing.

Why would there be a landing ahead? Who landed there? She quickened her pace, and Toby eagerly followed her. When they had gone less than a mile, she knew. It appeared through the trees, beckoning and taunting her: a house big enough for a planter's family. She drew in her breath. A planter would have slaves. Maybe even a slave street, a place to ask for food, if not for shelter. Perhaps they would know where to cross the river.

She suddenly felt exposed on the bank and slipped into the trees that bordered the property. Just beyond, cotton grew, the plants green and vigorous. No one worked the field. She realized how late it was. The slaves must be at their dinner.

The best way to approach a strange plantation, she had learned, was to waylay the cook. A house this size would have a kitchen building far from the house for safety. She skirted the cotton field, searching for the path to the yard. Yes, there it was: dirt trodden many times a day.

Toby whined. "I know you hungry," she said. She thought with longing of the smokehouse that must be somewhere on this place. She would be mad to even look for it. If it was like every plantation she had ever seen, it would be locked, and anyone who tried to break in would be whipped hard enough to never try such a thing again.

As she waited, a woman opened the kitchen door and stood on the steps. Pen edged closer and called out, as low a noise as a horned owl's, "Miss."

She was tall and angular, and over her dress she wore an apron, spotted and stained. Her face was slick and ashy, as though she'd been smeared with grease and flour. She turned. "What you doing here?"

"Just passing through," Pen said.

"You shouldn't be here."

Uneasy, Pen said, "Hoping that you might spare a bite to eat."

She dropped her voice. "Can't help you, and you can't stay here."

"Won't linger."

"No," the woman said. She gestured toward the woods with her chin.

"All right," Pen said.

The woman's eyes narrowed. She warned, "Patrollers all around here."

Pen turned to go. She had never been refused before.

Something wasn't right, and she wouldn't stay to find out why. She was tired and hungry, but she wanted to get as far from here as she could.

She wanted to go back to the river before sunset to try to find another landing and another plantation more hospitable than this one. She retraced her steps, and soon she and Toby were making their way, Toby sniffing for water birds, and Pen straining to look for a jetty.

It rested on a stony spit too small to be called a beach: a little boat just big enough for herself and Toby. Someone had left the oars in it. She clambered down the bank.

She had never sat in a boat before, much less rowed one. She couldn't swim. She gazed at the wide, darkening river and remembered the brush of the gator's tail in the river that morning.

Escape had presented itself, but she was unable to take advantage of it. Tears of discouragement trickled down her face. Thickly, she said, "Toby, we keep going."

She climbed back up the bank, her feet heavy, her heart heavier, and slipped back into the woods.

The sun set, and she was in a dark and unfamiliar wood full of live oaks that littered the ground with spiky twigs and acorns as big as marbles. The forest floor was hard and uneven. She nearly turned her ankle in the dark, and she had to bite her tongue to keep from crying out.

Patrollers all around here, the unwelcoming woman had said. Suddenly Pen was too heartsick to care.

Toby whined, his way of getting her attention, and then she heard what had alerted him. Footsteps.

Was it a hunter or a patroller?

She didn't move. Whoever walked here was stealthy,

someone who had learned to hide in this forest. She strained to hear. She moved her hand to her bag, feeling for her pistol. Did she need it? Did she dare use it?

Toby whined again, and she put her hand on his head. "Hush," she whispered. "Don't give us away."

The steps came closer. Pen found the pistol and curved her hand around it.

And a startled voice said, "Who are you?"

It was a woman. Her dress was wrinkled, as though she'd been lying on the ground, and her kerchief was askew. When she got close enough, she gave off a ripe odor.

The stranger had been in too much of a hurry even to wipe herself off before she left her man.

Pen let go of the pistol. "Who are you?"

"Live around here," she said. "What you got in that bag?"

Pen removed her empty hand and showed it to the stranger. "A dress and a shawl."

"You gave me a start," the stranger said.

Pen laughed. "So did you."

"Why you laugh at me?" Her hand went to her head, as she tried to straighten her kerchief. She was not much older than Pen herself, Africa and Europe mingling on her face: a proud straight nose and full, berry-colored lips. Under the kerchief, she wore her hair long, bound back, and when she pulled on it to smooth it, Pen saw that it was twisted into ropes. She had never seen a Black woman wear her hair like that.

"You been sneaking and creeping, haven't you?" Pen asked.

The woman hesitated, as though she wasn't sure she

should take offense. Then she grinned. "You run away, didn't you?"

Pen said, "You right, but how you know?"

"Look like you lost. You fall in the river? You smell like it, too."

"Hah!" Pen said. "You one to talk."

"Was it patrollers?"

"Yes," Pen said.

"Where you from?"

"East of here."

"Price on your head?"

"Haven't looked back to know." Pen said, "Why you ask me that? You in as much trouble as I am."

"I know where I'm going."

"So do I," Pen said. "Just have to get there."

"Where?"

"I'm bound for Mississippi." Pen gestured toward the direction of the river. "Have to cross that river first."

"What you look for in Mississippi?"

She said, "Your man, he right here. But my husband sold away before the war."

"You go all the way to Mississippi? To find the man you marry?"

"Yes," Pen said. "Still married to him. Always married. Is you married to that man you see?"

Suddenly the stranger looked as though she might cry.

Pen said, "I'm sorry. I love him, and I miss him so much it hurt me. Wasn't kind of me to talk like that to you."

"I married, and it don't do me any good. My husband live on the neighboring place. His massa know that we want to be together. But he hard, and he won't sell my man. And my massa's just as hard. Won't let me go there to see him regular. We take our turns, sneaking and creeping. And getting whupped for it."

"You braver than I am," Pen said. "Stay here for love, and get whupped for it."

"You crazy. Run away to Mississippi for love!"

"I have to cross the river," Pen said softly.

The woman wiped her eyes with her sleeve. "I been rowing on the river since I was a gal. I know where to find a boat."

"What's your name?" Pen asked.

"Mary. My whole name Mary Magdalene."

"Your mama name you after a fallen woman?"

"Oh, I fall, all right," she said. "Come on, I find us a boat."

Mary led Pen and Toby through the trees, where the half-moon shone with a silvery light. Even here, Pen could hear the water lapping against the bank. A horned owl called, and longing for Jonas rushed through her. *I come as soon as I can, sugar*, she thought.

As they got closer to the river, Mary moved with more confidence. She scanned the bank. "Ah!" she said, walking with purpose toward the edge of the water. On a strip of stony beach sat the little boat that had sent Pen into despair.

Mary laughed. "We in luck. That fool never do put his oars away."

"Whose boat?" Pen asked.

"Don't you worry. You gone by then." She gestured across the water. She slipped easily into the boat and waited as Pen clambered in and encouraged Toby to join her. Mary said, "Settle and be quiet." She pushed off and began to row with sure strokes.

Pen glanced at the water and shivered at the memory of the scaly snout. "Are there gators here?"

"Yes, we got gators here. Don't worry. They don't bother us."

The raftsman's words, in her dream.

The river, brown in daylight, was black, slashed by silver where the moonlight hit it. The water rippled. "Is that a gator?" Pen asked.

Mary pulled on the oars. "Look down."

Pen looked and met the bulging eyes, which blinked as though the gator recognized her. She said to Mary, "Get us away."

Mary pulled harder on the oars. The gator submerged, leaving behind a stream of air bubbles.

Toby whimpered. Pen put her arm around him and held him tightly against her side. "When we get across, how do I go toward Mississippi?"

"Go west across Clarke County."

"Is it far?"

"Twenty mile across. But you got another river on the other side."

"Another river?"

Mary maneuvered the boat close to the shore and expertly beached it. The bank inclined gently upward, and beyond the boggy shore, trees grew. Not pines. Something else.

Mary pointed. "You find a path in there. Follow that."

Pen hoisted her skirt to her knees and stepped on the

stones. Toby jumped out to join her. Mary said, "Tombigbee. Other river's called the Tombigbee. Due west." Before Pen could reply, she pushed the boat back into the river and sculled away.

Toby shook himself as though he'd fallen in the river and gotten wet. Pen said, "All right. We go." She turned toward the thicket of unfamiliar trees and began to climb the bank.

Somewhere, in that silver-lit darkness, a horned owl called, and it was as though Jonas beckoned, calling to her: *Come find me.*

PEN AND TOBY SLEPT in the woods that night. When she woke, she sighed and said to Toby, "I guess we eat rabbit again and look for that cress to go with it."

On this side of the river, they were in a new forest. To her left grew the familiar longleaf pines, with their tall canopies that sheltered magnolia and dogwood. To her right, the ground was wetter, with clumps of birch interspersed by a tree Pen had never seen before. It had gray bark and was broad at the base, tapering toward the top, and crowned by leaves instead of needles. The smell that wafted from them was sweeter than the pines, with an undertone of smoke.

Pen was in no mood to appreciate any kind of tree. She was sick of trees. She wanted to see a house. Preferably a plantation house that would have a slave street nearby.

Toby, sensitive to her moods, nosed her hand. She sighed as she scratched his ears. "One foot in front of the other," she said, not feeling encouraged by her own words.

She was tired of being wary. Tired of straining to see between the trees. Tired of quieting herself to listen. She wished she could find a wagon to cart her to Mississippi. A boat to cross the Tombigbee River, when she found it. A railroad car to hurtle her down the tracks. Hah! She snorted at her own thought. She might as well wish to fly to Mississippi.

That day they walked through the woods without incident. The smell of the tapering trees grew stronger and with it, an undertone of wet, rotting leaves on the ground. When they stopped for the night, Toby left her to hunt in the swampy grove. He brought back a rabbit. She rubbed his head and said, "Good boy," but without enthusiasm.

They spent the night on the piney side of the woods on dry ground that gave off a strong smell of crushed pine needles. Toby, trying to cheer her, curled up close to her belly. She said, "Look at you, trying to cajole me." Suddenly the tears came. Disturbing Toby, she sat up. She began to sob and didn't bother to muffle it. Who would hear? She felt a soft insistent tongue on her cheek. Toby licked the tears from her face.

She looked up. Toby sat with his head cocked, his eyes bright and intent on her. She had never seen a dog look worried and puzzled before. Sniffling, she reached out and hugged him close. Without thinking, she had used her left arm, which was not yet completely healed. He seemed to know that her shoulder was tender. He nestled against her gently.

Still hugging him, she said, "Now I know how crazy I am. Lost in the piney woods, man and beast after me, and I let my dog love me up." She kissed the top of Toby's head, which was a mistake because he was still muddy and smelly from his swim in the Alabama River. She wiped her face. "If you give me fleas, I don't forgive you."

He yipped softly and licked her face again.

IN THE MORNING, SHE and Toby shared the last of the rabbit, and after she had consulted her compass, she pointed them west.

She was used to the pines by now. Even their danger felt familiar. But the swamp oozed menace. The sun filtered even more weakly through the swamp than through the pines, making the woods dim even at midday. The smell of vegetation dying in mud overpowered the smoky scent of the odd trees that were draped with vines that looked like snakes. She heard slithering sounds, and she shuddered. In Georgia, the snakes that liked water were cottonmouths, and they were poisonous. She kept her face toward the pines.

By midafternoon, she was tired and thirsty. On this wet ground, the water puddled, silty and impure. She licked her dry lips. They needed to find sweet water.

From the piney side of the woods came a thudding sound, like a blacksmith pounding on an anvil. But it was loud and constant, as though many blacksmiths worked side by side. She couldn't figure it. *Who put a smithy in the middle of the woods?*

Curious, she walked toward it, Toby at her heels. It got louder, but she still couldn't discern what it was. She knew it wasn't an animal sound, and maybe she was wrong to feel reassured. But she kept going.

Without warning, a man rushed from the woods. He held an axe, gripping it with both hands. Running toward her, he yelled, "Watch out!" He was a Black man, very broad in the shoulder.

Her heart leaped into her throat.

He yelled, "We felling trees! You too close! Too dangerous!"

"Fell trees?" she said weakly.

He looked down at the axe and realized how he'd frightened her. He moved it to his right hand and held it by the handle, the blade pointing safely down at the ground. He scolded, "What you doing here?"

"Passing through," she said.

"No one pass through here. You lost?"

"No."

He looked her up and down. "You steal away," he said, and a smile crept over his face. He was only a little older than Jonas, but he was much darker of skin, and his arms and legs were thickly muscled.

She said, "You tell your overseer that? Your massa?"

"No," he said, and he grinned even wider.

"Then where am I?"

"Salt works. We fell trees for the salt works."

Puzzled, she asked, "Salt works? What are they?"

"Oh, I show you." He grinned again and bent down. "What your dog called?" He extended his hand toward Toby. Toby growled, and he straightened up.

"Toby. He a good dog." She was embarrassed to tell a stranger how much she loved Toby. "He hunt for me and find me water and keep me company."

The stranger said, "He protect you, too."

"Who are you?"

He gave her another grin. "My name Franklin Wiley. Most people call me Frank."

"Are you?" she asked.

He laughed. "When it suit me."

Now that she knew, she could distinguish the rasp of saws and the thud of axes. As they walked, the woods rasped and thudded in a ceaseless cacophony. "It so loud," she said.

He said, "It never stop. All day long, the woods ring with it."

"How big is your gang?"

"About a dozen men. But we got gangs and gangs here. Thousands of men."

"Thousands?" She had come from a big plantation with a hundred hands. She couldn't imagine that many people in one place. "Where are they?"

"Deep in the woods. We walk far away. Keep you safe."

"Why you cut down trees for salt?"

"Up at the works, they sluice salt water out of the ground, then they boil it down in big copper pans. Under every pan, they got a kiln made of brick, and in every kiln, they keep a fire going all the time. They feed all our wood into them fires. All the wood we can cut!"

"All this toil for salt?" Pen asked.

Frank said, "Can't live without salt. Have to salt everything to keep it. Can't get salt from the north no more, after the blockade. All over the countryside, people starved for salt. They willing to pay twenty dollar for a forty-pound bag. Salt worth more than money."

"Where do all these men come from?"

Frank said, "From the plantations around here."

"Your massa give you up?"

"No. He hire me out. He get twenty dollar a month for me. He hire out ten hands. That's two hundred dollar a month."

"Who have money?"

"Oh, he don't get paid in that Confederate paper that ain't good enough to wipe your butt with. He get paid in salt."

They walked away from the sound of axes and saws. Pen asked, "Where are we going?"

"I take you to the camp. Women work there. Cook and launder. Miss Tilly know what to do with you."

The camp was a vast cleared space, with long, low-slung buildings in rows on the packed dirt. "What are those?"

"Barracks. We sleep there. Twenty men in a building. It ain't bad. They give us rope beds and blankets."

She stared at the sea of barracks. She tried to imagine thousands of men living here. "Where are the women?"

"Kitchens. One for every five barracks."

"How do they feed so many?"

"You see."

She had never seen anything like the kitchen, either, a huge shed bigger than any plantation kitchen she had ever entered. It was fiercely hot inside and smelled powerfully of bacon grease. A dozen women labored there, mixing cornbread, stirring great iron pots on the stoves, and frying bacon in skillets.

Frank called to a woman who stood at the stove. "Miss Tilly!"

Miss Tilly was a stout woman with tawny skin. Her round cheeks made her look young, even though her hands betrayed decades of labor. She wiped her hands on her apron and said, with good humor, "Frank, you don't get enough to eat at your meals? You here to beg something in between?"

He laughed. "No, Miss Tilly. You feed us enough to fell trees all day. I bring you a new gal."

Miss Tilly's eyes rested on Pen. "Her massa send her along with a hound dog?"

"Not exactly."

Miss Tilly's gaze traveled up and down Pen and sideways to her dog. "You have a name?" Miss Tilly asked her.

"Pen. And my dog, Toby."

"You hungry?"

Toby yelped. Miss Tilly laughed. "Frank, you go on. I take care of this gal and her hound," she said.

Miss Tilly sat Pen at the corner of a huge, scarred pine table. Pen was in the way of a woman who scraped cornbread into a skillet and looked askance at Toby. Miss Tilly gave Pen a plate of peas with bacon, and Toby got ham scraps and a bone, which he attacked with gusto.

Pen asked, "They don't stint on food here?"

Miss Tilly gestured to the bustling kitchen. "A man who fell trees all day, he have to eat like a horse. No, we got plenty."

When they were both full, Miss Tilly said, "You can stay here for a while, if you like. We hide you in plain sight. Put you to work in the kitchen. Say you new here."

"I have to go," Pen said.

"Why? Where you go?"

171

"Have to get across the Tombigbee River."

Miss Tilly shook her head.

That night, Miss Tilly found her a rope bed in the women's quarters. Despite the name, it was a barracks just like the men's, with twenty beds in two rows. The place smelled of sweat, lye soap, and bacon grease, evidence of the work the women did. As Pen sat down on the bed, Miss Tilly asked her, "You want a blanket?"

"Not if it's trouble."

"It ain't."

Pen grasped her bag tightly. Miss Tilly asked, "You can put that down, if you like."

"I want to keep it by me."

"Why? What you got in there?"

She could imagine the fuss that the discovery of her compass and her pistol would arouse. She said, "All the clothes I got in the world."

Pen lay down on the bed, crowded equally by the bag, tucked under her hip, and by Toby, who curled up at her feet. She felt uneasy, surrounded by the sounds and smells of so many strangers. She fell into an uneasy sleep.

THE NEXT MORNING, AT breakfast, she asked Miss Tilly, "You ever go to the salt works?"

"No. Why should I? My task here."

"Could I see the works?"

"Frank drive up there sometimes, with a load of wood," Miss Tilly said. "Gals don't go up there. A lot of rough men up there."

And not down here? Pen thought. "Won't I be all right if I go with Frank?"

Miss Tilly sniffed. "Them men haven't seen a woman in weeks."

Pen thought of the pistol in her bag. She said, "What if I dress as a boy? Would that help any?"

"That wouldn't fool Frank," Miss Tilly said.

"Get me some boy's clothes," Pen said. "We'll see."

"You watch yourself," Miss Tilly said.

"You mean watch Frank."

"Yes, I do, Miss Steal Away."

One of the laundresses, amused by overhearing this, said, "Well, if you want to dress up to wander through the camp, I can help you."

She found Pen a shirt, trousers, and a cap. The clothes had been newly laundered and smelled of lye soap. In the women's quarters, Pen shucked off her petticoat and dress to button the shirt over her chemise and pull on the trousers. The nankeen itched, and she wished she'd thought to ask for a man's underthings. She pulled on the cap to hide her hair. She moved around in the unfamiliar clothes, which were too big on her. It was strange not to feel a skirt brush her legs. Toby sniffed her and whined at the unaccustomed smell. She reached out her hand for him to sniff. "It's all right, boy," she said. She left him in the kitchen, where he looked expectantly at Miss Tilly, who shook her head at both woman and dog.

She sauntered over to the men's barracks, where Frank stood outside, waiting for his gang. He glanced at her and said, "Who you work for, son?"

Pen laughed. "You don't know me?"

Frank stared. "You! Why you dress like that?"

"Want to see the works. I hear you go up there."

He was still surprised. "I do," he said. "But I can't take you there. Don't care how you dressed."

"Why not?"

"It too dangerous."

"More dangerous than here?"

He said, "Tree or an axe, them dangers I know."

"You much too good a lumberman to let a tree hit me in the head."

"All right. I spell it out for you. We hidden away here. Thousands of Black folks here and just a few white men. No one know or care about a stranger. The saltworks, that different. White men all over. Overseers. Bookkeepers. Superintendents. They take notice of someone who don't belong here."

"They see me for a runaway," she said slowly.

"And you know full well what that mean."

"You turn me in?"

"Why would I? What do I get for it?" He said, "Work hard here, and the overseer don't bother me none. Eat plenty for a change. Don't want anyone taking notice of me, either."

In protecting her, he was protecting himself. "It keep us both out of trouble."

"Yes," he said. "You smart. Don't act the fool. Put your dress back on and lie low. No one notice another gal in the kitchen."

STUNG, PEN RETURNED TO the women's quarters and put her dress back on. Her skirt felt heavy and damp around her legs. She shook it out and went into the kitchen, where the busy, burdened cooks stared at her. One of them said, "Look at young miss, who too good to do any work. You come here for biscuit, young miss?"

Angry, Pen said, "Young miss! I chop cotton all my life on my old place."

Another woman said, "Ask her how her dress-up go this morning."

The first woman taunted, "Them trousers keep you safe?"

"I ain't staying here, and I don't work here. Where's my dog?"

Miss Tilly looked up from her seat at the table, where she was peeling potatoes. "Leave her alone, all of you. Miss Pen, your dog right here, at my feet." She asked, "You all right with Frank?"

"Why you keep asking me that? He fine." She was much too embarrassed to tell Miss Tilly how Frank had chided her.

"He don't take you anywhere, I can tell. Trousers notwithstanding."

"It was fine," Pen repeated, lying. Miss Tilly shrugged.

THAT EVENING, PEN FELT too restless to stay put. She summoned Toby and went outside. The swamp—and the river, just out of her reach—filled the air with moisture. The evening was little cooler than the day. She gazed at the sky, pleased that no canopy of longleaf pine hid the stars. She quieted, hoping to hear birds. But in this deforested woodland, which sang with the rhythm of axes and saws, the birds had fled.

What an odd place, she thought, *with thousands of men and hundreds of women in slavery to salt.*

Toby nosed his way, and she followed him. She found herself near the men's quarters, where a group of men sat in a ragged circle, passing a jug around, and their laughter rose like a cloud of midges from river water.

"Miss Pen! Set with us." It was Frank, his voice a little unsteady.

"Don't want to *trouble* you," she said, hoping to needle him.

"You don't trouble me none, not now," he said, his teeth flashing white. "I know I was sharp with you this morning. Sorry to do it. I put it aside if you do."

"You mean that?"

"I do. Join us."

Toby pressed against her leg. "All right."

Frank made room for her. She sat, pulling her dress to cover her ankles. Toby settled at her feet, keeping his eyes on Frank.

The whiskey jug came to Frank. He took a deep swig and held it out to her. "You want some?" It wasn't his first taste; he smelled of liquor.

She shook her head.

"Thought you wanted to learn how to act like a boy," he said, grinning. In the dark, it didn't seem as friendly as it had been in daylight.

Toby raised his head and pricked up his ears. "Boy

or girl, I don't care for whiskey." She took the jug, and he made sure to let his fingers touch hers. She said, "You need to mind yourself," and passed the jug to the man next to her.

He was drunker than Frank. "I ain't seen my wife for a year. Is that any way to live?"

Rough men, Miss Tilly had said. "No," Pen said.

The drunken man grabbed for her arm, and whatever he meant, Toby raised his head and growled at him.

Frank said sharply, "You leave her alone."

"Why?" the drunk asked. "Do she belong to you?"

Thoroughly uncomfortable, Pen said, "I believe that up to me," and she rose.

Frank rose, too. "Let me walk you back to the women's quarters."

"I'm all right."

"Worry about you, alone in the dark," he said.

"Walked all the way from Georgia," she said. "I reckon I can manage to walk a few feet."

But he followed her and caught hold of her hand. "No reason to be so tetchy."

All the amity had fled. "Ain't tetchy," she said. "Just telling you."

He held her hand tight. Too tight. He said, "I want a little sugar. Sick of salt. I want sugar."

"No," she said, trying to break free, as Toby growled.

"Don't do that," he said to both of them. With his free hand, he grabbed her left shoulder, which was still not completely healed, and pulled her close. He put the other arm around her and clenched her tight. She could smell the whiskey on his breath and feel him against her, hard as an axe handle. She tried to struggle free. "Don't you do that," he muttered. He kissed her, a rough, unwelcome kiss.

Toby growled, a meaner sound than she had ever heard from him, and suddenly Frank yelled, "Damn!" Toby had caught Frank's trouser leg between his teeth. Frank shook his leg, trying to fend Toby off. "Your damn dog! Call him off!"

"Let me go," she gasped.

He loosened his grip and pushed her away. "Damn your dog and damn you, too."

"Toby!" she cried out. "Let go!" Toby growled again, but he obeyed her.

Shaking, she turned away. It was all she could do not to run.

INSIDE THE WOMEN'S QUARTERS, she sat heavily on her rope bed. She could feel Frank's heavy hands on her shoulders and his unwelcome kiss on her lips. Shame washed over her. Despite all her efforts to belong to herself, a man had taken her. She had trusted him. The betrayal was worse than the compulsion.

She thought of how much worse it could have been. She let herself feel the full weight of the threat she had lived under since she left Dougherty County. She wrapped her arms around herself, rocking back and forth as she began to sob. Toby leaped onto the cot and pressed his head into her lap. Crying uncontrollably, she hugged Toby tight.

Miss Tilly bent over her and touched her shoulder. She shied away.

"Damn that man."

Miserable, Pen said, "I tell him no."

Miss Tilly sighed. "When do a Black woman get to say no?"

Pen sobbed, oblivious to Miss Tilly's arms around her. Thousands of men, starved for women, enslaved by salt. She couldn't cross the Tombigbee River and leave this place behind fast enough.

THE NEXT MORNING, FRANK was sober, and his eyes were bloodshot. He said stiffly, "I wasn't all right last night."

"You weren't!" she cried. "Should have let my dog bite you to the bone."

He said, "Your dog a better man than I am."

"You just call yourself a dog?"

"Call myself worse than a dog," he said.

"If I plan to stay here, I make you beg forgiveness," she said, angrier because he had made her feel so weak. "But I move on, and next week I don't even remember you."

"Now that's harsh."

"You don't deserve any better."

"Thought you wanted help to get across the river."

"Don't trust you to help me."

He didn't grin. "If you want to cross the river, that ain't up to you."

She thought of the pistol, Denmark's gift. She could shoot anyone who got too close, and next time she would. "It is up to me," she said, and walked away.

Pen followed the smell of bacon grease to the kitchen

and found Miss Tilly at the stove. "Miss Tilly, can you help me?"

"Frank bother you again?"

"No. Done with that. Can you help me get across the Tombigbee River? Find someone with a boat?"

Miss Tilly's eyes lingered on Pen's face. She said slowly, "Have a better notion than that."

"What?"

"Hide in plain sight."

"What you mean?"

"Get a pass. Take the ferry."

"A pass? Who write me a pass?"

"Mr. Theodore," she said. "Butler to the superintendent. He know me. Do me a favor."

Pen thought of Dido, back in Georgia, who forged a pass in her mistress's name.

The superintendent lived in a place made to look like a plantation house, a big version of a country four-up-and-down with a wraparound porch. Not so different from the Dougherty County place back in Georgia. Miss Tilly went to the side door, tapping it to call for Mr. Theodore.

Mr. Theodore had a reverend's dignity. He was probably his master's son and had been a house servant all his life. From the look of him, Pen thought he would be the first to tell massa that someone had a plan to steal away.

Miss Tilly introduced Pen. Mr. Theodore said, "I hear about her." He nodded to Miss Tilly. "Will you let us talk private?"

He took her to the pantry. "I hear you've run all the way from Georgia."

"Yes," Pen said. "Who tell you?"

"I hear things."

Too many strangers here knew her secret.

Mr. Theodore leaned forward, as though he had a secret of his own. He dropped his voice to a whisper. "I've run away four times, and I'll keep trying until I don't come back."

She met his eyes. She whispered, "Do you know about the Proclamation?"

He nodded. "Forever free," he whispered. "You wait here."

She waited, feeling apprehensive, knowing that she didn't belong in the big house. She felt exposed. Any servant might stop to challenge her. Worse yet, the superintendent might. Or still worse, his missus.

Too many rivers to cross, she thought.

When Mr. Theodore returned, he held a slip of paper between his fingers.

"Let me see that," Pen said, relief washing through her.

"You can read?"

"A little."

He handed it to her, and she puzzled over it, but the handwriting was too different from the letters in the book about the cat, the mat, and the rat. She couldn't decipher it.

Mr. Theodore held out his hand for the paper. He read softly, "I grant my servant Pen my permission to visit her relations in Washington County. Signed, Mr. George Woolsey, Superintendent."

"Is it good enough for a patroller?"

"It will be," he said.

She looked into his limpid brown eyes. "Why don't you write yourself a pass, Mr. Theodore?"

He hesitated. Then he told her another secret. "Won't get me far enough."

"How far is that?"

"North. As far north as I can go." He let her see all the longing and all the rebellion under the house servant's veneer. "Fifth time, I want it to be for good."

Chapter 11

Jones County, Mississippi
June 1863

As Pen entered Mississippi, leaving the rivers far behind, she was in the piney woods again. That meant white farmers instead of planters and small farms instead of plantations with slaves who might be sympathetic to her. Or not.

She had spent enough time in woods like these to know that the militia, if they rode through here, would not be hunting runaway slaves. They would be looking for Confederate deserters. Her knowledge didn't console her. White deserters were a danger of their own. They might be decent to a slave on the run or they might hate a planter's nigger. Or they might be bushwhackers, who were half soldier and half bandit, rough men who wouldn't care if she said no or not. She moved her pistol to her pocket and often slipped her hand to it, touching it for reassurance.

Her fear deepened her loneliness. She wished she could rest. She wanted to find people she could trust. She found herself talking to Toby as though he were a person.

It was a sign of an unsound mind, and she didn't like it. But she didn't stop.

Despite her compass, she felt lost—and worse than that, adrift. She was in Mississippi at last. But Mississippi was a big place, and she still had no idea where Jonas might be. She began to feel like the Israelites in the desert, doomed to wander because they didn't deserve to find what they were looking for.

Spring had turned to summer, but the piney woods were still cool. Now she knew why Georgia planters, Low Country and Piedmont alike, had always decamped for the pines in the hot months. She trudged through the trees, Toby pacing her. Trees and more trees. A veritable sea of trees.

At midday—she had learned to gauge the filtered light—the trees thinned. Then they gave way to a field. Corn, knee high. No one in that field. Corn didn't need tending. She sighed. A white hog and hominy farmer, no doubt, more likely to shoot at her than to welcome her.

The trees thinned alongside the field, and she skirted it as she continued westward. She was about to melt back into the woods when she glimpsed the house in the clearing.

A log house. A farmer's house. Chickens and shoats in the front yard. A dog sleeping in the dirt. A porch, where someone sat. A woman.

Pen inched through the woods to take a good look. She told herself that it didn't matter if a white woman looked kindly. It was her husband she had to worry about.

But the woman wasn't white. Even though she was light of skin, she was unmistakably a woman of color.

Pen drew in her breath. As she watched, the woman

lifted something from her lap, not her mending but a newspaper. She raised it with a practiced air, as though used to reading.

A Black woman who could read, and who read openly, not caring who saw her.

Pen's mind began to race. She might be a free woman. Or she might be the slave of a master so lenient that he allowed her to read.

Would he be equally generous with a runaway?

Pen nodded to Toby, and the two of them emerged from the woods. Deliberately, Pen walked into the yard and up to the porch.

The woman put down her newspaper, and Pen saw the face of a woman who had always been a beauty. If she was a slave, she had lived with peril different from a field hand's or a runaway's. It was dangerous to catch a master's fancy and equally dangerous to lose it.

"Who are you?" she asked.

Pen said, "A traveler, all the way from Georgia."

"You a long way from home," the woman said.

"I am," Pen admitted. "We're thirsty, my dog and me. Hoped you might spare us some water."

The woman's eyes swept over Pen, taking in her bedraggled dress and her leather bag. "I can do better than that. I can give you something to eat."

"Be obliged," Pen said.

She said, "My name is Liza Fairburn. Who are you, traveler?"

For the first time in a long time, Pen gave her full name. "Penelope Mitchell." She patted Toby on the head. "And this is my dog, Toby."

"We feed him, too."

The door opened, and a man stepped onto the porch. "Liza? Who have you got out there? Is it another stray?"

He was swarthy in complexion, with keen brown eyes and a disheveled head of hair. He wore the coarse shirt and nankeen trousers of a farmer, soil-stained at the knees. He smiled at Liza, his affection for her clear.

Liza smiled back. "Not a stray. A guest. Penelope Mitchell. Miss Penelope, this is my husband, Carver Fairburn."

He was white.

"Welcome," he said.

Liza settled her at the kitchen table and fed her ham, eggs, and cornbread and poured her coffee to drink.

"Where you get coffee?" Pen asked, astonished.

Carver, who had joined them, grinned and said, "We have our ways."

None of them lawful, Pen thought, but it would be worse than rude to inquire. She asked the question that every landowner liked to answer. "Is this your place?"

"Yes," he said. "A hundred acres, some in corn and the rest in Liza's kitchen garden."

"Where am I? What is this place called?"

"Jones County, Mississippi," he said. "My family's been here for a long time. My granddaddy came here from North Carolina and settled here when he was a young man."

"Is he still with you?"

"No, he passed on," Carver said. "My uncle runs his old place now, and my daddy has a farm of his own."

"Like yours?"

"My daddy's is, yes. My uncle inherited from Grand-daddy. He has a thousand acres. He owns slaves." A shadow passed over his face. "My daddy and I, we don't."

Liza listened unperturbed, as though she had often heard the tale. Was she slave or free? Was she a wife in law or because she and Carver believed so? Pen couldn't ask.

Carver said to Pen, "Liza tells me you're from Georgia."

"Dougherty County, not far from Alabama."

"Where are you bound?"

She looked down at her plate. "Don't know yet. Come to find my husband." She glanced at Liza. "He was carried away to Mississippi before the war. Don't know exactly where."

"You come all this way for love?" Liza asked.

"I reckon so," Pen answered.

Liza and Carver smiled at each other in complicity. Liza said, "We ain't the only ones, Carver."

"Outside the law?"

"Fools for love, sugar."

Pen drew in her breath.

After the meal, Pen thanked them both, and said, "I should be on my way."

Liza said, "Won't hear of it. You stay with us tonight. You can stay for a bit, if you like."

Something was strange here. Pen wavered between wanting to know and wanting to be on her way. "Don't want to trouble you."

"You won't. I bet you'd dearly love to wash that dress of yours."

Pen weakened. The dress was stiff with dirt and foul with sweat.

"And yourself, too," Liza said.

Her scalp itched with the longing for a wash. "I really won't trouble you?"

"Of course not."

Liza drew her a bath, even though it was the middle of the day and the middle of the week, and left her to soak in the tin tub. Pen soaped herself all over. The soap was smooth in her hands and smelled like lavender. Fancy store-bought soap. Where would she get that?

Liza had laid out her spare dress, and as Pen buttoned it, she realized that her bag was gone. She ran into the kitchen. "Where's my bag?" she demanded.

Liza said, "It right here on the table. I clean it a little."

"You take my things out!"

"Had to. Don't worry. We keep them safe for you."

"My compass! My pistol!"

As though every visitor had one, Liza said, "If you want, Carver clean that up for you, too."

Pen said, "Is he a soldier? Who he fight for?"

Liza didn't reply. Pen leaned against the table, and even though it bothered her to raise her voice to her host, she said, "And what about you? What are you?"

Liza regarded her with unruffled calm. "It a long story," she said. "You stay for a while, and we'll tell you."

Later that afternoon, Pen found Carver sitting on the porch, her pistol in his lap. He said, "Liza asked me to take a look at it. It don't need cleaning. Looks like you haven't used it."

"I haven't."

"Do you know how to use it?"

Stung, she said, "I do. Been careful, that's all."

"How did you come by it?"

"Why you ask? You a militia man?"

He roared with laughter. "Dear God, no. Just wondering, since it ain't at all usual for a Black woman to roam the countryside with a pistol in her pocket."

She said, "You're a deserter, ain't you?"

"I am," he said, nonplussed. "What made you think so?"

"Met some deserters in Alabama. Traveled with them for a while. You put me in mind of them, that's all." She must be a little light-headed to talk to a white man like this. But he claimed a Black woman as his wife. He wasn't Pen's massa or inclined to be anyone's massa, it seemed.

"Were they Union men?" he asked.

"Don't think so. Just hated fighting. Wanted to go home."

"What happened to them?"

"Shot. All of us got shot." Her hand stole to her left shoulder. "I'm better now."

He watched her rub the spot that still wasn't right. "So that's why you have a pistol," he said. "Something you can fire with one hand."

She let her hand fall from her shoulder. "Something I can hide in my pocket."

THE NEXT MORNING, WHEN Liza poured her another cup of coffee, Pen said, "Wonder how you come to have real coffee."

Unflustered—Liza would be calm in the midst of a firefight—Liza said, "I might have a friend who's a Union man."

"Really? Do he give you that fancy soap, too?"

"You don't miss much, do you?"

"Been keeping my eyes and ears open all the time since I left Georgia." That was brazen. Where had it come from?

Liza said, "When Carver leave the Confederates, he take up with the Union men."

"He join the Union army?"

"He have an understanding with the local Union men."

Pen said nothing. She drank from her cup.

Liza asked, "You want any more coffee? There's a spot left."

After breakfast, Pen offered to help Liza with the dishes. Liza said, "You ain't here to work. You're a guest."

"Don't feel right setting when there's work to do."

"You can help me in the garden," Liza said.

Liza's kitchen garden was as large as the one on the Dougherty County plantation. She surveyed it with pride. "Everything coming along nicely," she said to Pen. "Beans, peas—green and black-eyed peas—tomatoes, and all kinds of greens. Ice potatoes and sweet potatoes both. Fruit, too. Strawberries just ripening now. We pick some for dinner."

The garden needed only a little weeding, light work for someone used to chopping cotton. Liza had lent her a straw hat against the sun, but the warm air felt good on her hands and arms. The heat had encouraged the rasp of the crickets and the calls of the birds. Birds always made her think of Jonas. She wondered where he was now and what he was doing. She thought of working close by him in the cotton field, watching how he used a hoe with such grace, and tears rose to her eyes. Where was he, in all of Mississippi?

When they had weeded to Liza's satisfaction and picked enough new peas and strawberries for dinner, Liza said, "Time to rest."

Pen laughed. "You indulgent for a driver."

Liza rose and brushed the dry dirt from her apron. "It all right when you drive yourself."

They sat in the shade of the porch, their chairs side by side, drinking water from the nearby creek, which was sweet on the tongue. Pen asked Liza, "Are you free?"

Liza said, "There ain't a straightforward answer to that."

"Tell me anyhow. Even if you have to go all around to do it."

Liza said, "I was born a slave on a place in Adams County, not far from Natchez. My daddy was my massa, as you can see plain in my face. I grow up pretty. I always know that it make trouble for me. When I was fifteen, old enough to catch a man's eye, my massa get into debt. He take me to Natchez to sell me." She didn't falter as she spoke. "There was a slave dealer in Natchez who like to sell pretty light-skinned slaves for fancy girls. Everyone know it. He get high prices. He sell me to a man who pay two thousand dollar for me."

Pen drew in her breath. "That's a lot of money."

"As though it would help me," Liza said. "I take his fancy, all right. In his house by day, in his bed by night."

"Fifteen year old," Pen whispered.

"I knew it wouldn't last. A fancy never do. The woman lose her looks or have too many children or Missus finally take notice that there are a passel of bright-skinned little'uns who look just like massa. So I go back to Natchez, and this time I wasn't sold for a fancy. I was sold as a housemaid. Only eight hundred dollar this time."

"Did you have children?"

"Of course I did. They stay on the place. Three babies, and I leave them all behind." Her eyes were stony. She was beyond grief. "A man named Fairburn buy me, and he bring me to Jones County. I work as a housemaid, but my fate follow me, and Marse Gideon use me just like my old massa did."

Pen asked, "Were he Carver's daddy?"

"No. His uncle. Like Carver tell you, two branches in the Fairburn family. His uncle well-off and own slaves. Carver's daddy scramble for a living, but his uncle don't. Well, even though the families don't get along, they see each other and know of each other's doings. Carver have reason to visit his uncle, and that's how he first see me. Later he tell me it was like the Lord hit him with a bolt of lightning. He was smitten. And he was furious at the way that my massa use me."

"Fool for love," Pen murmured.

"That's exactly it. I didn't understand at first because no white man ever bother to consider me. But Carver do. He court me. Treat me with kindness. He didn't force me, not even to kiss me. And then he tell me that he can't bear to leave me in his uncle's hands."

Pen said, "Marse Gideon wouldn't sell you, and his brother couldn't buy you."

"Oh, you see it, what a dilemma we have. But Carver figure how to fix it." She paused. Pen had listened to many a storyteller. Liza savored this part of the story, and she wanted Pen to know it. "He don't bother with the law. He took me to his daddy's place and kept me there. He say he rescue me, but he just steal me away." Her expression livened a little. "And when his uncle came by to take me back, Carver ready for him. He meet him with a pistol in his hand and point it right at him. He say, 'If you try to take her, if you touch a hair on her head, I'll shoot you through the heart.' Carver's daddy stand next to him. He have a rifle. And he say to Marse Gideon, 'I'm right with him.' After that, Marse Gideon don't even go to the courthouse to try to get me back. He hate Carver for what he done, but he let it go."

"Do it bother Carver that you were ill-used?"

Liza understood. "No, Carver don't care about my past. Know it were never my fault. Love me despite it."

"I never hear of a man like that," Pen said.

Liza laughed. "Carver do more than follow his heart. He live as a law unto himself, too."

"Ain't you still a slave?" Pen asked, puzzled.

"Carver can't truly free me. No one can. The laws of Mississippi make it too hard to free anyone. But that pistol set me free. Carver treat me like I'm free, like I'm his wife. Been that way for ten year now."

Pen said, "The Emancipation Proclamation—"

"Oh, I know all about it. Even the Jones County newspaper take notice of it. But the law don't matter so much in Jones County. What matter is who hold the pistol and the rifle and who willing to use it."

Pen asked, "Do you know how to shoot, too?"

"Of course I do," Liza said, as though it were the most natural thing in the world for a stolen slave to defend herself with a firearm. She asked, "Will you help me shell them peas? They'll be fine for our dinner."

THEY HAD A GUEST for midday dinner to share the new peas and the strawberries baked into a pie. It was Carver's brother, Emory, who embraced Liza like a sister. Emory looked askance at Pen. "Who's this?"

Liza said, "A friend of mine, come to stay with us for a bit."

Emory was a few years younger than Carver. He didn't say why he wasn't in the Confederate army, but Pen could hazard a guess.

After dinner, Carver said, "Liza, will you excuse us?"

Liza said, "Miss Pen, I believe the dishes can wait. We set a little first."

As they left the house, Carver closed the door. On the porch, out of earshot, Pen asked Liza, "What's that about?"

"Oh, they talk politics now. Bore us to death."

"Is Emory Fairburn a deserter, too?" Pen asked.

Liza said, "I believe you know the answer to your own question."

"Do he have an understanding with the Union army?"

"Miss Pen, why do you want to know?"

"The last time I travel through a county full of deserters, I got shot at." She flexed her arm and felt the hitch in her shoulder. "Just want to make sure it don't happen again."

"I like you, and so do Carver. But we all careful who we trust and what we say."

Pen said, "I run away. I been dodging patrollers and militia men all the way westward. I act like I believe the Proclamation set me free. What side do you think I'm on?"

"You don't sound like a runaway," Liza said.

"I ain't a Confederate spy, if that worry you."

"No," Liza said. "You sound like a contraband."

PEN HAD WORRIED ABOUT danger for weeks, but this was something different. Carver and Liza were in the middle of something, and Pen wasn't going to avoid it if she traveled through Jones County. She just didn't want to walk into it blind and stupid.

That afternoon, she sat on the porch steps, keeping an eye on Toby, who was sniffing around the Fairburns' dog. It was a hound built very much like Toby, with a brindled coat that mingled brown and yellow. The two dogs were careful around each other. She thought that she and Toby were becoming too much alike. Despite Liza's generosity in feeding Toby, he wasn't sure of the Fairburns, either.

Now alone, Carver returned, strolling toward the house. He stopped before the steps, smiling. "Miss Pen, it would bother Liza something terrible to see you sit on the steps."

Pen rose. "I'm all right," she said. "Just watching Toby."

Carver glanced at the dogs. "They making friends?"

"Getting acquainted, more like."

"He's a good dog. Looks like a hunter."

"Good hunter. Someone teach him right."

"How did you come by him?"

"He was lost in the woods. Took to me and wouldn't leave me."

"Faithful companion," Carver said.

"More than most people."

He laughed. "You don't trust me, any more than your dog trusts mine."

"Mr. Fairburn, what you up to?"

He said, "Let's walk a little. Bring your dog along."

"If anyone bother me, he bite."

"I thought as much," he said, reassuring her.

She called Toby, and the three of them took a turn for the woods.

The last time she had walked through the woods with a white man, she had been with Jasper. Carver Fairburn was nothing like Jasper, who had been young enough to be embarrassed by his unintentional meanness. Everything about Carver was intentional.

The trees here were longleaf pines, with the now-familiar smell of turpentine. They stopped beneath a pine that must have stretched thirty feet high. It was odd to look upward and think of it, to take its measure, like a lumberman for the salt mines. Toby found something at the foot of the tree that interested him and sniffed it.

Carver said, "So you think I'm up to something."

"You a Confederate deserter and Union man. Must be up to something."

He sighed. "There are deserters in every pinewoods county in Mississippi. Most of us were at Shiloh. Do you know of it?"

Jasper had been there, too. "I hear of it."

"A terrible battle. Twenty thousand dead. Terrible, bloody battle. And for what?" Like Liza, he had a point to make. "We poor men fought so that planters with more than twenty slaves could sit out the war. We died for that."

Pen thought of Carver holding a pistol on his slave-owning uncle. She said nothing.

"That's why I came home. I was done fighting for slavery. There are Union regiments in this part of Mississippi. After I came back, I found one and told them I'd help them."

"The coffee," she said slowly.

He said, "No, not for coffee. The Union men talk about freedom. Not just the freedom to break up slavery, even though you can see why that matters to me. The freedom to own your land, make your living, and maybe make your fortune without a planter's foot on your neck."

"Like your uncle's family."

"It's all of a piece," he said. "When I help the Union, when I hinder the Confederacy, I fight for my daddy and against my uncle."

"Don't want to walk through a battlefield," Pen said. "If I go west of here, might you point me around it?"

He said, "A dog and a pistol, that ain't enough to protect you. I can do better than that. Let me put a rifle in your hands and teach you how to use it."

"You mad," Pen said. "A runaway slave with a rifle? What do you think my chances are if I meet up with the militia?"

"I know better than anyone," he said. "The militia in Jones County hunts down deserters like they hunt down slaves. They send the dogs after us, too." He met her eyes, and she saw the ardor that he had lavished on Liza as a young man. It hadn't diminished now that he aimed it at the war.

AS PEN FELL ASLEEP that night, she thought, *I can't stay here.* She would thank them for their kindness tomorrow morning and go.

When she told Liza that she hoped to leave that day, Liza said, "Where you go to look for your husband?"

Pen couldn't reply. She didn't know. She just wanted out of Jones County.

Liza said, "Did Carver try to recruit you for the Union?"

"He offer to school me in shooting a rifle."

"He teach me how to shoot, too."

Pen said, "I want to be free, but I ain't sure I want to use a rifle to do it."

Liza laughed. "What do you think this war is about?"

In teaching her to shoot a rifle, Carver wasn't gentle with her, as Denmark had been. Carver didn't coddle her when she winced. He said, "If you use that shoulder, it won't hurt so bad." He didn't touch her to position her hands on the stock and on the trigger. He showed her, and he criticized her for doing it wrong. It didn't hurt her feelings. He had been a soldier, and he treated her like one. At her first attempt to hit a target, he said, "If that were someone who wanted to shoot you, you'd be dead already."

That hurt her pride. She forced herself to ignore the stiffness in her shoulder. In a few days, she got better. He said, "See? When you use that shoulder, you have a good eye."

"I ain't planning to be a sharpshooter."

"You never know," he said. "Keep at it."

SHE ITCHED TO GO, but she still didn't know where. Liza, who put her to work in the garden when she wasn't straining her shoulder by practicing her shooting, said to her, "I have a thought about where you might look for man carried away to Mississippi."

Pen looked up from her weeding. "Where?"

"Natchez."

"Why Natchez?"

"Because it full of slave dealers and auction houses. Some in Natchez proper and some in Forks of the Road."

"What's that?"

"Where the Natchez Trace and the main road into town meet. A host of slave dealers and houses there, too."

"How do that help me?"

"If your husband were sold there, they might have a bill of sale. Tell you who bought him, where he went."

With sarcasm, Pen said, "That just the thing for a runaway. Saunter into the slave market and say, 'How do, Mr. Slave Catcher. Do you have a paper that tell me who buy my husband and where he go?'"

"You might find someone to ask for you."

"And run the risk that they betray me for a runaway."

"Why you afraid all of a sudden? Natchez the place to ask. You smart. Know when to put yourself forward and when to hide. For someone like you, Natchez ain't any more dangerous than any other place you ever been."

She was abashed that Liza saw it so clearly. After months in the piney woods, the thought of a city rattled her. She didn't like her fear, and she liked even less that Liza saw it. She squared her shoulders. "How far is it?"

"About a hundred and fifty mile. Walk straight through, you get there in a week or two."

"What do I walk through? More battles waiting to happen?"

"Can you read a map?"

"Yes."

"Then we draw you a map." After a pause, Liza said, "I have another thought."

"Them thoughts of yours scare me," Pen said.

"Why don't you dress as a boy? You safer that way." She pressed her point. "Could even carry a rifle."

"Oh, that's fine. They shoot me instead of outraging me."

"Think about it."

PEN KNEW SHE SHOULD go, but she didn't. Liza shook her up, even as she charmed her with stories of her past and three ample meals a day. Pen felt weak to be beguiled by coffee, but she was. Carver drilled her, as blunt with her as any sergeant, and her shooting improved. Toby dithered along with her. Liza, who plied him with scraps, had finally won him over. He even tolerated the Fairburn dog, who greeted him daily with a sniff at the rear.

Carver watched the two dogs negotiating. He laughed and said to Pen, "You want to take those dogs out hunting?"

"They won't fight each other?"

"Won't let them," Carver said. "I'll lend you a rifle. You can shoot at something for real."

Pen didn't mind playing with the rifle to shoot at a target drawn on a dead tree. But she disliked the idea of carrying it with her when any white man might use it to challenge her, and she didn't like the idea of shooting her dinner, either. "Why? Liza glad to wring a chicken's neck for you."

"Sometime you'll have to shoot something living. It's better to try on something you can eat for dinner."

"You too fond of that rifle," she said.

He fetched her the rifle she'd used for target practice and handed it to her. She shook her head, but she rested it on her right shoulder, her good shoulder, to humor him and followed him into the woods.

She had been in the piney woods for weeks. She knew the thick smell of these trees, the grayish quality of the sunlight, the calls of the daytime birds. She had walked woods like these with a pistol in her bag. But the weight and the pressure of the rifle against her shoulder made her stand differently and walk differently. It interfered with her ability to step quietly and listen. The rifle distracted her.

"Stand up straight," Carver said.

"The rifle get in the way."

"You'll have to get used to it."

He was used to the threat of death, and now, the

possibility of capture. So he might be right. She straightened up. "Like this?"

"Better. But you ain't a soldier yet."

They walked deeper into the woods without speaking. He was nearly silent when he walked. He held himself still, listening. He was either a good hunter, or he'd been a scout.

Carver's dog growled softly, and so did Toby. Carver halted. He said, "We have company."

"Militia?"

"Not during the day."

A gravelly voice called, "Who's there?"

Carver didn't move, but he showed no evidence of fear. He let the man find him. When he came into view, Carver said, "Uncle Gideon! Don't shoot at me."

He was grizzled and rough—not at all Pen's idea of a successful planter. He lowered his gun and growled at Carver, "Who's that with you?"

Despite the firearm in her hands, Pen's heart pounded in fear, and her mouth went dry. As though they were making introductions after church, Carver said, "Friend of Liza's."

Gideon Fairburn stared at Pen. "Nigger gal? Why has she got a gun?"

"She can shoot, just like Liza," Carver said. His hand rested easily on the rifle stock.

The old threat hung in the air. *If you touch a hair on her head…*

"Niggers with guns," Gideon said. "Is that what they teach you in the Union army?"

"I ain't in any army, Uncle Gideon."

"I hear different."

"You hear wrong."

Gideon spat. "You stay away from my place. Or I'll shoot you."

Carver's voice went cold. "We'll see who shoots first."

Gideon spat again and walked away.

THEY BAGGED NOTHING, NOT even a rabbit, and Liza fed them ham for dinner. Carver didn't tell Liza about their meeting with Gideon Fairburn, and Pen was more uneasy than ever. Union against Confederate, Fairburn against Fairburn: it wouldn't matter when the bullets began to fly. She didn't want to be there for it.

That night, Pen said, "You been kind to me, both of you, but I plan to leave tomorrow."

Liza said, "Tomorrow? Don't have clothes for you."

"Clothes?" Carver asked.

"Boy's clothes. I figure she'll be safer dressed like a boy."

"She'd be safer with a proper firearm."

Pen let herself feel the fear she'd tamped down during the showdown with Gideon Fairburn. "No. Man or woman, I'd be a nigger with a rifle. I'd be in a world of trouble because of it." Liza was getting ready to protest. Pen said, "Don't tell me that you get away with it. You under the protection of Carver Fairburn, whether you his wife or not. That ain't true for me. Nigger gal? Runaway? If I had a rifle in my hands, I'd be dead."

For the first time since Pen had met her, Liza lost her

look of calm. Worry furrowed her brow and deepened the lines on either side of her mouth. She said, "Carver, don't dispute with her." To Pen, she said, "Give me time to fix up some clothes of Carver's." She turned to Carver. "You don't mind sparing her a shirt?"

Carver shook his head. He didn't have to say it. *No, I don't mind the shirt. But I despair of the rest.*

"Day after tomorrow, then," Pen said.

LIZA PILED THE CLOTHES neatly on the guest bed. She had the foresight to include drawers and a pair of socks. Thankfully, everything was clean, smelling neither of lavender nor sweat but of harsh laundry soap. Pen took off her woman's clothes, down to her skin, and she started with the shirt. The cloth was worn and soft. Carver hadn't relinquished anything new. Well, that was right; she should look as though she wore massa's castoffs. She pulled on the drawers. They were tight on her hips, but that didn't matter. The trousers were nankeen, threadbare at the knees. That kind of wear was all right, too. Liza had found her a cap and a kerchief to wrap her hair beneath it. Pen felt uneasy all over again, thinking of the people who knew so well how to put together a disguise. Playactors and spies.

Her leather bag was there, too, noticeably cleaner and more supple. Pen pulled everything out to make sure it was all there. Dresses, chemises, petticoat, shawl. At the sight of the shawl, which she hadn't worn for months, she thought of her sister, Cassie. She pressed the shawl to her face before she put it back in the bag.

Compass. Pistol. She palmed the pistol in relief. The handkerchief with the silver dollars in it. She hefted it. It seemed to weigh the same as before.

The book. "*Leaves of Grass*," she whispered, tracing the words on the cover.

And a few things that were new. A big box of matches. She'd been down to her last few. A map, showing her the way westward, tracing the distance to Natchez, a hundred and fifty miles, a week's steady journey. Covington County. Lawrence County. Franklin County. Adams County. Whoever drew the map—she guessed it was Carver—had made a note that the Pearl River in Lawrence County was, in some places, too wide to wade across. It was good to be forewarned.

She repacked the bag and slung it over her shoulder, relishing the familiar weight. She flexed her left shoulder. It no longer hurt. If she had any reason to pick up a rifle, she could use it.

She walked into the front room and onto the porch, where Liza sat in her chair, her newspaper folded on her lap. Pen asked, "How do I look?"

Liza said, "You'll do."

Pen laughed. "Sometimes it good not to be a beauty."

Carver waited at the foot of the steps. He said, "I'll be damned. I wouldn't know you were a girl. What will you call yourself?"

It came to her in a moment, a boy's name to match the clothes. "Mitchell Penn."

"That will do, too." He held out his hand. "Best of luck to you, Penelope Mitchell. You won't reconsider the offer of a firearm?"

She met his eyes. "Have to fight my war without it." She called: "Toby!"

Toby, who had been resting in the dirt of the yard, stood up and shook himself. He looked expectantly at Liza, wagging his tail. Liza said, "Goodbye to you too, Toby."

Pen turned, facing west, and set off with Toby at her side.

Chapter 12

JONAS WOKE TO THE smell of coffee. He lay quietly as the morning light filtered through his tent, and relished the feeling of the bedroll beneath his head and the blanket draped over him. Around him, soldiers emerged from their tents, splashed water, spat, and joshed each other. The horses, also waking for the day, whickered as they waited for their breakfast. Jonas stretched and sat up. Far away, as distant as a summer thunderstorm, the bombardment of Vicksburg continued.

He put on his trousers and shoes, glad to be dressed in clothes that were whole and clean. The laundresses, all of them contraband, had a soft spot for the contraband men who served the Union army.

Jonas strolled to the cook tent, where the aroma of coffee was joined by that of frying bacon. Two men sat at the table under the canopy, eating.

The cook, also a contraband, greeted him with a smile. "Got fresh eggs today," he said. "Fry you some along with the bacon."

He asked, "Where do them eggs come from?"

One of the men at the table, a contraband named Titus, said good-naturedly, "Quartermaster Corps *emancipate* a hen or two from a plantation nearby."

Jonas sat at the table, laughing. "They read her the Proclamation?"

Titus's companion, a white private named Thatcher, said, "Whether we do or not, I'm sure she's eating better than she has since the war started."

The cook set a filled plate before Jonas: fried eggs, bacon, and the white bread that was still a marvel to a man who had been grateful for an extra bite of dry cornbread. "There's more if you want it," the cook said.

His mouth full, Jonas nodded.

The cook said, "Major Leverett ask us to fatten you up."

Major Leverett had found him one of the quietest spots in the Union encampment at Vicksburg. He had situated Jonas with the Quartermaster Corps responsible for transporting men and supplies, which was as far from the front lines as a man could get and still be in the army. The Corps had a multitude of wagons drawn by a horde of horses. Jonas had been assigned to work in the stables with Titus and Thatcher. Since the Quartermaster Corps mingled soldiers with contrabands, the men had decided to call each other by surname rather than rank. It was respectful, if not absolutely soldierly. Their sergeant didn't mind it.

Titus had been with Grant's army since he ran from his plantation after the Battle of Shiloh. His master had kept a stable of racing and carriage horses, and Titus had been his ostler, overseeing his master's beauties. Now, as an employee of the Union army, Titus introduced Jonas to his new duties and his new charges. Titus asked, "Is you used to horses?"

"No. Chopped cotton on my massa's place and built fortifications for the Confederates."

Titus chuckled. "Today you meet some." He led Jonas to the temporary stable, a rough series of stalls under a canvas canopy. The smell of hay drifted out, as did a whiff of manure and the smell of the animals themselves, strong but not unpleasant. Titus stopped at the first stall.

Jonas said, "That a mighty big horse."

"Big, strong horse," Titus said, laying his hand on the horse's neck. Titus's arm and the horse's coat were the same rich brown hue. "Even temper. Has to be, not to shy when the guns fire." He stroked the brown coat. "Name Ulysses," he told Jonas. "After General Grant."

"Ain't that disrespectful?"

"No. We all think the world of General Grant." He said, "Now put out your hand."

"Why?"

"Let him get acquainted with you."

Tentatively, Jonas did so, and the horse nudged him. Titus chuckled. "He want sugar," he said. "He don't get it. But he get a carrot." He drew it from his pocket. "You give it to him."

Jonas took the carrot with hesitant fingers. "He don't bite me?"

"He as gentle as a kitten. Hold it out for him."

Ulysses raised his head to get a good look at Jonas and the proffered carrot. He gently took the carrot between his teeth, and once it was in his mouth, he nosed Jonas's palm in a touch as gentle as a woman's.

"You can pet him, if you want," Titus said. "On his neck, like I do. He like that."

Jonas touched Ulysses's neck. "He feel soft," he said in surprise.

"We groom him, and he have a good coat. I show you how to do that, once you get used to him."

In this calm place, free of the burden of bombardment, Jonas was suddenly overcome by all the anxiety he'd tamped down for weeks. His head swam, and his legs were too shaky to hold him. He said, "Can I set down?"

Titus took his arm and settled him on a clean patch of straw. "You want a cup of water?"

"No." He took a ragged breath.

Titus said, "I recall when I first run to the army. I walk around in a daze. Couldn't believe I was safe. Took me a while to get used to it." He put his hand on Jonas's arm, as he'd touched Ulysses's neck, and said, "Major Leverett tell us to be easy on you. Didn't need him to say so. You look like a colt that's been starved and overworked and beat."

THATCHER SHOWED JONAS HOW to feed and water the horses. Like his charges, the Union draft horses, Thatcher was big and burly, with an even temper and a sweet nature. As they worked together, he told Jonas about himself. He was a farmer from Chester County, Pennsylvania, and grew fruit and vegetables that he sold in nearby Philadelphia. "That's why I'm in the Quartermaster Corps. I spent more time on the road driving my team to market than I did farming. Never minded it. I always liked horses."

Despite the difference in their status, Thatcher treated Titus as his equal, and he did the same for Jonas. Jonas couldn't bring himself to ask Thatcher why, but he did ask Titus. Titus said, "You can talk to him direct, you know."

"I ain't in the habit of being direct with a white man."

Titus nodded. He said, "Thatcher have a Black man for a neighbor in Chester County. He a farmer, just like Thatcher. Born a free man and own that farm outright. And that neighbor of his, he married to a white woman. So he won't mind it, not at all."

JONAS CAME TO LIKE the horses, just as Titus had predicted. Titus showed him how to curry a horse, using the good-natured Ulysses as an example. Ulysses liked to be groomed, and when Jonas used the comb on him, the horse turned his head and nosed Jonas's face. Jonas stopped to stroke Ulysses's neck.

In Ulysses's stall, so far from the battlefront that he no longer heard it, Jonas thought of the life that he might choose for himself. He knew that he was unlikely to go anywhere as long as the Union army continued to besiege Vicksburg. It seemed strange to be happy in the midst of war, but in the company of Titus and Thatcher, befriended by the horses, he was happy for the first time in months.

In the wake of happiness, he felt guilt. He hadn't thought much of Pen. Thinking of her had been a loss in his life, along with a night's sleep, enough to eat, or a day untroubled by the danger of mortar fire. Now that he was safe, his daze lifted, and he thought of her often with pain and regret.

He dreamed of her. He saw her standing on the bank of a river, fog swirling around her dress and over the water. He reached out his arms to her, and she did the same, trying to close the gap of an expanse too wide to cross over. He woke with tears running down his cheeks.

One night, after dinner and before tattoo—the army's word for the bugle call to end the day—Jonas sat on the ground with Thatcher and Titus. Thatcher smoked a pipe, which Titus and Jonas teased him about.

Titus said, "That tobacco smell worse than horse manure."

Jonas said, "If we capture some secesh, maybe we *emancipate* some good tobacco for Thatcher."

"Hope so," Titus said. "You in better spirits. You feel better?"

"Better in some ways, worse in others," Jonas said.

"How is that?" Thatcher asked.

Jonas had taken Titus's advice about Thatcher to heart. He spoke as freely as he would to Titus. "Titus tell me that he in a daze after he first become a contraband. I was, too. Not anymore. Free to think about things. To remember things. Don't always like what come to mind."

Titus nodded. Thatcher puffed on his pipe. Neither man spoke. They were used to horses, whose moods they read in the flick of a tail or the flattening of an ear. They would let Jonas speak as he wished to.

Jonas asked, "Are you married? Either of you?"

Thatcher said, "I am. My wife is running the farm

back in Chester County. I miss her and the children, but she's all right."

Titus said, "My wife die just before the war."

"You have a family?" Jonas asked.

"God never blessed us that way."

Jonas said, "When I was sold away, I left my wife behind. Pen. Penelope. At first I miss her and grieve for her. But the war eat me up. And it shame me that I put her aside in my mind." He took a deep breath. "Now I think about her all the time. Recall how much I love her, and I miss her."

"Where is she?" Thatcher asked.

"She in Georgia. Dougherty County." He rubbed his chin. "I ain't likely to go back there anytime soon."

Titus said, "Maybe she a contraband, too. Maybe she ain't in Georgia no more."

"How would I find her?" Jonas asked, feeling despair well up in him. "If she run away and she gone only God knows where?"

Thatcher said, "You ask after her, wherever you go. And you keep her alive in your heart and your soul."

Jonas nodded. Now, in addition to the guilt, he felt an overwhelming sadness. He was still married to Pen. He would always be married to Pen. And as much as he yearned for her, he didn't know if he would ever see her again.

WHEN JONAS HAD BEEN with the Union army for about two weeks, Titus pulled him aside early in the morning.

"Happy day! Paymaster here! We collect our pay today. You lucky. Don't get paid regular, not when we in battle like this."

"Pay?"

Titus looked at him as though he'd gone back into his fugitive's daze. "You work for the army, they pay you," he said. "They pay me, even though I ain't a soldier. Pay all of us contrabands the same. Ten dollar a month."

"Ten dollar?"

"Soldiers get more. But I ain't complaining. Ten dollar more than I ever get in slavery."

"How do I get my money?"

"Go to see the paymaster. He dole it out. Come with me. I show you."

Jonas stood in line with Titus, surrounded by soldiers and contrabands both. At the paymaster's desk, the paymaster asked for his name and consulted a list. "Jonas Mitchell. With the Quartermaster Corps."

"That's right, sir."

"It hasn't been a full month, so we pay accordingly. Five dollars. Next month, we'll start to figure it at ten dollars." He handed Jonas an envelope.

Jonas fingered the envelope, expecting to feel coins. Perplexed, he went to find Titus. He asked, "What in that envelope? Don't heft like money."

Titus grinned. "Open it and see."

Jonas looked. "Paper! Nothing but paper!"

"Greenbacks. US government money. As good as silver or gold."

Jonas squinted at the portrait on the front of the

note. "Who that a picture of?" He held it out for Titus to examine.

"Don't know. I get a ten-dollar note. That have a picture of President Lincoln."

A FEW DAYS LATER, on the first of July, the afternoon quiet of the Quartermaster encampment was rent by the sound of an explosion so loud that Jonas ran from the stall where he worked, yelling, "What were that?"

"Easy," Titus said, putting a calming hand on his arm. "It far away."

Thatcher said, "We'll find out soon enough what it was."

By late afternoon, the camp was abuzz. The Union engineers had succeeded in exploding a mine under the Jackson Road Redan, making an immense crater that breached the fortification. The seven men who worked in the shaft had been killed, but one man—a Black man named Abraham—had been ejected by the blast and had landed unhurt behind the Union lines. He was dazed but otherwise all right. Titus said, "He say he was blowed to freedom!"

Jonas felt dazed himself. He thought, *I help to do that.* He wondered what Major Leverett thought.

Abraham became a spectacle. Thatcher was disgusted to hear it. "They should give him a proper job with the army, not show him off like an exhibit in Barnum's museum!"

"I want to see him," Jonas said.

"Not because he's a spectacle!"

"No," Jonas said. "Because I work on that mine before I get behind the Union lines. Maybe he know what become of the men I work with."

Still disgusted, Thatcher lent him a nickel, the price of admission to see Abraham. Jonas made his way to the exhibition tent; it was easy to find because the soldiers had thronged to see the marvel. Jonas was the only Black man in the crowd, and the soldiers who surrounded him didn't have Thatcher's delicacy. One of them asked him, "How did you get here? Were you blowed to freedom, too?"

Jonas let himself get angry at a white man, and he let himself show it. "I work for the secesh before I come here. And I walk through the lines like a man, not like a ball shot out of a cannon." His interest in seeing Abraham was spoiled. He didn't need to spend a nickel to hear which men had died in the explosion. Even if Huntoon had been among them, he no longer wanted to know. Despite his spark of decency, Huntoon was the enemy now. He was a damned secesh.

Jonas returned to the stable and put the nickel back in Thatcher's palm. "What's this?" Thatcher asked. "Didn't you see the exhibition?"

"Didn't want to see a Black man made into a spectacle." He was still angry. "I work on the countermine, and when I come to the Union army, I tell Major Leverett everything I know about it. The Union men, the sappers and miners, they blow it up because I help them. Blowed to freedom!"

Thatcher laughed.

"What you laugh at?" Jonas asked.

"A free man is free to get mad," Thatcher said.

THAT EVENING, AFTER DINNER, their sergeant came looking for Jonas. Jonas rose as he approached. "Mitchell?"

"Yes, sir," he said. He was schooling himself to say "sir" crisply, as the soldiers did, and not the slurred "suh" of slavery.

"You're to come with me."

"Do I do something wrong?"

"No, not at all," the sergeant said. "Someone wants to see you."

Before the quartermaster's tent sat an officer, his eyes wearier than before, but his face curved in a smile. He rose as Jonas approached.

"Major Leverett," Jonas said.

"Mr. Mitchell. My men exploded their mine under the Jackson Road Redan today."

"We hear the sound of that explosion, even here. And then we learn all about how it happen, sir."

"I wanted to thank you, Mr. Mitchell. Your help was of great value to us."

"Glad to hear it, sir."

"How are you faring here?"

He knew that Major Leverett had done him a favor. "I do fine, sir."

"Do you like it?"

"I do, sir."

"I haven't forgotten the other matter. The matter of your preference."

"Thank you, sir."

"It will have to wait until the siege is over. But I have a feeling that it won't be too long now."

"I hope so, sir."

MAJOR LEVERETT WAS RIGHT. On July 4 of 1863, Independence Day, General Pemberton surrendered to General Grant. Jonas, who had learned that the Union men called the general "Unconditional Surrender" Grant, was disappointed to hear that he offered parole to the men who had defended the city. He told Ulysses the horse that he wished that Ulysses the general had squashed the secesh of Vicksburg like a bug.

That night, as Thatcher smoked and Titus tolerated it, Jonas said, "It so quiet." For the first time since the middle of May, the sound of war was silenced. No roar of mortars, no whistle of shells, no scream of bullets. Jonas listened to the silence. Someday, when this war-torn ground healed up, birds would sing here again.

As the men celebrated General Grant's triumph at Vicksburg, news of another victory came to the camp. Just after the battle ended, they got the news from Gettysburg. Thatcher said, "They won that one on Independence Day, too."

"Were it close to your farm, Thatcher?" Titus asked.

"No, thank God. But it was on my home soil, which is something I never thought I would say about this war."

Major Leverett summoned Jonas a few days after the news from Gettysburg. Jonas marched to the major's tent in the company of a private who looked at him sidewise, surely wondering what business the major and the contraband might possibly concoct together.

Major Leverett seated him and offered him coffee. Jonas said, "Thank you, sir. Never thought I would say this, but for once I've had enough coffee!"

"You look well, Mr. Mitchell."

"Thank you, sir." Jonas wished he could say, as to a friend, *So do you.* In the way that slaves put it, Major Leverett looked as though he had laid his burden down.

The major said, "I haven't forgotten what I promised." He handed Jonas an envelope. "This is a letter for Colonel Webber, who commands the First Mississippi. I've told him how brave and how loyal you are and that I know you'll make a fine soldier. If you want to muster in, he should be glad to have you."

Jonas was overwhelmed. He felt a little dazed again, and in his confusion, he said, "Major Leverett, why do you do this for me?"

Major Leverett said, "I'm a Boston man. My family has been opposed to slavery since the Revolutionary War." His eyes crinkled as he smiled. "Since that first Independence Day." The officer extended his hand, and the former slave shook it.

THE UNION ARMY CAMP at Lake Providence, fifty miles up the Mississippi River from Vicksburg, had always been a supply depot, and the steamboats that made the journey had to be carefully laden with artillery and horses as well as men. In the cargo hold, Titus moved among the horses, patting noses, stroking necks, and murmuring softly into ears. Jonas, along with Titus and Thatcher, sailed in the cargo hold with their horses.

Thatcher sat on the floor to lean against a trunk. "The horses are fine. Titus isn't. He doesn't like the water."

Jonas angled himself to get a good view of the water. He breathed in the smell of the river, a muddy odor, and gazed eagerly at the cloudy water. As the boat got underway, the engine roared, and the river smell was lost under the stink of coal burning. It wasn't like the sound or smell of war, which promised death. This was the sound of movement. Jonas touched the letter in his coat pocket. It felt warm, as though it were a living thing.

He'd seen the Flint River, which flowed through Dougherty County back home, but it was nothing like the Mississippi. The Flint was narrow enough to spit across. The Mississippi made him feel that he could stretch his arms wide. "How far across is this river?" he asked Thatcher.

"I don't rightly know. I never saw a river like this before I came south. I see why they call it a mighty river."

Jonas craned his neck to watch the spume the boat left in its wake. Happiness surged through him. *I feel free*, he thought.

THE ARMY CAMP, LIKE the siege encampment, was orderly, a town of canvas tents interspersed with cook sheds. The enclaves of the larger tents were reserved for the officers. The supply wagons and temporary stables were orderly, too. Behind the camp, sprawling westward into

Louisiana, was a shabby shadow of the army's neatness. Rickety buildings crowded against each other. Jonas asked, "What's that mess over there?"

Titus, who had recovered now that he was on land again, said, "That's the contraband camp. Every army camp have one. I live in one when I first run to the army."

"Why don't the army clean it up?"

Titus said, "Well, they got that little matter of winning the war to take care of. That keep them mighty occupied."

Jonas was billeted with the Quartermaster Corps in one of the neat canvas tents of the army, but he still thought about the ramshackle camp that had attached itself to the main camp like a leech to a leg. He wandered over there the day after he arrived.

Amid the ramshackle houses were people. Swarms of people. Mostly men but also a surprising number of women with their children. The sight of a little boy, ragged and hollow-eyed, made him stop. He asked the child's mother, "How old is he?"

"Just three."

The baby Pen had been carrying would be three now. He wondered if it were a girl or a boy. "What he called?"

"Freddy."

Jonas knelt and said gently, "How do, Freddy," in the soft tone that Titus had taught him to use around horses.

The boy hid his face in his mother's skirt. She said, "He ain't all right. We have a bad time running to safety." Her face was exhausted and ashy.

Jonas stood. In the same soft voice, he said to her, "Sorry to hear it."

After that, he saw only the women. Young mothers with babes in their arms. Women old enough to be grandmothers, with their daughters close by. And a woman by herself, sitting on the ground, her skirt pulled over her ankles and her kerchief neatly tied, even though her face registered the new contraband's daze. She was lighter-skinned than Pen, but the set of her head and the shape of her lips reminded him of Pen. The thought of Pen constricted his chest. He stopped and said, "Are you all right, sister?"

"Who are you?" Her voice had an unfamiliar lilt.

"Contraband," he said. "Came to the Union lines three week ago. Was in a daze at first, so surprised to be free."

She lifted her eyes to his. They were a surprising shade of green. "You all right now?"

"Not in a daze no more."

"You free yet?"

She'd gotten to the heart of it. "No," he admitted. "Not yet."

"What you plan to do?"

"Been working for the army. Intend to muster in as a soldier, if they'll have me."

"Black man? A soldier?"

"Black regiment. First Mississippi. Right here, at Lake Providence."

"Believe it when I see it."

"What you hope to do?" he asked her.

That startled her, just as being asked had astonished him. "Don't know," she said. "I was a housemaid on a place just west of here. Don't imagine there's much call for a housemaid here."

"Why did you run away?"

"Couldn't bear it no more. Weren't it the same for you?"

"What's your name?"

"Coralie," she said. "You?"

"Jonas Mitchell."

She said, "Don't have a surname I like. Won't be called by Missus's name. Don't know what to call myself."

"Ponder it. It come to you."

For the first time, she smiled. "I'll do that. Where do you stay? Is it with the contrabands?"

"I hope with the army," he said, gesturing toward the camp proper.

"Can I come to see you?"

He saw anew the echo of Pen in her face and her body. "Don't think they'd like that."

"You might come to see me."

Desire, so long dormant, swelled in him, and he felt his cheeks grow hot. "I'm a married man," he said, sounding foolish even to himself.

"You flirt just fine for a married man. Where is she?"

"Back in Georgia, last I knew."

"You're here, and she ain't." The daze had cleared, and her eyes were limpid. "Come to see me, if you can."

As he returned to the army camp, he told himself that the desire was for his wife, to whom he was still married and would always be married. He carried the shame of his betrayal all day. That night, he dreamed that he lay with a woman. He couldn't see her face; all he had was the pleasure of her body. He didn't know whether she was the beguiler from the contraband camp or his beloved faithful wife, Penelope.

THE NEXT MORNING, THE dream clinging to him, he shook himself awake. He reminded himself of his purpose in coming to Lake Providence. He dressed and put Major Leverett's precious envelope into his coat pocket.

He told Titus, "Today I see about mustering in. Tell Thatcher."

"Say goodbye to Ulysses."

He went looking for the great, sweet-tempered horse, and he leaned his head against the strong, silky neck. He whispered, "Ulysses, you be a good soldier, you hear me? Do your best to beat them secesh. And stay in one piece doing it." He put his arms around the horse's neck, and if Ulysses was surprised to be embraced, he didn't show it.

Jonas moved through the camp, asking where he could find the colonel who led the First Mississippi, and when he did, he was greeted with the sight of a Black private standing smartly before the colonel's tent. A Black man in a blue coat. He said to Jonas, "State your business."

"Come to see the colonel," he said. "Army business. Have a letter for him from Major Leverett of the Corps of Engineers. He the chief engineer at Vicksburg."

"You wait here," the private said, and he poked his head inside the tent. "Colonel Webber, sir?"

A Yankee voice, clipped but not unkind, said, "Private, I've heard the whole thing. Send him in."

The officer within the tent was surprisingly youthful. Like Major Leverett, he was sober of expression and smudged under the eyes with fatigue. He asked for Jonas's name and invited him to take a seat. He asked, "May I see your letter?"

Jonas drew it from his pocket. He had cherished it in his pocket like a hen setting on an egg. He found that he was reluctant to give it up.

Colonel Webber read it swiftly. When he looked up, he was smiling. He said, "I'm not personally acquainted with Major Leverett, but he speaks very highly of you. I heard about that explosion at Vicksburg. It helped to secure the surrender. And you had a hand in that."

"I hope so, sir," Jonas said.

"We would be glad to have you join us in the First Mississippi, Mr. Mitchell."

Jonas was overcome again. "You'll take me?"

"If you want to muster in, we will."

They ask me, he thought fiercely, *what I want.* "Yes, I do," Jonas said.

JONAS WAS IN A daze again as his name was added to the regiment's muster roll and his measurements were taken for a uniform. He would be issued a rifle, too, but the uniform came first, in a supply tent with a spot partitioned off by a sheet. The sergeant who handed him the uniform said, "If you want privacy, you can put on your uniform in there."

He doffed his civilian clothes to don the uniform. They had issued him a white shirt, not so different from the shirt he shed, and an ordinary-looking pair of blue wool trousers. But when he put on the blue coat, buttoning it all the way despite the summer heat, he looked down at the bright buttons that read "US Army," and tears slid down his cheeks.

The sergeant, watching him emerge, didn't mock or criticize. In a kindly tone, he said, "Along with that uniform, we issue you some handkerchiefs, too."

Chapter 13

Jefferson County, Mississippi
July 1863

THANKS TO CARVER'S MAP, Pen anticipated crossing the Pearl River. She found an oarsman and a boat. The water was full of gators, but she gritted her teeth and didn't look down. She kept her eyes on the farther shore.

She and Toby were surprised when they had to stop dead on the eastern bank of a river that wasn't on the map. Narrower than the Pearl, it was still too wide to wade across. She gazed over the muddy water and tried not to think about gators.

"What do we do, Toby?" They were in the pinewoods, and the likelihood of finding someone to sneak her across the river was slim. She glanced at the slow-moving water. "How do we go?" The current flowed lazily south. If she followed it northward, she might find an easier crossing. She shifted the bag on her shoulder. "We go north," she said to Toby.

As Mary Magdalene had taught her, she followed the river from the safety of the woods, but it took the better part of a night to find where the water narrowed to a silty creek. Pen sighed. She was dressed like a boy, but she couldn't bring herself to get dirty like a boy. She took off her shoes and socks and rolled her trouser legs up to her knees. Toby bounded into the muck, but Pen stepped carefully. Muddy water was usually full of leeches. On the other side, she pulled the leeches off her ankles in disgust.

She left the piney woods behind to enter the landscape of cotton, where groves of live oak and birch mingled with the pines and grew adjacent to cleared cotton fields. The open country made her uneasy. She stayed wary all day as she traveled.

Cotton fields meant plantations with big detached kitchens and slave quarters. At dusk, Pen glimpsed a big house through the trees. Dougherty County had its share of two-story white plantation houses, but this one had a greater grandeur than any Georgia place. Newly painted a dazzling white, a porch shaded the second story as well as the first. She didn't linger to see if the ladies of the house reclined there to fan themselves in the evening air. She had no truck with Missus. She wanted to find the kitchen and the cook who labored within.

From her hiding place, she spied a kitchen as big as Liza and Carver's house, built extravagantly of brick. *How many acres did this massa have? How many hands?* When the cook left the kitchen, Pen slipped from the trees to accost her. "Can you help me?"

The cook started. "Who are you? Strange man who don't belong here?"

Pen hadn't realized that her disguise might alarm

anyone. She softened her voice. "I ain't from around here. Might you spare me a bite to eat?"

The woman put her hand to her chest. "You scare me to death," she said. "I should tell you to get away."

"I'll be gone tomorrow," Pen said softly.

"Where you from?"

"Far away."

The woman took this in and drew the obvious conclusion. She whispered, "Come with me. Walk easy. Act like you belong here."

Pen followed her to the slave quarters, set far away from the house, behind the stables and the sties. The slave cabins, like the kitchen, boasted of the owner's pride of place. Five cabins lined each side of the street of tamped-down dirt, and even though the cabins were small, they were solidly built of pine boards and had wooden stoops. The people on this place used the stoops like Missus would use the shaded porch. They sat there to take the air and talk.

"How many people live here?" Pen asked.

"Over a hundred hand in the field. That don't count the people who work in the house."

"Decent massa?"

The woman snorted. "Rich massa."

A man on the nearest stoop called out, "Dinah, sugar, who you got with you?"

"Runaway," Dinah said matter-of-factly.

"Contraband? Bound for Natchez?"

Dinah said, "Didn't ask."

"Why not?" the man said. "Now that the Union army

take Vicksburg, they come down the river to Natchez, and contraband swarm there like bees to a hive."

"The Union army take Vicksburg?" Pen asked. "And they occupy Natchez, too?"

The man said, "Confederate army surrender to General Grant on Independence Day. Hah!"

"All around here, the woods full of militia looking for anyone who run away," Dinah said. She eyed the man and scrutinized Pen for good measure. "You watch yourself. You ain't free yet."

Natchez was twenty-five miles away, and it was in Union hands. But the road to Natchez was thick with militia men trying to seize anyone who yearned to be contraband of war. Pen thought, *So close, and yet so far*.

THE NEXT NIGHT, AS Pen made her way through the woods, she heard the slap of feet on the dirt and the crash of a body through the brush. Something wasn't right. Anyone who shouldn't be there would know to sneak and creep. Someone was desperate. Someone was in flight.

She burst through the trees, her dress torn and bloodied, her face bruised and bloody, too. When she caught sight of Pen, she screamed.

She was just a girl. Pen said, "Easy."

"Don't hurt me," she sobbed.

"I won't," Pen said. Her mind raced. She was in plenty of danger all by herself, dog and pistol and trousers notwithstanding. If she helped a local runaway whose massa would soon have the patrollers on her trail, the peril was even greater. She might go to Natchez in shackles, whether the Union army was there or not.

She looked at the bruised, bloody, sobbing girl, and her heart twisted. *Could have been me*, she thought. *Could have been Cassie.* She said softly, "What's your name?"

"Lucy."

Pen held out her hand. Lucy stared at it as though it were a trap. Pen asked, "Do you know the land around here?"

The girl nodded.

Pen said, "Come with me. And be as quiet as you can."

Lucy tried to lead them, but she stumbled so badly that Pen took her arm. Lucy flinched. Pen thought, *She think I'm a man.* This was no time to disabuse her. She said, "Steady," and the girl sagged in her grasp.

"I'm wore out," she whispered.

Pen said, "So am I. Is it far to water?"

"Why we need water?"

"Wade in the water," Pen said.

Lucy raised frightened eyes to Pen's face. "What you mean?"

"Dogs," Pen said. "Whoever come after you bring the dogs."

Lucy covered her face with her hands.

Pen pulled on Lucy's arm. "Do you want to get to Natchez? Or not?" She tugged harder. "Look at me."

Lucy took away her hands. Her bruises had begun to turn purple. Pen said, "You stay here, if you like. If you want to get hurt a lot worse."

Lucy whispered, "Let go of me." With her free arm, she pointed through the trees. "This way."

The creek was a trickle, the kind that Pen had welcomed for drinking water when she first left Dougherty County. She scuffed her boots in the water and said to Lucy, "You, too. You get your feet in that water." Lucy obeyed her, and Pen hoped that they had confused the dogs enough.

Too slowly, they got going. Lucy, more tired than ever, found it hard to keep up. Pen wanted to press her, feeling that they hadn't gone far enough. But Lucy faltered so badly that Pen decided to stop for the night. She found them a glade to hide in.

Lucy sank to the ground. She buried her face in her hands and began to shake as though the warm Mississippi night held the frost of a Georgia winter. Pen knelt. Without thinking, trying to reassure, she put a hand on Lucy's shoulder.

Lucy started as though she had been slapped. "Don't touch me!"

She look at me, she see a man, Pen thought. She took her hand away. "I won't hurt you."

Lucy shivered. Dully, she said, "They all hurt me. Couldn't take it no more."

"What happen?" Pen asked gently.

"Young Marse."

"He hurt you?"

Lucy raised her head. "He take advantage of me. Missus find out. She beat me for it." She shook as though she had a fever.

Pen said, "No call to be afraid of me."

Lucy didn't reply. She wrapped her arms around herself and rocked back and forth, still shivering.

Pen took a deep breath. "I ain't a man. I just dress like one." She pulled off her cap and shook out her hair. "See?"

Lucy didn't look. She shook uncontrollably.

Pen opened her bag and felt for her girl's clothes. Her hand rested on the shawl that her sister Cassie had given her. She shook it out. "Would a man carry this? I swear that it belong to me."

Lucy stared at the paisley pattern in the wool. Then she stared at Pen's unbound hair.

Pen said, "Back in Georgia my sister give it to me. I carry it to remember her."

Still shivering, Lucy touched the shawl. She stroked it, her face wistful. She asked, "What your sister called?"

"Cassie," Pen said.

Her shivering subsided. "You take me with you tomorrow?"

"Yes," Pen said.

"Where you go?"

"Toward Natchez, if you help me," Pen said.

"What in Natchez?"

"The Union army," Pen told her. "You get to the Union army, they take you in as a contraband, and no one can take you back again."

PEN WASN'T MUCH RESTED by morning, but she wanted to get away. She roused a weary Lucy, and they made their way in daylight.

Lucy started at every sound, and even though her fear annoyed Pen, she could forgive it. She remembered the terror of her first few weeks of flight. But Lucy was noisy in the woods. Pen was sharp. "If you want to get to Natchez, you try harder to walk quiet."

Late in the day, Pen saw that someone had preceded them. Someone had built a fire. The logs were charred but not consumed. "Cook fire," Pen said.

"Who stop here?" Lucy asked in panic.

Pen fought down her own fear. "Think about it. Militia men all live around here. Go home to dinner. Anyone out hunting at night ain't stopping to eat." She felt better as she reasoned it out. "Probably someone who run, like us."

"How you know?"

"I don't. But I hope so."

Pen strode ahead as Lucy trailed behind. "Can't walk so fast," Lucy muttered. "Got a blister." She stopped to pull off her shoe and relieve the offending spot. As Pen waited, she glanced through the trees. She saw the flash of a shirt, then a kerchief. A man and a woman with their children, all stepping cautiously, muffling their steps. Relief flooded her. They were slaves. They were runaways.

Pen ordered Lucy, "You stay here."

"Alone?"

"Toby watch you." She bent and rubbed Toby's ears. "Stay," she said, with much more tenderness than she felt for Lucy.

Pen moved swiftly. The sound alerted the man, who turned and froze. Pen stepped into his sight. She let him take her in, her brown skin, her boy's dress, her leather bag.

He looked her over carefully and asked, "How you find us?"

"Saw your fire. You take quite a chance. You lucky I saw it and not the patrollers."

His look was sharp, as though he didn't expect a youngster to chastise him. "Is you alone?"

"No. Got a dog. And there's a girl with me."

"What kind of dog?"

"Yellow hound. Good hunting dog. Why you ask?"

He said, "It help to have a dog along."

"You know the land around here?" Pen asked.

"Been hunting it all my life."

"Where you bound?"

"Natchez."

"Us, too. We go together?"

"We help each other," he said.

Pen retrieved Toby and Lucy, and introductions were made. They were the Smiths, Isham and Ellie, and their children, two boys and a girl. They had all been slaves on a big place nearby. The Union army's arrival in Natchez, after Vicksburg's fall, had prompted their flight. "Been thinking of it for a while," Isham said.

As Ellie hugged her daughter, she added, "All of us."

Pen allowed herself a moment of envy for a family that was together.

Ellie Smith turned to Lucy, and with a mother's concern, she asked, "Child, what happen to you?"

Lucy shook her head and bit back tears. Ellie Smith put her arm around Lucy's shoulder to hug her close, as she'd held her own girl. Lucy laid her head on Ellie's shoulder and wept.

One of the Smith boys said, "If we bawled like that, Daddy would whup us."

His sister said, "She all beat up! Don't be mean!"

The boy said, "If she come along with us, she better be quiet."

Pen smothered a laugh.

"We move on," said Isham, father and now leader. Pen and Toby joined him in the lead. Behind them walked the Smith girl, holding Lucy's hand, and Ellie Smith and the two boys brought up the rear. After weeks of being wary, it was a relief to share the burden of being the eyes and ears.

Isham led them to a creek. He said to Pen, "We cross here."

"Wade in the water," Pen murmured.

He looked at her with new respect. "You know that?"

"Yes."

After they stopped, and Isham and Pen settled the rest for the night, Isham took Pen aside to ask, "Can we take your dog hunting tonight?"

"You have a firearm?" Pen asked.

"No, I'd be crazy to have one. We just run him."

Pen said, "I have a pistol."

He gave her a searching look. "Where you get that?"

She thought of Denmark with a pang. "Good friend give it to me."

"Don't you go brandishing it. You get nothing but trouble."

She was suddenly angry. "I come all the way from Georgia, and I still in one piece! Don't need some Mississippi field hand to tell me how to conduct myself."

"Easy," he said.

"Ain't been easy for weeks."

He regarded her again. "I can tell you ain't a boy."

She nearly said, "Don't you needle me," but there was no reason to make him mad just because she was. "How do you know?"

"Been a hunter all my life," he said. "Learn to pay attention."

"Don't tell anyone," Pen said.

"I won't. Figure you have a good reason for it. Know how to keep a secret, too."

AS THEY APPROACHED NATCHEZ, Pen began to hear the sound of movement in the woods more and more often. Sometimes it was a practiced rustle, and sometimes it was a hapless crash. Each time, it was another group of runaways bound for Natchez and the Union army's protection. Their band swelled to ten, then to twenty. When more people joined them, a man called out good-naturedly, "Won't fit in the woods no more! We take to the road!"

For the first time in weeks, Pen set her feet on a paved road. The crowd grew. Men and women. Old and young. Field hands in rags and house servants in neat aprons. Faces glad, proud, dazed. People who had been marched in coffles and forced into order now thronged and seethed, delighted to make their own disordered way.

Toby, not used to crowds, pressed close to Pen's leg. She craned her neck, trying to see down the road, and got a glimpse of a cluster of buildings ahead. She asked Isham, "What's that up there? Is that Natchez?"

"No. That called Forks of the Road. You never hear of it?"

She remembered what Liza had told her. "Yes."

He said, "Biggest slave market in Mississippi. Near every slave brought to Mississippi sold here."

Had Jonas been among them?

The crowd's movement slowed to a crawl. "Can you see up there?" Pen asked Isham.

"No." He asked a man ahead of him, "What slow us down?"

"I hear that Union soldiers stand up there to guard us as we go by."

When Pen was close enough, she drew in her breath. Union soldiers stood on both sides of the road as the crowd inched by. Men in blue, resting their hands on their rifles, not intending to use them but proud to have them.

All the soldiers were Black.

Pen stared. "Why the army here?" she asked the nearest soldier.

He grinned in a most unmilitary way. "We close down the slave market," he said. "Put all them slave dealers out of business."

"No more slave dealing here?"

"Not on the army's say-so."

If the slave dealers gone, how do I find Jonas?

The soldier said, "Happy day! I was sold here before the war. Came here in shackles and sold like a pig. And look at me now!"

Had he been here at the same time as Jonas? Before she could ask, the soldier laughed. "Bottom rail on top now!"

Chapter 14

TOBY WHIMPERED AS HE pressed close to her leg. He disliked crowds even more than Pen did, and they had both been part of a crowd since Forks of the Road. The crowd had borne them into Natchez and to the contraband camp at Natchez Under-the-Hill. Now the crowd pressed on them in the camp itself.

The lumber camp at the salt mine had been large and crowded, but it had been orderly. The contraband camp was not. Makeshift tents grew like weeds on the muddy ground. People crammed into this place, sitting outside the tents, standing in clusters, and eyeing the newcomers. The place stank of woodsmoke, bacon grease, and human waste.

Isham, who had kept the secret of Pen's disguise, now treated her like a capable young man. He took her along to ask about food and shelter. They waited with another crowd, some of them in terrible condition. The family next to them in line, their faces haggard and frightened, were in rags. All of them were barefoot.

Pen didn't have the heart to ask, "How you come here?" As a hunted runaway, she had rarely felt fortunate. Now she did, and she was overwhelmed by the suffering that she saw here.

She and Isham waited a long time, the sun hot on their faces and necks. The children in the ragged family began to whimper for water. Pen said to Isham, "I come right back," and she went in search of a bucket. She was lucky enough to receive a tin pitcher full of water. She said to the woman with the parched children, "This for you." Without a word, the woman took it.

She and Isham returned with the knowledge of where to receive the weekly rations, where to get material for a tent, and where to apply for work. The soldier who spoke to them looked as though he hadn't slept for a week. He regarded the crowd of contrabands with the exhaustion of a man given a broom to sweep back a flooding river.

Ellie's face fell when she saw the tattered square of canvas in Isham's hands. "This our house," he said, trying to joke.

She looked even more dismayed when Pen handed her the cornmeal and salt beef. "This our meals?"

Pen and Isham put up the tent. Pen stood back and asked, "How we all fit in there?"

Isham was remarkably cheerful. "Your dog sleep outside."

Ellie found a neighbor with a skillet, and she managed to make corncakes for their dinner. Pen took the cake and sighed. All this way to eat johnnycake again.

After dinner, Isham left to see about getting work. "You want to come with me?" he asked Pen.

"Not just yet," Pen said, grateful that he still hadn't betrayed her disguise.

He came back, smiling. "Ellie, the army hire me. Ten dollar a month! Imagine!"

Ellie had news of her own. "Our neighbor tell me that the army hire washwomen. Five dollar a month for washing!" She glanced at Lucy. "You, too!"

And me, Pen thought, *if I put my dress back on.* Her heart sank at the thought of being a washwoman. She felt as confused and lost in the contraband camp as she had first felt in the woods. She sat outside the tent, talking to Toby like she had when she was alone in the pines. "Toby, how we find Jonas? Where we start?"

One of the Smith boys snickered as he said to her, "You talk to your dog like he a man?"

Pen flared. "He a better friend to me than many a person, man or woman."

SHE DIDN'T THINK JONAS was in Natchez proper. It was more likely he'd been sold here and taken elsewhere in Mississippi. She hoped that the slave dealers of Natchez, unlike those in Forks of the Road, had not been shuttered.

But even as a contraband, she could hardly make a direct inquiry of a slave catcher. She would ask the Union army to help her.

She wasn't ready to give up the freedom of being dressed as a boy. In her trousers and cap, she returned to the crowd of new arrivals, bringing Toby with her, and stood in their miserable midst.

A little girl sidled up and asked her, "Why you bring your dog with you?" She wore a filthy dress, and her hair was long and wild around her head.

"My dog go everywhere with me," Pen said.

"Is he mean?"

"Oh no. Got a sweet temper."

"Can I pet him?"

"Let him sniff your hand first."

The girl extended her hand slowly, as though she were used to dogs, and let Toby set the pace. She reached to scratch him between the ears, which he liked. "When we run away, we leave our dog behind. I miss my dog."

Why did the little girl's sorrow make her eyes sting?

A woman called, "Essie! Don't talk to that strange man!" The girl gave Toby a final scratch, turned away, and disappeared into the crowd.

When it came her turn, Pen found herself facing the same soldier who had looked so weary a few days before.

He said, "Yes?"

"Don't need a tent or a meal. Have an inquiry."

"Yes, what?"

She reminded herself not to say, "my husband." "Want to find a someone who were sold away to Mississippi before the war. Want to figure who to ask. How to ask."

He stared at her. "We don't find missing persons."

"Don't ask you to find him for me. Ask you to direct me to someone who help me make my inquiry."

"Can't help you," he said curtly.

Pen turned away. As they returned to the Smiths' tent, she said to Toby, "I guess we go into Natchez and ask there."

Her disguise had served her well in the woods, where it protected her. In the camp and in a place like a town, it might not. She thought of the way that Essie's mother had cautioned her against the "strange man." If her disguise alarmed Black folks, who shouldn't have a reason to fear her, how would white folks feel? She didn't like to think that a skirt and a kerchief would be a better disguise than trousers and a cap.

To go into Natchez, she would put her dress back on.

When all the Smiths were elsewhere—Isham digging holes, Ellie and her girls washing, the boys making mischief somewhere—Pen appropriated the tent for her transformation. She struggled out of her shirt and trousers. Reluctantly, she pulled on her dress, doing up her buttons with difficulty. She crawled out and stood, shaking out her skirt. In the shifting crowd outside full of strangers, no one noticed that she had gone into the tent as a boy and come out as a girl.

She made her way to the spot where the laundresses gathered and found Ellie at the washtub. She stirred the clothes as Lucy watched. Ellie greeted her. "Who are you, sister?"

Ellie had never seen her in a dress. Pen said, "You know me."

Ellie looked puzzled. Lucy smirked but didn't speak. Pen said, "When you meet me in the woods, I wear trousers and call myself Mitchell. My real name Penelope."

Ellie said, "You fooled me."

"I knew," Lucy said.

Pen gave Lucy a disgusted look. "You never could be quiet."

Ellie asked, "What you do, now that you properly yourself?"

"Look for my husband." She told Ellie the story. "I plan to go into Natchez to try to find him."

Ellie asked, "Didn't you ask here?"

"Asked the army. No help from them."

"The washwomen all talk to each other. Know everyone in this place. I can send the word out. What he called?"

"Jonas Mitchell," she said. "From Dougherty County, Georgia."

IN THE CONTRABAND CAMP, people came and went all the time, unguarded. When Pen left that afternoon, Toby at her heels, no one noticed. Outside the camp, she tried to orient herself, as she had so many times in the woods. From here, she could see the Mississippi River and the boats moored at the docks. She had followed a river before. She walked toward the water.

A man's voice called out, "Hey! Where you going?"

She turned. He was a short, stocky man, dark brown and weather-beaten. She said, "Why you ask?"

"Don't want anyone falling into the river."

"Do that happen?"

"Yes," he said. "Sometimes by accident and sometimes by design."

"People that desperate? Fling themselves in the river?"

"You'd be surprised."

"Nothing like that. Just wanted to get my bearings. Where the road into town?"

"You contraband?"

"Come from the camp, yes."

He pointed and said, "The road that way. You follow that."

She shaded her eyes to look. "Is it far?"

"Less than a mile."

She thanked him and set out. She felt foolish and nervous. She wondered what she would find and whether anyone in this place—which was so much more foreign than the woods or the cotton fields—would want to help her.

So this is a town, she thought, looking at the brick buildings that lined either side of the road. They were a little ramshackle, and nothing indicated what might be within. She slowed at the sight of a big white building, two stories tall, with a porch in front. It looked just like a big house. She hadn't realized there were big houses in towns. It would have a kitchen and a cook who might be able to help her. Reassured, she went searching for the back door.

She knocked, and a woman opened it. She was light of skin, still handsome, and she wore a cook's apron. She said to Pen, "You ain't pretty enough to work here."

"What?"

"You contraband?"

"Stay at the camp, yes."

"Contraband! You smell like it." She glanced at Toby

as though he offended her, too. "Dog! Won't have a dog in the house. Flea-ridden contraband dog."

Pen was irate on Toby's account. "He don't have fleas. He sleep with me, and I don't have no fleas, either."

The woman rolled her eyes. "Contraband. Come here day after day, hand out. Don't have a thing for you. Go on."

Pen was still mad. "I don't need no charity. Didn't come for that. Came to make an inquiry."

"Inquiry!" the woman spat.

A musical voice drifted from the kitchen. "Emma, who are you talking to?"

"Some contraband and her flea-bitten dog."

"Why is she making an inquiry?"

"She making a nuisance of herself."

The speaker floated toward the door. She had the ivory skin that bespoke of having one Black grandparent, and her dark hair had been curled on purpose, like a white woman's. Even though it was afternoon, she wore an ecru silk dressing gown that matched the color of her skin and was lavishly trimmed with lace. She was covered, but somehow it made her look naked. The skin above her bosom was the same pearly color as her face. In the heat, she gave off a scent, like lilacs in bloom. She said, "Miss Emma, I know that you fight off beggars all day long, or so you tell us. We don't get many contrabands who want to ask a question." She addressed Pen. "What is it that you want to know?"

Pen said, "I look for my husband, who were carried off to Mississippi before the war. I want to learn if he were sold in Natchez. Can't go to a slave dealer myself. Want to know if someone can help me."

"Where was he carried from?"

"Georgia. That's where I come from."

"How did you get all the way to Mississippi?"

Her eyes weren't right. Her pupils were huge in the light brown of her irises.

"Put one foot in front of the other."

She said, "You walked all the way from Georgia for love?"

"I reckon so."

"What a tale, Emma. We should help her." To Pen, she said, "Inquiry? Slave dealers? Madame Bella would know."

"Don't you bother her, Eveline," Emma said.

"Bother? She won't mind."

Emma said, "Don't you take her into the parlor!"

Eveline laughed. "I'll square it with Madame Bella," she said. "Even the dog."

Pen followed Eveline into the parlor, where red brocade paper covered the walls, and red velvet swathed all the furniture. Pen asked, "What is this place? Is it a big house?"

Eveline laughed. "It's a bawdy house."

"What's that?"

"They don't have bawdy houses in Georgia?"

"Not in Dougherty County, where I come from. What go on in a bawdy house?"

"You really don't know?"

"Why would I fun you?"

She smiled and spoke with a lady's daintiness. "We young ladies give our favors to gentlemen. For which they give us a consideration."

Pen understood. She blurted out, "Like a fancy girl. Only you get paid for it."

Eveline gazed at her with the eyes that were all pupil. "Yes."

"Who Madame Bella?"

"We all work for her."

"She your missus?"

"A madame is not a missus," she said, in her lady's tone.

Pen shook her head in confusion, but Eveline didn't explain. She disappeared. Pen didn't sit. She was afraid to get the velvet seat dirty. She remembered feeling out of place in the butler's pantry in the house at the lumber camp in Alabama. This was even worse. She didn't like to think what Madame Bella would do to someone she thought had fleas.

Madame Bella was a statuesque woman tightly laced into a black silk dress that matched her black hair. There was nothing of the bedroom about her. She looked businesslike and shrewd. She said to Pen, "Eveline has told me quite a romantic tale about you. She has a soft spot for love stories." Her dark eyes swept over Pen. "She insisted that I listen to you. You have a request for an inquiry? What is it about?"

Pen swallowed hard. She explained herself, feeling the weight of Madame Bella's appraising gaze. A missus in a bawdy house, it seemed to Pen, was just like a slave dealer for judging human flesh.

Madame Bella said, "I can't help you. Everything that happens here is a matter of confidence. Do you understand?" She talked like a real lady, not someone playacting at it.

"You keep it a secret," Pen said. "Because it shameful."

Madame Bella looked surprised, as though Toby had given her an answer. "You look like a field hand, but you're smart."

Pen thought, *Didn't come here for insult.* She clenched her skirt in her hands and said politely, "Ma'am, I didn't mean to trouble you."

"She isn't a trouble. Won't you help her?" Eveline's voice drifted into the room along with her perfume.

"Eveline, why aren't you dressed yet?"

"I'll be dressed when I need to be." She contemplated Madame Bella, and Pen saw the power and the pain of the connection between the two women. She wished that she weren't in the middle of it. Eveline said, "I can think of someone who knows everyone and who doesn't have to keep secrets like we do. Our dry goods merchant, Mr. Levy."

When Madame Bella didn't reply, Eveline said, "Your cousin."

Madame Bella compressed her lips. Pen knew that tiny gesture. One that Missus would use just before she got mighty angry. "That's enough, Eveline." To Pen, she said, "His shop is just down the street. Levy's Dry Goods."

Pen's throat was dry. She wanted to leave, very badly. She said, "Thank you, Missus Bella."

She found her way back to the kitchen, where she hesitated. "Miss Emma, what's wrong with Miss Eveline?"

"Why you ask?"

"Her eyes."

Emma snorted. "Laudanum."

Pen knew that white ladies took laudanum for pain. "Do her head hurt her?"

"She say her life hurt her," Emma said, opening the door. "Go on, you and your dog."

As Pen walked down the street, the buildings began to look better kept. The sidewalks outside had been swept. The plate glass windows had been washed. The wooden signs had been brightened with paint.

A cart rumbled down the street, driven by a Black man who took no notice of her. But the sidewalk was empty.

Some of the windows had gold lettering. She stopped before one, sounded out the letters, and deciphered the word *grocery*. She peeped inside. A white man stood behind a wooden counter, and at the sight of her face, he scowled. She backed away.

Another shop. More gold lettering. This was easier to read. "Levy's," she read. "Dry Goods." She was pleased with herself. It was like being able to find cress in the woods. She could navigate a little in a town. Still, she hesitated before she pushed open the door. She peeked inside. A young white woman sat behind the counter, and she was reading.

A bell jangled, announcing her arrival, and the young woman hastily hid her book. Pen looked around. Behind the counter, on shelves that reached nearly to the ceiling, were bolts of cloth in a wealth of colors. The case sported ribbons, trims, and all kinds of lace, as ornate as the lace on Miss Eveline's dressing gown. The ribbons and trims, like the bolts, presented the eye with a rainbow. Pen thought of the ten silver dollars in her bag. In this shop, could she buy lace or ribbons for herself?

In the contraband camp, Pen felt decently dressed, but here she knew she was not. The young woman wore a white dress striped with blue. The white trim at her neck and her wrists was as pretty as anything in the case. It had likely come from the case.

The young woman spoke. She asked, "May I help you?"

Polite, Pen thought. She didn't dare lean against the counter. "I come to see Mr. Levy, if I can."

"He isn't here at the moment. Perhaps I can assist."

"I come to talk to him," Pen said.

"Oh, he's my father, and I know all about the stock here. If your missus wants ribbons or laces or lengths, I'm sure I can find something to suit."

That explained the courtesy. The young woman thought she was here on Missus's say-so. Pen said, "It ain't about ribbons, and it ain't for my missus. It's for me, and it's a matter of business."

Her eyebrows were dark and delicate, and now they rose. "Not about dry goods? Did someone send you here?"

"Missus Bella tell me to ask here."

"You don't work for her, I hope."

"No," Pen said.

Toby snuffled. The young woman stood up and leaned over the counter. "A dog," she said, but she had begun to smile. "My father would have a conniption to see a dog in the shop."

"He a good dog," Pen said. "He lie down and sit quiet."

She laughed. "And he'll shed!" She said, "My father won't be long. Would you like to wait?"

"If you don't mind."

"I don't. It's so dull in the shop these days. Having the Yankees here has frightened everyone off the streets. I hate it when we don't do any business."

Pen asked, "Is that why you read?"

She blushed. "Papa doesn't like me to read in the shop."

"What book do you read?"

She met Pen's eyes. She was younger than Pen had first thought, just out of girlhood. "Can you read?"

Was it all right to admit? Pen thought of Kate and of Liza and took the leap. "A little."

She held up the book. "Poetry."

"Like Mr. Walt Whitman?"

She was shocked, but she was also delighted. "*Leaves of Grass*? Have you read that?"

"I try to," Pen said.

She held out the book for Pen to see. "Heinrich Heine. A German poet. It's in German. My father was born in Germany, and I speak it and read it, even though I've never been anywhere in my life but Natchez." She hid the book again. "Where are you from?"

"Georgia," Pen said.

"That's far away. Did your massa move here to Mississippi?"

Pen smiled at this young woman who had spent her whole life in Natchez and who now spent all her days behind this counter. Was she mad to trust this girl because she read poetry? "I brought myself."

The young woman leaned on the counter. "What was it like to come all the way from Georgia like that?"

"It's a long story," Pen said.

"I like long stories," she said, her face full of yearning. "My name is Rosa. What's yours?"

"Penelope."

PEN WAS HOARSE BY the time the bell on the door jangled and a man entered the shop. He wore a black wool suit, and his hair was silky and dark like Rosa's. He rested his hat on the counter. "Has there been any custom while I was gone?" he asked, looking askance at Pen.

"Papa, this is Penelope, and she's had such a journey from Georgia to Mississippi. An odyssey!"

He looked down at Toby, who slept on the polished wooden floor, and shook his head.

Rosa continued, "Miss Henriques sent her. Penelope has business to talk with you. She has an inquiry!"

"Ah, my distant rogue cousin, Miss Bella Henriques. What business could it possibly be?"

"She wouldn't tell me. She insisted on waiting for you."

"What else calls me today?" he asked. "No custom, not since the Yankees overran us." He sighed. "All right. Penelope, tell me your business."

She wasn't sure of him, as she now was of Rosa.

He grew impatient. "Speak up and tell me."

She didn't like being prodded, but she wanted his assistance. "Here to make an inquiry about a man sold to Mississippi before the war. Wondered if he were sold here. Hope to ask your help to make an inquiry about him."

"What kind of help?"

"Miss Bella say you know all the men of business in

Natchez. Slave dealers among them. Can't go to them slave dealers myself. That's why I ask you, sir."

"Who is this man?"

"Name of Jonas Mitchell. My husband."

He suddenly looked as tired as the Union soldier in the contraband camp. He rubbed his forehead with his fingers. "Why would I do such a thing? For a stranger who's most likely a runaway slave herself?"

"Papa," Rosa said. "*Avadim hayinu b'eretz mitzrayim.*" Rosa looked at Pen but spoke to her father. "From the Bible. We Israelites were slaves in the land of Egypt, too."

"Ah, Rayzel," he said, the unfamiliar name suffused with affection. "What a troublemaker you are."

"We should help her."

He touched his daughter's cheek with his elegant fingers. "For you, Rayzel."

Rosa covered her father's hand with her own.

He returned to Pen. "I'll need some particulars to make an inquiry."

"Yes, sir," Pen said, wondering what he meant, but he began to ask about Jonas—his color, his height, his age—and those were easy questions to answer.

"I'll see what I can do."

He might find Jonas. Gratitude swept through her. "Thank you, Mr. Levy, sir," she said, tears misting her eyes.

He said to Rosa, "I'll be in back. Call if you need me." He picked up his hat, leaving the two of them alone in the front of the shop.

Pen said, "Been wondering about something. You said I had an odyssey. What do that mean?"

Rosa said, "It's from a poem. Written in Greek, in ancient times. It's about a long, difficult journey."

"Like the forty years in the desert?"

Surprise registered on Rosa's face. "Not so different," she said. "Where are you staying?"

"In the camp down the riverbank."

"I hear that's an awful place."

"Yes, it is," Pen said. "Wish I could find someplace better."

"I know of someplace better." Rosa's expression was mischievous. "Why couldn't you stay here? You could help me in the shop and sleep in the back." She leaned over the counter to check on Toby, who was still asleep. "He can stay in the yard."

"I believe all that up to your daddy," Pen said.

Rosa held up her little finger. She mimed wrapping a ribbon around it. "Let me talk to him," she said, smiling.

WHEN PEN RETURNED TO the contraband camp, Ellie Smith said, "You smiling. You hear something good today?"

"Found someone to inquire with them slave dealers."

"I tell the washwomen to ask about your man," Ellie said. "So far no one know of a Jonas Mitchell. But we keep asking."

PEN KNEW THAT MR. Levy wouldn't have anything for her so soon, but she went to visit Rosa a few days later. This time, Rosa boldly held up her book.

Pen asked, "Still them German poems?"

"Yes. I read German very slowly, so they last me."

"Did your daddy learn anything yet?"

"No, but there's other news." She grinned in the most unladylike way. "He said that you could stay in the shop to help me. As long as you didn't insist on being paid, since he hasn't got anything but Confederate paper."

With a pang, Pen thought of the five dollars a month the Union army paid the laundresses. "I don't mind."

"Oh, I'm so glad," Rosa said, and her face suffused with happiness.

"Where do you live, Miss Rosa?"

"Upstairs. Over the shop."

"You don't have a house somewhere?"

"Why would we? We own this building, and we live in it, too."

"Where do your servants stay?"

"It's just Bessie, our housekeeper and cook, and she lives upstairs, too."

PEN TOLD THE SMITHS that she had found a place in town to work and stay for a while, and she moved in. Bessie brought Pen upstairs to eat in the kitchen. Even in the Levys' small apartment, with only a parlor, a dining room, and two bedrooms, the etiquette of slavery had to be observed. In the dining room, the Levys ate chicken with their rice; in the kitchen, Bessie served Pen black-eyed peas with theirs.

Pen said, "What's in them peas? Taste different."

"Chicken grease," Bessie said.

Pen wrinkled her nose. "Why not bacon grease?"

"They Israelites. Don't eat ham, bacon, or lard. It's their religion and their custom."

"Israelites? Like in the Bible?"

"Not really," Bessie said. "They ain't too different from any other white folks."

"How long you been with them?"

"All my life. Used to be with Miss Rosa's mama and her family. The Henriques family, who live in New Orleans. When young miss marry Mr. Levy, she take me with her."

"Where is Miss Rosa's mama?"

"She gone. She die of fever before the war. Miss Rosa was just a little chit, twelve year old. Mr. Levy torn up with grief and never remarry. I take care of Miss Rosa, like I take care of her mama."

Pen thought, *Bessie bring her up, and she keep the Levy family going. Even if no one say so.*

Bessie set her fork on her plate. "Miss Rosa like you. Haven't seen her so cheerful for a long time."

"She still miss her mama?"

"Won't she always? But she get engaged just before the war break out. Her beau join the Confederate army and die at Shiloh."

"So she miss him, too."

"Well, it a little peculiar. She tell me that she like him, but she don't love him. She get engaged to him to please her daddy, who want her to marry an Israelite. She sad that he die, but it don't break her heart."

Pen said, "I think she want to get away more than she want to marry."

"She tell me quite a tale about you, how you walk all the way from Georgia for love. Say that it a better tale than she read in a book, and she love her books."

BESSIE FIXED PEN A makeshift bed in a tiny room behind the shop, scarcely more than a closet. She also ordered Toby into the yard, where he whined until he found birds and squirrels to divert him. He was banned from the shop, but at night Pen slipped him into her room to sleep on her bed.

Pen's duties in the shop were light. She swept the floor, dusted the counter and the case, and helped Rosa straighten the bolts of cloth. Dry goods evidently needed a lot of straightening. Pen suspected that it was all make-work to keep Rosa company. Business didn't improve, and whenever Mr. Levy left, Rosa retrieved her book.

On Pen's third day, a new book appeared, a big, slender volume in dark red with something stamped in gold on the spine. "What you read today?" Pen asked.

Rosa said, "Not poetry. This is a book of accounts."

"What's in there?"

"It's a record of our business. What we spend and what we bring in." She opened the book.

Pen leaned over the counter to see. "Them marks. They ain't letters."

"They're figures."

"Can a person learn to read them, too?"

Thoughtfully, Rosa said, "Yes."

"Could I?"

Their eyes met, the woman on a journey and the girl who longed to go away. Rosa said, "Watch the shop for a moment. I need to fetch something from upstairs."

Pen eyed the door and hoped that no one would come in. What could she say to a missus who wanted a ribbon or a gentleman who wanted a handkerchief? To her relief, Rosa wasn't gone long. She returned with yet another book in her hand. "I learned from this when I was a little girl. I'm glad I kept it."

Like a book of poetry, it was small enough to fit into a dress pocket. Pen took it and sounded out the title on the cover. "*The North American Arithmetic, Part First, Containing Elementary Lessons.*" She opened it and was immediately delighted. "It has words and pictures!" Pen exclaimed. "To learn about figures!"

"Would you like to start now?"

"Don't your daddy want you to work on your own figures?"

"Later," Rosa said.

DESPITE THE CRAMPED SLEEPING room, it was pleasant to take refuge in Levy's Dry Goods. Pen soon realized that Rosa didn't need any help in the shop, which continued to have no business. Pen ate the peculiar food, chatted politely with Bessie, and learned how to figure. Rosa also encouraged her to read. Together, they perused the *Natchez Gazette*, which was venomous about the occupation by the Yankees and the contrabands who came in their wake.

The bell on the door interrupted them, and Rosa quickly put down the paper as Pen rushed to take up her broom.

It wasn't Mr. Levy. It was a customer, a dark-haired young white man in a Union coat. Rosa was so surprised that she lost her manners and stared at him before she stammered, "How can I help you?"

He asked, "Do you sell handkerchiefs?"

Still having difficulty, Rosa managed to say, "We do. We have some made up, and we have all kinds of cotton and cambric, if you have someone to sew for you."

He laughed. "I have an army of contraband seamstresses at my disposal."

Rosa opened the case and removed the tray of handkerchiefs. She laid it on the counter and asked, "Are you at the camp down the road?"

"In the army camp. I'm with an Ohio regiment."

Rosa's manners were returning, along with her composure. "You're an officer?"

"Yes, a captain."

"You command men."

"A company with shovels," he said, smiling. At Rosa's startled look, he added, "My men are all contrabands."

"Where are you from?" she asked, as though she hadn't heard that his men were Black.

"I'm from Cincinnati."

Rosa's hand shook as she gestured to the handkerchiefs. "Do you see anything that will suit?"

He bent over the tray. Decisively, he picked out three plain squares of cloth. "I'll keep the seamstresses busy." He smiled. "I'll ask them to embroider my initials on them."

Rosa wrapped the handkerchiefs in brown paper and wrote on a slip of paper. Pen wondered what she wrote. Rosa said, "To whom am I selling? I'd like to put your name on the receipt."

"Marcus Cohen," he said. "Captain Marcus Cohen."

Rosa's hand shook again. "You're an Israelite!"

"Yes, I am. I'm glad to give my custom to fellow Israelites." He held out his hand for the parcel and the receipt. "Who am I addressing? In case I return?"

"Miss Rosa Levy."

He touched his cap and smiled again. "Pleased to meet you, Miss Levy." And as he left, the bell jangled, now sounding cheerful.

Pen asked, "How do you know he an Israelite?"

Rosa still looked astonished. If she weren't a young lady, Pen would say she looked like she'd been poleaxed. "Everyone named Cohen is an Israelite."

MR. LEVY BROUGHT NO news. Pen grew restless. When she lay on her bed at night, breathing in the smell of wool and lavender sachets, she veered between hope and despair. Mr. Levy would find where Jonas had gone. Or he would not.

After a week, Mr. Levy said to Pen, "Come talk to me in back."

She put down the broom. "Yes, sir."

He said, "This place has never been so well-swept."

"Thank you, sir."

She had never been in the back room that was Mr. Levy's office. It was as tidy as the shop, the papers neatly piled on the desk, and on the shelf behind him, red account books, too many to count, lined up like soldiers. He straightened some papers that didn't need to be straightened. He cleared his throat. Pen began to feel dismay. If he had good news, he'd be swift to tell her. He said, "I've inquired at all the auction houses and with as many dealers as I could find. I'm very sorry. I haven't been able to find anyone who might be your husband."

She waited.

"It's quite possible that his was a private sale, from his former master in Georgia to the new one in Mississippi. In that case, the dealer would have transported him but not recorded the sale."

"Why do it take so long to find out?"

"The bills of sale don't have names. I had to go by his age and description."

Pen hid her hands in her skirt and balled them into fists. Disappointment felt like a splinter in her eye, and she tried to blink it away. She reminded herself that Solomon Levy was not like his daughter. He was a white man of business and a slave owner. With all the self-control she could muster, she said, "I thank you for trying to help me, sir."

When she emerged from the back, Rosa said, "What was the news?"

She untied her apron. "I have to go."

"Bad news, then."

"He ain't here, and I have to go away to find him."

"Was Papa rude to you?"

"No."

Rosa reached for Pen's hand. "Oh, Penelope," she said, and Pen heard a voice different from Solomon Levy's. The voice of the girl who had been mothered by a slave. Who had listened to the story of a slave's journey with a whole heart. Who had reminded her father that Israelites had once been slaves, too. "I hope that you find him. Wherever you go next."

Pen nodded.

Rosa let go of Pen's hand and reached beneath the counter. "Take this with you."

It was the book that taught about figures. "It's yours," Pen said. "I can't."

Rosa seized the pen from the inkwell. She opened the book and wrote forcefully on the first page. She looked up. "It says, 'To Penelope, to remember me as she continues her odyssey.'" She held out the book. "Please, take it."

Pen took the book, which fit as comfortably in her palm as the book of poems. She measured her words. "Maybe someday, you go on an odyssey of your own."

WHEN SHE RETURNED TO the contraband camp, the smell hit her in the face like a slap. She had gotten too used to lavender. Ellie Smith said, "You back."

"Inquiry in Natchez didn't turn up anything."

"We washwomen have been asking after your man. We don't turn up anything, either."

She sat on the ground outside the Smiths' tent, her chin on her knees, Toby's presence at her feet no comfort to her. She resisted the temptation to ask Toby what to do.

She was in no mood for mockery from one of the Smith boys.

When the thought came to her, she said aloud, "I been a fool." Captain Cohen was in the Union army, and his company of contrabands was likely full of men from Mississippi. She would go to army camp to ask about Jonas. She looked forward to meeting Captain Cohen's men. She rose and dusted off her skirt for the walk to the army's camp.

THE ARMY'S CAMP, UNLIKE the contraband camp, was not easy to enter. The guards, both white, stopped her. One was tall, and the other was stocky.

She said, "Could I speak with Captain Cohen?"

"What's your business with him?" the tall one demanded.

When she explained about Jonas, they shook their heads. "We don't find missing persons," the tall one said.

"Please, sir, let me ask Captain Cohen if he knows of my husband. Or if his men do."

"Captain Cohen?" the tall soldier asked his companion. "The man who oversees the contrabands?" He was just short of rude.

The stocky man corrected him. "He's the officer who commands the contrabands. He's a good man. Polite to everyone. He might speak to her." He said to Pen, "I can ask him."

"Thank you, sir," Pen said.

The tall man shook his head as his companion left in

search of Captain Cohen. As she waited, the tall soldier said, "Contrabands. Nothing but trouble."

To her surprise, the stocky soldier returned with Captain Cohen in tow. At the sight of Pen, he looked puzzled.

She said, "Sir, I was in Levy's Dry Goods when you come in and fluster Miss Rosa so much."

He stared at her, trying to remember.

"You buy three handkerchiefs."

He said slowly, "You were sweeping."

She nodded.

"So you've come to find a man named Jonas Mitchell."

"My husband," she said.

"I know my own men, but there are other contraband crews. They might know of him. I can make a quick inquiry. Would you wait?"

Was Jonas here? Might I find him? Her throat was dry. "Thank you, Captain Cohen, sir."

It wasn't a long wait, and Captain Cohen returned alone. "I'm sorry. No one has heard of him."

She was too disappointed to thank him. She nodded, feeling tears start in her eyes.

To her surprise, he noticed how crestfallen she looked. With more gentleness than he had shown before, he said, "If your husband isn't here, he might be at the camp north of Vicksburg, at Lake Providence. There's a big contraband camp next to the army camp." He thought for a moment. "He may have mustered into the Black regiment up there. The First Mississippi."

She nodded, thinking of the guards at Forks of the Road. "Vicksburg? Is it safe to go there?"

"It is now," Captain Cohen said. "Now that it's fallen, you can travel right up the river."

"How do I get there?"

Captain Cohen smiled as though he were glad to do her a good turn. "I know a man who pilots a boat."

Chapter 15

The Mississippi River
August 1863

To FIND THE MAN with the boat, Pen made her way back
to the river's edge, where the stranger had admonished her
not to throw herself into the water. This time, she knew to
skirt the docks. She was looking for a boat called *Liberty*
and a man named Robert Mayhew.

She expected a riverboat pilot to be old, grizzled,
and bowlegged, but Robert Mayhew was none of those
things. He was only a little older than Pen herself, and his
wiry hair, smoothed with pomade, was thoroughly black.
His legs, as much as she could see of them in his Union-
issue trousers, were long and straight. She had never seen
a Black man with his coloring. His skin was golden; he
seemed to glow.

He stood on the dock beside the boat as though he had
been expecting her. His smile, like his face, conjured the
warmth of the sun. He didn't call out to her. He waited until she got close enough for conversation and said, "Don't
get many ladies visiting me. What can I do for you?"

"My name Penelope Mitchell, and Captain Cohen, a Union officer and an Ohio man, send me here. I have a long story. Is there somewhere to set where I can tell it?"

He said, "Yes, you and your dog. What he called?"

"Toby."

"We can set on the boat."

"Is that all right?"

He laughed, a musical sound. "It surely is. A pilot can set on his own boat whenever he like."

"Thought it was the army's boat."

"It is, but it don't go anywhere unless I pilot it."

She followed him over the gangplank, and once on the boat, up a narrow flight of stairs. Toby's nails scrabbled on the polished wood of the risers. Robert Mayhew opened a wooden door of honey-colored wood and led her and Toby into an enclosure where the ceiling and the walls were all glass. He spread his arms, indicating the whole glass enclosure. "The pilothouse."

A huge wheel, taller than Mr. Mayhew himself, dominated the space, and facing it were two wooden chairs made of the same honey-colored wood as the steps. He gestured toward the chairs in invitation. "This is where the pilot set, when he ain't at the wheel." She sat, and he joined her.

Just outside the windows stretched a vista. Once upon the water, the pilot could take in the water for river ahead. Breathless, she exclaimed, "You see everything from up here!"

"Ain't it something? Never tire of it, no matter how many times I go up and down the river."

"How long you been a pilot?"

"Been on the water all my life," he said. "Grew up on a plantation on the river."

"How you learn to pilot?"

"Massa send his cotton to New Orleans by boat, and he let me go with it when I was eighteen. I have a knack for it, and in a few years, he let me pilot the boat all by myself."

"How you come to pilot for the army?"

"Contraband," he said. "Hopped on an army boat. They glad to have me. I was at Vicksburg on one of them boats that General Grant run through during the siege."

"Is it safe now? To go up the river?"

"Now? The Union army hold the river from New Orleans to Memphis and all the way north. It as safe to run from Natchez to Vicksburg on this boat as to set here." He settled in his chair. "I reckon you want to get to Vicksburg."

"To the army camp near there. The contraband camp."

"That Lake Providence." He rubbed his chin. "I go up there all the time for the army. Take supplies, horses, guns. But I don't take passengers."

"Captain Cohen himself suggest it to me." She smiled at him, wishing she were better at beguiling.

He leaned forward and tapped her knee. Toby, who had been quiet at her feet, suddenly stirred. He drew back and said, "Tell me your tale."

"I fear that I look for a needle in a haystack," she said, and she explained what she hoped to find up the river.

He listened. Under his swagger, he had a calm that would be good on a boat. He said, "Can't promise that you find your husband. But I can certainly take you up the river."

"Don't the army have to say yes?"

269

"They do. But they don't usually say no to me."

She was suddenly tired of his conceit. "You full of yourself, you know that?"

His sunny face was suddenly overcast. "You been a slave, just like I was, ain't you?"

"Yes, I was."

"Might take a lifetime of being full of yourself to help you get over it," he said.

A FEW DAYS LATER, just after sunrise, Pen stood on the dock, waiting to board Pilot Mayhew's steamboat. She rested her hand on Toby's head. He was calm, but she was not. The Mississippi River, so much wider and deeper than the Alabama, the Tombigbee, or the Pearl, was sure to have gators in it.

"Miss Penelope!" called Mayhew from the deck, beckoning to her. "Got a place for you on this boat, and your dog too!"

She boarded the boat. "Where do we go? How we travel?"

He shone. "With the pilot, in the pilothouse."

In the pilothouse, she met the copilot, a lanky, dark-skinned man named Chester. Chester sat with her. Mayhew stood at the great wheel, resting his hands on it, gazing at the river. The dark water was still, and the sun rose in a cloudless blue sky.

Pen fidgeted. Mayhew turned. "You all right, Miss Penelope?"

"Are there gators in this river?"

"Gators bother you?"

"I hate them."

"Well, the river full of gators, but they don't bother a steamboat none. You on the river in a pirogue or a canoe, that a different story. But steamboat churn up the water. Scare the gators away. You won't even see them."

"You promise that?"

He nodded. "I do promise that."

The engine roared to life, once Mayhew steered the boat away from the dock. They got underway, and Pen tried to settle into her chair. Toby stood beside her, his ears cocked, not liking the vibration or the rumble that pulsed two decks below. She scratched his head, trying to soothe him. "It all right, Toby," she said.

Chester flashed her a smile. "It all right, Miss Pen," he said. "Look out them windows, you see something fine."

She wished she could obey as easily as Toby, who quieted under her hand. On the water, the vista promised in the harbor was breathtaking. Pen had thought the Tombigbee was a wide river, but the Mississippi put it to shame. Two Tombigbees could fit into the Mississippi's span and have room left over. The river stretched ahead, curving a little as far as the horizon. "Chester, where do this river go?"

"All the way north, Miss Pen. Vicksburg, Memphis in Tennessee, St. Louis in Missouri. Flow right between Illinois and Iowa. Keep going into Minnesota, even though I ain't never been there. I hear tell that where the Mississippi start, up in Minnesota, it a little trickle your dog could jump over."

Pen said, "You funning me."

"No, he ain't," Robert Mayhew said. "Father of waters

down here start out as a little creek way up there." He didn't turn, but he seemed to have eyes in the back of his head. He asked, "You hungry, Miss Pen?"

How did he know? "We got food?"

"Army food," Mayhew said. "Salt beef, but the bread fresh. Chester, you want to oblige Miss Pen? Fetch some?"

She didn't think that she would enjoy salt beef, but she did. She put down her plate to give the leftovers to Toby, too.

Pen looked northward, as Mayhew did, to see that the sky ahead was an ominous gray. "What down there?" Pen asked.

Mayhew didn't even turn his head. "Rainstorm. Come up all the time on the river. Don't worry."

The farther north they went, the darker the sky became. The clouds massed in the heavens, and the air began to smell wet and a little sweet. Thunder rumbled somewhere north, and Pen began to feel nervous. "More than a rainstorm."

"We all right," Mayhew said.

It began to rain, at first a drizzle against the windows, then a trickle, and then a harder downpour. The sky darkened even more. Northward—Pen had no idea how far away—lightning flashed. The thunder grew louder.

They were steaming right into a thunderstorm.

"Is it all right?" Pen asked, not caring whether Chester or Mayhew answered her. "That we go through a storm like that?"

Chester said, "I pilot with Mr. Robert before, and I see him come through many a storm."

A bolt of lightning hit the water, and Pen started in her chair. The crack of thunder upset Toby so much that he put his paws on Pen's leg, begging her for comfort. Pen scooped him up, and even though he was too big to fit on her lap, she let him jump up there. She put her arms around him and hugged him tightly.

She was terrified to watch and afraid not to. Lightning struck the water again, and the boom of thunder drowned out the roar of the engine. Rain lashed the windows so hard that Pen didn't know how Mayhew could see to steer the boat.

Would lightning strike the boat? Would it catch fire, or worse, explode? She hoped that she and Toby would die quickly. She couldn't bear the thought of being hurled into the water for the gators to find, encircle, and eat. Someday Robert Mayhew's luck would run out, and it might very well be today.

She bent over Toby, clutching his fur, and began to sob. "We die," she sobbed. "Oh Lord, we die here."

Chester whispered something to Mayhew, and Mayhew nodded. He spoke in a voice as calm and as sure as he'd been on the dock. Without turning around, he said, "Miss Pen, sing to me."

"Sing? You crazy!"

"No, I ain't. Just sing. Pilot's order."

"Sing what?"

"Whatever come into your head."

Suddenly the refrain of fear and escape all along her journey sprang into her head, and she couldn't make it go away. She had told herself over and over to wade in the water. Weakly, she opened her mouth to let the words out. She couldn't sing while crouched into a ball. She sat up, her voice so thin and reedy, she was ashamed of it.

Chester joined her. He had a fine, rich, low voice, and his notes twined around hers, lifting them and strengthening them. Together, they sang about the way that God troubled the water. She looked out the window, trying to see past the sheet of water that cascaded over the windows. She had always known that this song was about escape, wading in the water to cheat the militia's dogs. But she had never thought about its other message, salvation.

When they finished, Chester asked her, "Do you know 'One More River to Cross'?"

"Of course I do." As the lightning flashed around them and the thunder roared, Chester led her to sing about one more river to cross, a wide river, as God made the earth tremble and the heavens rattle. *He do his work here*, she thought, her eyes darting over the expanse of the Mississippi roiled by God's fury.

Watery death, she thought, and she said, "'Throw Me Overboard.' Do you know that?"

Chester smiled. "I do," he said, and they sang it together, the story of Jonah. Pen sang of the storm on the sea, of God's wrath at Jonah, with particular fervor. She was still terrified, and she poured all her dread into the song. Chester knew every verse, and they got Jonah to the bottom of the sea, into the whale's belly, and safely spat out upon the shore.

Chester chose the next song before she could suggest something grim. As Mayhew piloted the boat through the storm, he sang, "Sail, O Believer," taking them yonder down the river, yonder to someplace better.

Maybe we get there, Pen thought. Just as she began to feel a little less afraid, lightning struck the water so close to the boat that she screamed, and when the thunder followed, as loud as an explosion, she bent over again, burying her face in Toby's fur.

"Miss Pen," Chester said. "Keep singing, Miss Pen."

The refrain pounded so loud in her head that she didn't realize she had begun to voice it. It had been a funeral shout back in Georgia. "Shall I die?" she sang, her voice a gasp. Chester took it up. His voice transformed it. When he sang, the bleakness faded away, and she heard the hope in the words. As little as she felt it, Chester's voice reminded her that Jesus was coming, that he was here, that he was stronger than thunder, stronger than lightning, stronger than gators.

Without asking her, Chester swung into "Don't Be Weary, Traveler," encouraging her to come home to a place where the world would look fresh and new.

When they finished, Mayhew lifted his voice for the first time, never wavering from the wheel as his voice rose. Pen and Chester joined him. "Come and go to that land," they sang together, travelers bound for a place that held nothing but peace, nothing but love, nothing but freedom. And then they were silent.

Pen realized that she could once again hear the roar of the engine. She could see out the windows. The storm had slowed, the rain had abated, and the black clouds had given way to the gray of an ordinary overcast sky. The sound of thunder had become faint. Pen sat back in her chair, worn out, and Toby jumped from her lap and shook himself.

Mayhew said, "What did I tell you? Come through the storm."

"You still full of yourself," Pen said weakly, too exhausted to move.

"Hah!" he said. "Chester, you hear that? She insult me. She feel better."

"Look," Chester said. "We go past Vicksburg."

"I pilot this boat through here when Vicksburg under bombardment," Mayhew said. "Quiet now. Siege over."

"Someday your luck run out," Pen said, feeling slightly revived.

"Not today," he said, and she didn't have to see his face to know that he was grinning.

By the time they steamed into Lake Providence, the water was still and the sky was a cloudless blue. The sun shone, as golden as Robert Mayhew's skin and as bright as his smile.

Chapter 16

Lake Providence, Louisiana
August 1863

PEN WANDERED THROUGH THE contraband camp at
Lake Providence. She looked in vain for the tents familiar
from the camp at Natchez. Lake Providence had ramshackle buildings, some of which looked as though they
had belonged to a settlement and others as though they
had been thrown together overnight. It didn't have the
order of a street in town or even a slave street. The improvised buildings crowded between and behind the older
ones, and in every possible open space, people crowded,
too.

In the heat of the afternoon sun, the air seemed more
humid than Natchez, and more fetid. The stink of human
waste was even stronger than at Natchez. *So many people*,
Pen thought. No wonder the latrines were overwhelmed.

Men lounged on the steps of the buildings, and women
and children sat in the dirt wherever they could find a
space. Men and women alike wore ragged clothes, and
Pen was disturbed to see that many of the children were as
barefoot as they had been as slaves. *Freedom should mean*

whole clothes and shoes. She reminded herself that many of these people had fled with nothing but the clothes on their backs, and they had suffered as they journeyed to end up at Lake Providence.

As she had so many times in the woods, Pen tried to orient herself. The sky above couldn't guide her. There was no river to direct her. Her compass would point north, but it wouldn't help her. She wiped her face with her sleeve and resisted the impulse to talk to Toby. She didn't need a stranger to jeer at her for conversing with her dog.

A man's voice accosted her. "You new, miss? You look lost."

He sat on the steps of the nearest building. He was her stepdaddy's age and had a friendly look.

She said, "I am new. Just got here. Don't know if I'm lost or not."

"What you look for?"

"Just came from Natchez, where people live in army tents. Don't see a tent anywhere. How do a person find a place to live?"

He chuckled. "Fit in wherever you can. We a mite crowded here."

"I see," Pen said, feeling worse and worse. "How do I find a spot? Who do I ask?"

He tapped the step he sat on and said, "I live in this house. We all bachelors together." He used the slavery term for young, unmarried men, even though he was far from young. "Right next door, it all women and children." He gestured. "They might be able to squeeze you in."

"Should I ask?"

He said, "Let me ask for you." Before she could thank

him, he rose and walked to the adjoining house to knock on the door. It was a small two-story wooden house, and once—perhaps before the war—it had been painted white. Now the paint was cracked and peeling and gray. A weary voice drifted from within. "Who that?"

"Hector here. Just meet someone new. A gal who need a spot."

The weary voice said, "You know we ain't got any room in here."

"She won't take up much room," he said, humor warming his tone. "She a skinny thing."

Feet padded to the door, and the weary speaker appeared. She looked as though she had once been stout, but now her skin seemed too loose for her. Her cheeks were ashy. She rubbed her head, dislodging a kerchief that was no longer white. "Hector, I mean it. We already full to bursting."

He gestured. "The whole place full to bursting. Sadie, you take her in, you get another ration of meal and meat."

Sadie looked askance at Pen. "Is that a dog you got?"

Pen said, "He don't take up much room, either."

"Do he have fleas? With every other misery we got here, we don't want fleas, too."

The last person who had asked her that had been the cook in Madame Bella's well-kept bawdy house. "No," Pen said.

Hector asked, "What you say, Sadie?"

She sighed. "We make room."

Pen came inside, bringing Toby with her. The house was empty of any furniture, but it was crammed with people. Women sat on the floor, their older children clustered around them, any younger ones in their arms or at the breast. Each family had staked out a spot with a sheet. That was a room, and a home. The house smelled of sweat, unwashed clothes, bacon grease, and unwiped babies. Pen asked, "How many people stay here?"

"Thirty. No, with you, thirty-one."

"How do you cook? How do you eat?"

"We share what we get from the army, and we cook together. Sometimes we cook for them men next door." She laughed without mirth. "They can't hardly take care of themselves."

"Where do I get food?"

"I show you. You can register for work, too. The army prefer that you work."

"What is it? Is it laundering?"

Sadie looked at Pen as though she weren't very bright. "The men, they get shovels and they dig ditches," she said. "We women and girls, we work at picking cotton on a place nearby."

"Do you get paid?"

She snorted. "We supposed to. But they ain't paid us yet, not a dime."

Pen felt despair. "Like in slavery time."

"What do you expect? That President Abraham Lincoln come here, shake your hand, and give you a hundred dollar?"

"This is some kind of free," Pen said.

Sadie said, "You tell me when you find something better."

PEN STOOD IN A long line to get her allotted ration: a peck of cornmeal and a pound of salt pork. *Just like slavery time*, she thought. She remembered the bounty at Kate's table in the refuge for runaways and the taste of new peas and fresh strawberries in Liza's kitchen, and felt her despair return.

Toby, always cheered by the smell of meat, trotted by her side, looking hopeful. She murmured, "Glad that someone happy in this place."

That night, she tried to sleep without bothering anyone who had claimed a sheet's worth of floor. She tucked her bag under her head to keep it safe, but it made a hard and painful pillow. The house was unbearably hot, and the smell grew worse after dark. She lay awake, telling herself that she hadn't come here to return to slavery. She was here to look for Jonas. *Needle in a haystack*, she had told Mayhew. She was afraid that she had been right.

THE NEXT MORNING, SUNDAY, dawned hot and bright. The women in the overcrowded house stirred, woke, chastised older children, wiped off and swaddled babies, and went outside to fry salt meat.

Pen straightened her skirt and hefted her bag over her shoulder. She asked the woman nearest to her, "Where can I find some water to wash?"

She didn't reply. She lay on her sheet, her knees pulled up to her chin, her hands wrapped tightly around her shins. Her eyes were closed.

Pen asked gently, "Sister, are you all right?"

A girl, her face sharp and shadowed and so fair of skin that she had a spray of freckles over her nose, said to Pen, "She ain't. She lose her baby when she get here, and since then, she don't talk no more."

Indignantly, Pen said, "Ain't there a doctor here?"

"Hah!" the girl said. Her shape said that she was about fourteen, but her face was much older than that. "We do what we can. She ain't sick in her body, but she sick at heart."

Pen bent her head. She blinked away the tears that came with the memory. The loss, and the oblivion afterward.

She walked outside, where the air was a little cooler, if not sweeter, and reminded herself, *Jonas. Think about finding Jonas.*

But in this seething, unwashed, disorderly place, she didn't know where to start. There was no sociable group of washwomen to spread the word. The army, so obvious at Natchez, turned its face away here. There was no town to help her with an inquiry. Nothing she had learned in Natchez would help her at Lake Providence.

Hector, the neighbor, waved to her. "Still look lost, miss."

"My name Penelope," she said. "Penelope Mitchell."

"Hector Price. Where you from, if I may ask?"

"You may." She gave him the short answer, Georgia, and told him about Jonas.

Hector looked thoughtful. "He may be here, and you ain't got an idea how to find him."

She nodded.

He said, "You wouldn't know to look at me, but I help out the Union army from the time that General Grant come to Tennessee to fight at Shiloh. You know what a scout do?"

"Not for the army."

"Ride out ahead and see what out there. Go in a group, all in uniform, all armed. Might as well carry a sign to announce the Union army come."

Pen laughed.

"I do it different. I go out in advance of them scouts. Pretend to be a runaway. Sneak and creep and get people to trust you and tell you what they know. And dodge all God's dangers doing it."

Pen thought, *That's what I done since I left Georgia.*

"Then I tell the army what I find out before they move forward and get themselves into a mess. Help them out more than they realize."

"Being a runaway ain't much different," she said.

"You wiser than you know," he said. "Unfamiliar place, full of strangers."

Pen understood what Hector told her: *This just like a wilderness full of peril. Find your way through it.*

She asked, "Can I trust you, Mr. Hector Price?"

"To do what, Miss Penelope?"

"To help find my husband, Jonas. Not to scout, or whatever you call it in the army. Just to send out the word. Just to ask."

"I reckon I can, Miss Penelope."

She hadn't known that her talent as a runaway might help the Union army fight the war. That gave her something to ponder.

After breakfast, she told Toby, "We get our bearings. We take a stroll around this place to *scout* it."

As they walked, she began to see more than a jumble. The spaces between the houses were like miniature slave streets, where these temporary neighbors gathered. She wondered if the contraband camp might have a space for a Sunday meeting. It didn't need a space for Saturday night pleasure, since contraband men could drink just as easily on their stoops here as on the slave street on a plantation.

She hadn't gone to meeting much since she left Georgia, and she had been so intent on her journey that she hadn't missed it. She had talked to God in snatches. *Lord, help me. Help me avoid the militia. Help me confuse the dogs. Help me not to get shot or outraged. Help me find a place where there's food, whether it's a bunch of cress under a tree or a kitchen on a big house where I can get scraps. Help me find Jonas.* Those prayers had been heartfelt, but they had been selfish, too.

On the boat, singing with Chester and Mayhew to keep her fear at bay, she had been closer to God than she had in months.

Curious, she stopped to ask a group of people who sat on a nearby stoop, "Is there a meeting at this place?" They looked to be a family, husband and wife and children, like the Smiths. She felt a pang. Free or not, they were together.

"Sometimes," the woman said. "It depend on whether Lieutenant Morgan can manage it."

"Lieutenant?"

"He a minister before the war. Hated slavery so much he couldn't stay behind, even though he a man of the cloth."

"Where might I find him?"

"You lucky today. He offer the service. Just finishing up. I take you."

"Why don't you go?"

"They don't sing much," she said. "Can't abide a meeting without singing."

The meeting had dispersed, and a few people, better dressed than the usual contraband, clustered around a man in a Union coat. Pen approached the group, smiling and hanging back a bit, showing that she was polite enough to wait.

The minister noticed her and beckoned. "Come, join us." He was very young, with sandy hair that flopped into his eyes, which were a deep blue. He said, "Were you looking for the service?"

"Just heard about it," she said. "Sorry I didn't know sooner."

"I try to come every week," he said. "But I'm a military man here, not a minister. I have other duties now."

"We do as much as we can."

"I wish I could do more," he said. "The contrabands need so much. Not just food and clothing and medicine, although their need for that is great."

"God's word."

"Even more than that," he said. "I have a good friend from divinity school who works in the Sea Islands. He teaches the contrabands to read and write. That's God's work, too."

"I can read. And figure. And write, just a little."

"How well do you read?"

What an odd question. She said, "I show you."

"From this?" He lifted the book he held.

"I have my own book." She reached into her bag and pulled out her book of poems. It still felt comfortable in her palm.

He leaned to look—like Rosa, he was drawn to the sight of a book—and said, "I don't believe I've ever met a contraband with her own copy of *Leaves of Grass*."

"You know this book?"

"Yes, very well."

She opened the book, turning the pages with pleasure. "Song of Myself," she read. She made her way through the lines slowly. The words were no more difficult than anything in the *Natchez Gazette*, but they resounded differently. It was as though Mr. Walt Whitman stood next to her, talking to her. She liked that thought so much that she read the second stanza of the poem, savoring the words, and she was sorry to stop.

Lieutenant Morgan had the most peculiar expression on his face. He asked, "Do you understand what you read?"

She met those bright blue eyes. It was still hard to look into a white person's eyes. She said, "Yes, I do. It about being free in your soul. Seeing and feeling the truth for yourself. And glorying in it."

He smiled, and that smile was better than a prayer.

PEN KNEW THAT INQUIRIES took time, but she was impatient. She waited only a day before she cornered Hector to ask if he'd heard anything.

He said, "This a big place and a confusing place, and

more people come every day. Haven't heard anything yet."

"What if he in the army? The Black regiment?"

"Don't know if the army would know, either. They in a mess here, with all these contrabands."

"Who could I ask?"

"It ain't safe for you in the army camp."

"Union army camp? I have trouble, surrounded by the Union army?"

"Not every man who fight for the Union army hate slavery and love Black folks. Don't let that Union coat blind you."

LIKE HECTOR, SADIE WARNED Pen about the soldiers. "They white men, and they ain't been with a woman for months. They ain't likely to ask if you mind what they do."

"They bother anyone?"

"I don't go out at night, and you shouldn't, either."

But it was so close in the overcrowded house that Pen couldn't bear it. She had to go out for air. She took her bag with her, as she did all the time, and as she sped down the steps, she thought of the lumber camp at the salt mines and slipped her pistol into her pocket.

It was barely dusk. The air was still hot and humid, and the proximity to the river meant that the mosquitoes came out in force. The contraband camp was too restless to settle for the night, even though the men who dug ditches and the women who picked cotton would have to get up early the next day. Pen wanted to be somewhere else. She wondered if she could make her way down to the river. At least to the docks, where Mayhew had left her.

But she got lost, and as night fell, she was disoriented again. "Which way we go, Toby?" she murmured, but he only wagged his tail and waited for her to decide.

She looked up. The clouds were wispy overhead and didn't hide the crescent moon. She stilled herself. She hadn't listened for birds in the human din that accompanied the contraband camp. Did owls fly here? Did they call?

A drunken voice said, "Look what we found."

Two Union men, both white, one taller than the other. The taller one was drunker, too. He said, "A nigger wench."

She wanted to growl like Toby.

The drunk said, "If she's out at night, she must be looking for a little fun." He came closer. "What do you say? A little fun?"

No, damn you.

He came closer. She could smell the whiskey on his breath. She reached into her pocket, and when he lunged forward, trying to grab her, she raised the pistol to point it at him.

She held the gun in her right hand and kept her left on Toby's head, ready to release him if she had to. "You come any closer, and I shoot you."

The drunken man said, "You wouldn't."

She could feel Denmark's hands on her arms, guiding and supporting her. "Don't test me."

The shorter soldier, less drunk, more cowardly, yanked on his companion's sleeve. "She means it."

"A nigger gal shoot a Union man?"

She aimed the pistol at the drunken man's heart.

The coward said, "Come on, you damn fool. We can

find a gal to tumble who doesn't have a pistol in her hand."

Pen didn't lower the pistol.

The coward dragged his companion away. The drunk said, "Damn you, you're wrenching my arm!"

Pen waited until they staggered away. The coward glanced over his shoulder, and he saw Pen still pointing the pistol at his drunken friend.

She thought, *It ain't sporting to shoot a man in the back. Even if he deserve it.*

She kept the pistol in her hand until she found her way back to Sadie's house to sit heavily on the steps, her legs trembling. Inside, she lay down and tucked her bag under her head, feeling the pistol dig into her temple. She began to shake, as Lucy had. She wrapped her arms around herself, trying to stop the shaking.

That night, she dreamed. She fell into a river, the water vast and muddy. As she flailed in the water, the gators came. They encircled her, staring at her with their odd froglike eyes. They opened their mouths to show her their teeth. They closed in on her, jaws agape, and she could either drown or let them tear her to pieces.

THE NEXT MORNING, PEN changed back into her boy's clothes. The girl with the old woman's face said, "Why you do that?"

"It ain't your business, but I'm on a journey. Bound to go. This is how I dress when I travel."

The woman who didn't talk lay on her sheet. Her eyes were open today. Pen knelt down at her side. She said, "Sister?"

Her eyelids fluttered.

Pen's heart seemed to stick in her throat. "I lose my baby, too. I fall into grief so wide and so deep that it like the Mississippi River. Thought I would drown in it. But one day, I get to the farther shore. To dry land. And I go on."

The woman spoke. "I'm so cold."

Pen rummaged in her bag. She took out the shawl. She said, "This a gift from my sister. It comfort me many a time after I run away. Take it."

To her surprise, the woman raised her hands. With tremendous gentleness, Pen laid the folded shawl in them. The woman touched the shawl to her cheek.

Pen said, "You wrap yourself up good in it."

"Thank you," the woman whispered.

Pen touched the woman's forehead. "God bless."

She rose, hoisted her bag to her shoulder, and nodded to Toby. She left the house and walked deliberately down the steps.

Hector sat on the stoop next door. As she came close, he said, "That ain't a bad disguise. Had to look twice to recognize you. Where you going?"

Pen said, "I want to shoot a man."

"Thought you wanted to find a man."

"That, too." She gestured around the contraband camp. "Can't do it here. This ain't freedom. I taste it, and I know. None of this is just. No house to live in and no proper food to eat. Work at picking cotton and don't get paid for it. Suffer insult from a white man, and you right, a Union coat don't make a man hate slavery."

"What you do about it?"

"Take the next step in the journey."

"That mean, look for your husband?"

"Yes," she said. "And it mean that I muster in to the First Mississippi."

Hector gave her a quizzical look. "Don't have to join the army to find him," he said. "Just make an inquiry."

"Tired of making an inquiry. Tired of not learning a thing from it." She took a deep breath. "Tired of being interfered with."

"In the army, the secesh interfere with you. They shoot you dead."

"I keep searching for Jonas. And while I look, I fight."

Hector chuckled. "You sound crazy, you know that?"

"Ever since I leave Georgia, people tell me that I crazy to do what I do. Maybe they right. But I keep going, whether they right or not." She touched the strap of her bag as though it held a rifle. "Next step in the journey."

He shook his head. "You got a boy's name to go with them boy's clothes?"

"Mitchell Penn."

He gave her the searching eye that had made him a good scout. "Well, whether you call yourself Penelope Mitchell or Mitchell Penn, you take care, and I hope with all my heart you find what you look for."

THE SOLDIERS' CAMP, UNLIKE the contraband camp, was orderly. White canvas tents in neat rows stretched as far as she could see. It smelled a little better than the contraband camp. They must muck out the latrines every day.

These were white soldiers, and they gave her unfriendly looks. She reminded herself that she was in trouble here because she was Black, not because she was a woman.

Someone called out, "What are you doing here?" The hostility in his tone suggested the mean word she disliked so much.

"I'm looking for the First Mississippi Infantry. The Black regiment. Plan to muster in to it."

The soldier jeered, "Your dog muster in, too?"

"Shut up," another soldier said.

"I don't like contrabands," the first soldier said.

The second soldier ignored him. He said to Pen, "The Black regiment is a ways off. At the back of us." He pointed.

"Thank you, sir," Pen said, not for the courtesy but to mollify anyone who might want to sling a mean word at her.

She trudged through the camp, seeing a sea of white soldiers. *Where was the Black regiment? It must be like a big plantation, where the slave quarters were far away from white eyes.*

The ground turned boggier, and the mosquitoes seemed thicker. The air was wetter here. It smelled like the Mississippi River, of mud and decaying vegetation, with the faintest whiff of cypress and pine.

More canvas tents here. Orderly.

But the men who sat outside them, who drank from tin cups, polished their boots, and cleaned their rifles, were Black. She drew in her breath at the sight of so many Black men in Union coats.

She stopped at a group of men sitting cross-legged on

the ground. One of them asked, "What brings you here, son?"

She pitched her voice low. "Come here to muster in. Where do I go?"

The soldier laughed. "Have to rouse the lieutenant from his breakfast first."

Another soldier laughed, too. "Let him finish his coffee."

The first soldier said, "I take you." He rose, and he saw Toby. "Is he a soldier, too?"

"He come with me since I run away."

He had an easy, loping walk. "When was that?"

She fell in beside him. "Right after the Proclamation."

"Took it serious, didn't you?"

"Yes, I did."

The lieutenant sat in the cook tent, his tin cup before him. His boyish face had been wearied and saddened by war. When the soldier said, "Got a boy who want to muster in," he set down his coffee cup and sighed. "Let me get the muster list."

He returned with a ledger book not so different from Rosa's accounts. She hadn't thought that a regiment would keep accounts.

He opened it and said, "I'll need to take your particulars."

Thanks to Mr. Levy, she knew what to expect. He asked for her name, and she had the lie ready. "Mitchell Penn, sir."

"Your age?"

"Eighteen," she said, to explain her smooth cheeks.

"How tall are you?"

"Don't know," she said.

"I'll hazard a guess," he said and wrote something down. "Eye color? Shall I say brown?"

"Yes, sir."

"Hair color? Can't see for your cap."

She pushed back the cap to reveal the kerchief beneath it, which completely covered her hair. He asked, "Why do you wear that?"

"Keep off the lice, sir. Lice a trial."

"Does it work?"

"So far."

"Your hair color?"

"Black, sir."

"Complexion," he said. "Shall I say brown?"

"That's right, sir. Why you ask how I look?"

"Descriptions distinguish the men."

She wondered how a regiment of men, all described as having brown eyes, black hair, and brown skin, would be distinguished from one another.

"Where were you born?"

That was easy. "Dougherty County, Georgia."

"That's quite far away. Most of the men here are from Mississippi or Alabama."

"Traveled a ways to end up here, sir."

"Occupation?"

"I'm a contraband now, but that ain't an occupation. Before I run away, I was a field hand."

"Where do you reside?"

Where was her home? The question filled her with a sudden longing, and she had to tamp it down to keep her voice even and low. She said, "I guess I live here, at the contraband camp."

"Are you married or single?"

She hadn't anticipated that question. She paused, not wanting to explain her dilemma or reveal her real reason for being here. She swallowed and said, "Sir, I believe you know that slaves can't get married proper."

He looked abashed. "Excuse me," he said. "I've just mustered in to the regiment myself. I didn't realize." He wrote some more and looked up. "You're on the muster list now," he said, regaining his composure.

"Sir? When do I get my uniform and my rifle?"

"We need to make a request of the Quartermaster Corps. That will take a while. It won't be today. They're in charge of your pay, too."

Toby, who had been quiet and patient, suddenly barked. The lieutenant leaned over his table. "Have you brought a dog?"

"Yes, sir."

A broad-shouldered white man said, "What's this, Lieutenant?"

"A new recruit, sir."

"Did you muster in his dog, too?"

"Captain, sir," the lieutenant said, turning red.

"I don't see how a dog will be a problem, since we're on garrison duty here," the captain said, smiling a little, and even Pen could tell that he was teasing. "What's your name, soldier?"

"Mitchell Penn, sir."

"We're glad to have you. Can you shoot?"

"I can, sir."

"Would you like to show me?"

Suddenly her mouth went dry. She told herself, *This what I come for*, and she worked to keep her voice level. "Yes, sir."

The lieutenant found her a rifle to test her shooting, and the captain, with the lieutenant in tow, brought her to a big, open spot. "Our parade ground," the captain said. "You'll get to know it well. We keep targets at this end to teach the recruits who don't yet know how to shoot."

"Yes, sir," Pen said.

The parade ground began to fill. "Roll call soon," the captain said. He walked her toward the targets. "Lieutenant?"

The lieutenant handed her the rifle. It was heavier than the hunting rifle she was used to, and the barrel was much longer. It felt strange in her hands. Suddenly she heard Carver's voice, as clear as if he were standing beside her. "Get used to it."

She balanced the rifle in her hands, getting her bearings.

Behind her, a crowd had gathered. Someone called out, "Who have target practice?"

The captain called back, "New recruit. Says he can shoot. We'll put him through his paces."

She lifted the rifle to her shoulder. She positioned her hands, as Carver had taught her. It was as though she could feel his fingers and hear his voice, with its rough affection. She steadied the rifle.

"Ready, soldier?" the captain asked.

"Yes." She aimed. She let her whole body ease, as Carver had taught her, and she fired.

The captain said, "Not a bull's-eye, but not bad. So you want to try again?"

"Yes, sir," she said, and fired again.

"Better," the captain said. "Closer. Another try?"

She nodded, aimed, and fired.

"Bull's-eye this time!" the captain said, pleased. Behind him, the men applauded and cheered. When they quieted, the captain called to a man in the crowd, "Sergeant! Come meet our newest recruit. He has the makings of a sharpshooter."

The sergeant detached from the crowd. Pen turned to look at him. He asked her, "What's your name, soldier?"

She saw the muscled arms first, tight in the sleeves of his coat, and the broad shoulders. Then the eyes, which had changed. Like the lieutenant's, they were sadder. The mouth had changed, too. That mouth, which had always been so quick to smile, was now resolute.

"Private Penn." She met his eyes, letting him look at her closely. She didn't take her eyes from his face.

She saw the surprise and the joy and the way that he muted them both, as a soldier on duty. He whispered, "Pen," but he said aloud, "Welcome to the First Mississippi, Private Penn. After roll call, we talk." Then he asked, "How you come to us? How you find us?"

She heard the private question under the public one. She met his eyes again and said, "Walked through the war to find you. And here I am."

Chapter 17

Lake Providence, Louisiana
August 1863

JONAS LED HER FROM the parade ground, being careful to keep a soldier's stride and a soldier's distance. She matched him. Toby did, too. Jonas found a spot behind the tents, sheltered by a clump of trees, secluded enough for private conversation. He turned to her and stared at her. The stalwart sergeant dropped away, and instead she saw a man whose expression mingled astonishment and delight. "You're really here? I ain't dreaming?"

"I dream that we meet again. Never dream that it would be like this."

"Wherever I go, in slavery and in war, I think of you, Pen. I long for you."

She was a little dizzy at the way he whipsawed between man and soldier. "So do I."

He shook his head. "So you really here." He laughed low in his throat. He had always laughed like that after love, when they lay together, sated and spent. "Sorry to ask you, but can you be a soldier for a moment?"

"I reckon so."

He took a deep breath and said, "You put me in a bit of a spot. As they say in the army, we got a situation here."

"Never meant to," she said. "How bad a situation?"

"Not so bad," he said, smiling. "Have an idea of how to fix it. With your help, soldier."

She heard the affection in his voice. "Do you tease me?"

He spoke as though he didn't care who might overhear. "I surely do, sugar."

Colonel Webber looked up from his improvised desk. He had the appearance of many of the Union officers—extreme youth hardened by the burden of command and death in war. Pen had not seen a colonel's insignia before. On both his sleeves gleamed eagles embroidered in gold thread.

He smiled at the sight of Jonas. "Sergeant Mitchell! What brings you here?"

"Got a dilemma, sir, and thought you might help me." His stance was straight and easy at once. He was courteous but not deferential. A soldier was very different from a slave, and an officer very different from a massa.

"Who is with you?"

"Our newest recruit. Got a dog, but don't mind the dog, sir. It ain't a usual circumstance, sir."

"Is he underage?"

"No, sir, that ain't it."

"Unfit somehow?"

"In a manner of speaking, yes, sir."

Colonel Webber said, "What's the matter, Sergeant Mitchell?" The colonel was calm and respectful. Even a private merited that.

"Sir, this private muster in with us as Mitchell Penn. But when the captain bring him to me, I know that ain't right." He took a breath. "This ain't a boy. This is my wife, Penelope Mitchell."

The colonel rested his eyes on Pen. She took off her cap and her kerchief and shook out her hair. She let him see the woman's features on her face. She said, "It true, sir."

Colonel Webber asked, "Sergeant, did you know that your wife was here?"

"No, sir. When I see her, it was the biggest surprise of my life."

"Mrs. Mitchell, why did you muster in to my regiment?"

"I come to the contraband camp to find my husband, sir."

"Surely it would have been easier to make an inquiry."

"I try, sir. But the contraband camp in such disorder that finding someone like finding a needle in the haystack. And I ask the army too, sir. But they so burdened with the contrabands that they can't help me, not a bit."

"I've heard many a young man lie to muster in to the army," he said. "I'm hearing something like that now. Truly, why did you muster in, Mrs. Mitchell?"

"Sir, I want to fight, too."

He sighed. "Mrs. Mitchell, you can't be a soldier in my regiment, as you're well aware."

"I'm sorry, sir. Didn't mean to cause trouble, sir."

Jonas said, "We get married before the war and then I was sold away to Mississippi. She come to find me, sir. Come all the way from Georgia to find me."

Colonel Webber said, "Mrs. Mitchell, it's quite a distance from Georgia to Lake Providence. How did you get here?"

"After Jonas sold away, I grieve and never forget that we married. When the Proclamation come, I decide to go to find him." She took a deep breath. "I walk through Georgia and Alabama and Mississippi until I come to Natchez, where the contraband camp is, and there I hear of the Black regiment up the river. So I come to Lake Providence, with hope in my heart. But the rest was fate."

"Contraband? I assume you were a runaway?"

"I was, sir."

He said, "So you braved slave catchers, militia men, Confederate men along the way?"

"And gators, sir. Crossed many a river full of gators."

"How did you manage? A woman alone?"

"Wasn't alone. Had my dog with me." She looked down at Toby. "And many people help me along with the way. That's how I learn how to shoot."

The colonel asked, "Sergeant Mitchell? Is this right? Your wife has walked through the war for love of you?"

Jonas said, "I reckon so, sir."

The colonel said, "That's a tale worthy of the ancient Greeks. Of Homer. I never thought to see it in my regiment."

She asked, "Homer? From ancient times? Did he write that poem about the long and difficult journey?"

He looked at her in surprise. "You know of it?"

"I do, sir." She glanced at Jonas. He was surprised, too.

The colonel said, "Sergeant Mitchell, your wife is a very courageous woman. And a very loyal one. You are a fortunate man."

Jonas dropped all pretense of being a soldier and looked at Pen with a husband's love and longing.

The colonel continued, "Let me talk to the lieutenant and the captain. They made an understandable mistake. Your wife was so clever in her disguise. Do you know if the muster list has gone to the quartermaster yet?"

"It shouldn't have, sir, since it happen just this morning."

"No harm done, then," he said. "Mrs. Mitchell, while I applaud your spirit, I'll have to cross your name off our muster list. We'll have to find you another way to fight." He looked at Jonas. "No one will be disciplined for this. Not even chastised."

"Thank you, sir," Jonas said. "What about the rest? That Penelope my wife? How do we explain that?"

The colonel smiled. "We tell the truth," he said. "That Penelope made an odyssey for love."

When they left the colonel's tent, Jonas took her for a stroll around the camp. They ended up at the very edge of the tents, where the air smelled of the river. "Can you see the water from here?" she asked.

"Not from here. If you like, I take you down to the docks to see it."

"I come up the river from Natchez. Came through a storm. God troubled the water for us."

"You came through all right."

"All right. But different."

Jonas faced her, and it was a pleasure to recall that they were nearly the same height. He touched her cheek. "You thinner."

"Catch as catch can when you run away," she said. "You ever eat something called cress?"

"No. Is it good?"

"It make you long for greens."

"I was a laborer at Yazoo City and at Vicksburg for the secesh," he said. "They didn't feed us right, either."

"You in the siege?"

"Yes," he said. "Shells all around me like hail."

"You come through, too."

His face was shadowed again with war's shadow. "Pen, how you learn to shoot?"

"Met a runaway who taught me to shoot a pistol," she said. "And a deserter who schooled me with a rifle. They both wanted me to be able to take care of myself, and now I can."

She thought of them all: Jasper and Mary Magdalene, Kate and Denmark, Liza and Carver, and Rosa. She realized that they would always be with her. She would always carry their gifts, no matter where her life took her. She thought of the baby she had lost, which she would also carry in her heart. She would tell Jonas about him, but not yet.

She said, "I ain't the same as I was."

Jonas reached out to touch her and seemed to think better of it. His hand dropped to his side. Neither of them were ready yet. "I ain't either."

She grasped the hand that Jonas had withdrawn and clasped it. His touch was familiar, as though they'd never been parted, the palms and fingers rough, the skin warm. "Do you recall what we said to each other on our wedding night?"

Her heart ached at the sight of the old, sweet smile. "I recall everything," he said. "What was the particular thing you remember?"

"To take it slow."

They stood hand in hand. "We'll do that," he said.

As though he were jealous of this stranger, Toby nosed Jonas's leg. Jonas laughed and bent to touch Toby's head. "What he called?"

"Toby."

He looked up, surprised again. "Toby? You name him after your stepdaddy?"

She brought her free hand to her mouth. "Didn't even think of it."

"How could you not? His name Tobias."

She laughed and reached down to pet Toby's head. "I guess I bring him with me, all the way from Georgia."

COLONEL WEBBER HAD GIVEN them a tent of their own, and Jonas had pitched it a little away from the rest of the camp to give them a bit of privacy. Pen left Toby outside, to his chagrin, and the two of them crawled inside. It was a cozy space for two people who didn't mind being close together. Moonlight filtered through the canvas, giving them enough light to see each other.

Pen listened to the frogs chirping and booming in the boggy forest beyond the camp. She let her body ease and listened for the birds, too. "Are there horned owls here?"

Jonas turned onto his side to look her in the eyes. "Yes, there are."

"Do you hear them?"

"Listen."

The call drifted through the night, that unmistakable combination of a hoot, a bark, and a coo. She said, "Whenever I hear an owl call, wherever I am, I always think of you." She smiled. "Because you tell me they stay together all their lives, faithful to one another."

She propped herself on her elbow to look at him. He touched her cheek, then let his fingers travel down her neck and to her shoulder. He found her scar. "You do walk through the war," he said. "What happen?"

"I tell you all about that, but not just yet," she said. "I take that slow, too."

He hesitated. "Pen, I know it can't be good, but tell me. What happen to the baby?"

She put her hand to her face, because it pained her anew. "I lose the baby after you taken away."

"Oh, Pen," he said, and a tear trickled down his cheek.

She touched his face to brush the tear away.

He reached out his arms, and she came into the shelter of his embrace. He kissed her, and she returned the kiss, at first slow and sweet, then more and more urgent. His hands slid over her body, his touch hungry. She didn't mind that hunger at all, in Jonas. She felt his heartache in it.

They pressed close, with nothing to keep them apart, and their two bodies joined as one, hungry together. They moved in unison, their desire diminishing their grief, laughing softly with the effort of trying to love each other quietly. And then it came, the joy so fierce and complete that it was hard not to cry out. They were married again.

IN THE MORNING, PEN woke first, and she watched Jonas. Asleep, all the sadness and weariness of war washed away, and he looked like the man she remembered. His eyes fluttered open. "Didn't dream it," he said. "You really here."

She smiled. "Journey over."

"Not yet."

She reached for his hand. "What you mean?"

He laced his fingers with hers. "Pen, do you want to get married proper?"

"Do marriage mean freedom to you, Jonas?"

"Of course it do. Along with being able to fight."

"Agree with you about being able to fight." She smiled. "That's why I muster in, cause you all that trouble."

"Hard to believe that you really want to be a soldier."

She laughed. "I'm a good shot."

"Do you recall what Colonel Webber say? That there more than one way to fight?"

"I do recall that." She let go of his hand and sat up. "Jonas, I want to be free. Want to belong together. But I want to belong to myself, too. Not sure that marriage help with that."

"We love each other. Want to be together. Took God's own trouble to be together again. You afraid of something. What is it?"

She didn't reply.

"Is it the baby?" he whispered. "Are you still heart-broke about the baby?"

"Oh, Jonas," she said. "I'll take that sorrow to my grave. Won't you?" She blinked away tears, and when she met his eyes, he did too. "I do want another baby. A family. But I know that ain't all I want. Freedom ain't just a husband and a baby, Jonas."

He touched her cheek with a gentle finger. "Then what is it, sugar?"

"I see so many different things once I run away to find you. The world so much bigger than I ever know, living in slavery in Dougherty County. Wider than the Mississippi River."

"I know," he said. "I come up the Mississippi from Vicksburg. Felt free on that river."

"Jonas, I know how to read now. Can read the newspaper. Can read from a book of poems. The world in them books is even wider than the Mississippi." She thought of reading "Song of Myself" and hearing the poet's voice in her ear.

"I can't read."

"Not yet. You can learn. Anyone can learn." She spoke with a passion she hadn't known that she carried. "Everyone should. Every contraband. Every slave. Every soul who used to be a slave. Think of it, Jonas! All of us, able to read! Able to see how wide the world is!"

He hugged her close. "I think you know what make you feel free, sugar."

A little while later, Jonas said, "We tell the colonel that we want to get married."

"Don't have to. He ain't like a massa."

"No. But he my commanding officer. I tell him out of respect."

The colonel was delighted with the news. "I've never met two people more married in their hearts and souls than the two of you. But I assume that you're talking about a religious ceremony and a marriage license."

"Yes, sir," Jonas said.

Colonel Webber said, "You have more than my blessing. The army can issue a marriage license, if a minister officiates. We'll all celebrate with you. And whatever I can do to help, I will do."

LESS THAN A WEEK later, a woman Pen had never met appeared at the door of her tent. She had a creamy complexion the color of ecru lace and wavy hair tamed into a knot on her neck. She wore a dress of striped calico with the most ornate sleeves Pen had ever seen on a Black woman's dress. Under her arm she held a big brown paper parcel. "Miss Penelope?"

"Yes, ma'am?"

"I come to measure you for your wedding dress."

"What is that? I never ask for a wedding dress."

"Colonel Webber ask me to sew it for you. And he promise to pay for the cloth and the lace, whatever you want. I favor satin for a wedding dress. It drape so nice."

Pen said weakly, "I can't take such a thing."

"Oh, he expect that you act prickly about it. He say that it's a wedding present. Hope that you like it." She pursed her lips. "Wouldn't be seemly to refuse it."

"Who are you?" Pen asked.

"No call to be impolite. My name Antoinette Richard, and before the war I was a seamstress to a lady in Vicksburg. I make all her dresses, and dresses for her daughters, too. She tell me I sew just as fine as any modiste in New Orleans."

"What you have in that parcel?"

"Muslin. After I measure you, I cut out the dress in muslin and fit it. Satin too expensive to fool with."

Pen said, "This an awful lot of fuss for a fool dress I won't wear but once. Why don't you sew me a nice dress I can wear to meeting after I get married?"

Antoinette said, "This dress ain't just for you."

"What you mean?"

Antoinette's self-assured expression faltered a little. "It for all of us contraband women. All of us, who lose our men and don't know where they are. Who love them and long for them. Who pray that we find them again, so we can marry proper. So that nothing ever part us again." Her self-possession was gone. She looked up at Pen, her lashes webbed with tears.

Pen thought of Forks of the Road, its purpose as a slave market ended, and her own eyes prickled, too. She said, "Satin, you say?"

Antoinette blinked her tears away. "White satin, as fine as any white lady's wedding dress. Some lace for the trim and the rest for a veil. You look like an angel in it. I promise."

"Hah! I ain't a white lady, and you don't have to flatter me. You make me look presentable, that's miracle enough."

Antoinette rummaged in her pocket and pulled out a tape measure. "We get right to work."

PEN WENT TO VISIT Colonel Webber to thank him for his kindness.

He smiled to see her. "How does the dressmaking go? Does Mrs. Richard suit?"

"She a fine dressmaker, and the dress going to be beautiful, sir. More than I deserve."

"Oh no," he said. "It's exactly what you deserve, Mrs. Mitchell."

She inclined her head. It was still difficult to hear this kind of consideration from a white man. "Don't want to seem ungrateful, sir," she said. "But I meet a minister when I was in the contraband camp. Hope that he still here, and that he might offer the marriage service for us."

"Who is he?"

"He an officer, but he a minister, too. Lieutenant Morgan."

The colonel's face lit up. "Alonzo Morgan! I know he takes an interest in the contrabands, but I didn't know he was a minister. A fine man. Should I speak to him?"

"Sir, if you don't mind, I'd prefer to. The army camp so big. How do I find him?"

"I can ask him here to speak to you. The army camp isn't very friendly to the women who are contrabands."

"I know that, sir. If you recall, I'm a good shot."

"We can't issue you a rifle, Mrs. Mitchell."

She drew the pistol from the bag she always carried. "I have this."

The colonel said, "Why am I not surprised? You'll find Lieutenant Morgan with the Massachusetts men."

TO MOVE THROUGH THE white section of the army camp, she took Toby along, and she slipped her pistol into her pocket. If she ever saw those interfering brutes again, she wouldn't hesitate this time. She'd shoot them.

She found Lieutenant Morgan in front of his tent, writing at a rickety table. He was delighted to see her. He invited her to sit and said, "I heard the news, that you found what you were looking for." His eyes sparkled. "And that you mustered in to the First Mississippi to do it."

"Do you hear that Colonel Webber make a big fuss over giving us a wedding?"

"No, I hadn't heard that, but it doesn't surprise me that he would. Colonel Webber is very dedicated to the welfare and the happiness of his men. It was a matter of conviction for him to lead a Black regiment."

White folks, Pen thought. They were always patting themselves on the back if they acted decent to Black people. She reminded herself that she had sought Lieutenant Morgan out. She said, "Came to ask if you would read the marriage service."

He looked as though she'd given him a gift. "Of course I will. When is the wedding?"

"Don't know yet. Every time I turn around, there's more fuss over it. But as soon as I know, I tell you."

He reached out his hand to touch her wrist, a gentlemanly touch. "I am very happy for you."

Pen said, "One more thing, Lieutenant Morgan. If you don't mind."

"What is it?"

"Been thinking about what you said. About teaching the children to read and write. That it God's work to help the contrabands that way."

"I still think so," he said.

"I learn to read from a book for beginners about the cat and the rat." She remembered Kate's pleasure in teaching her. "The children here could learn, too. If we could get some of them books."

"Primers," he said slowly. "My sister is very active in the Boston effort to aid the contrabands. They send books to my friend in the Sea Islands. But we need teachers, too. That's an even greater need."

So this was the task God had prepared her for. Spared her for. "You know I can read," she said. "I could surely teach the little ones to read from that book."

He didn't reply. He was pondering, as Rosa had when Pen surprised her by caring about poetry. He smiled. "Yes," he said. "You could."

"Your friend who teach. Do they pay him?"

"Yes. They do."

"Will the army pay me to teach?"

His smile grew broader. "I can ask. You can ask."

"Whatever they would pay a man. I'll ask for that."

Morgan began to laugh. "I wish you could meet my sister Olivia. The two of you are just alike. Equally *forceful.*"

THE WEDDING DAY DAWNED sunny and pleasantly cool for late summer along the Mississippi River. Colonel Webber vacated his tent for Pen and her attendants, since it was the only space big enough for several people to stand up in. Toby, to his great unhappiness, had been left in the camp. As much as she loved Toby, a wedding was no place for a yellow hunting hound.

Antoinette buttoned Pen into her wedding dress, and her daughter arranged the veil over Pen's hair. Antoinette picked up the colonel's hand mirror. "Look at yourself," she said. "You look beautiful, Miss Penelope."

Holding the mirror, Pen had a memory so vivid that it caused her pain. She had looked into a mirror on her first wedding day, too, as her stepfather and her sister exclaimed over her. She put the mirror down. "Wish I could have my family with me."

Antoinette handed her a handkerchief. "Dab your eyes," she said. Her eyes were wet, too. "We ain't your kin. But we feel like a family to you and your husband. We do our best to rejoice with you."

When Jonas came to collect her, he was resplendent in his Union coat, the buttons polished to a blinding brightness. At the sight of her in the white dress, his face filled with joy. "Never saw you looking so beautiful." He held out his arm for her, and she took it.

Smiling, she said, "Can't believe we do this."

He smiled back. "It ain't a dream."

From behind them came a sound of panting. Snuffling. Then a sharp bark. Toby sat on his haunches, his ears pricked up, looking expectantly at Pen.

Jonas said, "I like that dog, but a dog don't belong at a wedding!"

Toby trotted to Pen and stood at her side, wagging his tail. Pen smiled and rubbed his head. She laughed. "He don't, but he can't stay behind!"

The bride and groom walked together, arm in arm, and by the bride's side, close enough to shed on her lustrous skirt, walked Toby.

THE WEDDING GUESTS FILLED the parade ground. Together, with so many eyes upon them, they walked to the spot where the officers stood to conduct drill. Today it would serve as a pulpit for a marriage ceremony.

Lieutenant Morgan waited, his prayer book in his hand. When he saw Pen and Jonas, he smiled with joy. He took in Toby, and his smile grew even brighter.

The crowd hushed as the two of them faced Lieutenant Morgan—Reverend Morgan today—as he opened his book and began to read: "Dearly beloved, we have come together in the presence of God to witness and bless the joining together of this man and this woman in holy matrimony..."

Pen's eyes never left Jonas's face as Reverend Morgan recited the familiar words of the service. Anyone who married for the first time took a leap of faith in saying those words. Pen thought, *We already know they're true.*

She remembered the words so well from the first time, vowing to have and to hold from this day forward, for better and for worse, for richer and for poorer, in sickness and in health, to love and to cherish, until parted by death.

Not distance. Not for a debt. Not for a fancy. No man, no woman, no massa, no missus could tear them asunder.

Pen pulled back her veil, and as Jonas pulled her close to kiss her, she forgot that the First Mississippi Regiment and half the contraband camp watched them. There was only herself and Jonas. They were bound only by love. They belonged only to themselves and to each other, and they would never be parted again.

Historical Note

I used to write careful, thoughtful essays about the history behind the story, but I now realize that readers really want to know how much of the story is true. This is how much.

While Pen's journey is fiction, the impulse behind it—to find family members stolen away by slavery—is well-documented in every account of the contraband camps and the Freedmen's Bureau records. The newly free trudged long distances and made inquiries wherever they went to find their lost parents, children, siblings, and spouses.

The use of slave labor at the Yazoo City navy yard in 1862 is based on fact, as is the presence of the enormous slave labor gang impressed into the 1863 effort to build the fortifications at Vicksburg. Conditions were especially poor at Vicksburg, where the laborers were dragged away from plantations and callously overseen by the Confederate army, much to the fury of slave owners, who hated the appropriation and abuse of their valuable property.

The presence of deserters in Dale County, Alabama, is also based on fact. The bigger conflict erupted in 1864, when the ranks of the Confederate deserters swelled, but desertion began in 1863 as the initial two-year enlistment period ended and the reality of war had fully set in. The horrific Battle at Shiloh, with twenty thousand casualties, was an emotional turning point for many a Confederate deserter. And while there are no mountain lions ("painters") in Alabama today, they were common in the pinewoods in the nineteenth century.

The salt mines on the Tombigbee River in Clarke County are completely gone today, but during the war, they were one of the biggest industrial operations in the salt-starved South. The men who cut down the trees to feed the fires at the salt works were all slaves hired away from their masters. And yes, the masters were paid in salt.

The tale of Unionism and a family feud in Jones County is based on the notorious history of that place, which was the scene of an out-and-out shooting conflict in 1864. The leader of the Unionist band, who has been characterized as both a hero and a bandit, abandoned his white wife for a Black woman who he treated as a wife. There are photographs of her as a young woman. She looks imperturbable, and I bet she was a good shot.

The engineering effort at the siege of Vicksburg is well-documented (although not highly celebrated, since the Union bombardment of the city and the civilian retreat to caves is better known). Both armies, Confederate and Union, used Black labor to dig trenches and mines. The story of the confusion in the picket lines that Jonas slips through is taken from the accounts of both Union and Confederate officers. The story of the man "blowed to freedom" by the Union mine is also taken from historical record.

The existence of contraband camps at both Natchez and Vicksburg is taken from historical record, as is the presence of a Black Union regiment in Vicksburg. The First Mississippi Infantry Regiment, in which untrained Black soldiers fought valiantly against the Confederate army at the Battle of Milliken's Bend, was responsible for showing the North that Black men could and would fight.

During the Civil War, Natchez Under-the-Hill, the city's riverfront and red-light district, was home to the Union army camp, the nearby contraband camp, bawdy houses, and shops owned by Jewish merchants, many of whom sold dry goods.

I bent the truth on a few things. While there were runaway communities—they called themselves "maroons"—in the Florida swamps, there's no record of a runaway refuge in Alabama.

The Black men who guarded Forks of the Road were indeed there, but not until a little later in the war. They built the barracks and then mustered in to the Fifty-Eighth, Seventieth, and Seventy-First Infantry Regiments, USCT at Natchez, but not until 1864. It is true that they were Mississippi men, all of them slaves, and many of them had been sold there before the war.

The rest is fiction.

If You Enjoyed This Book...

Discover the Novels

I've written a number of books that share a theme: stories of white and Black, slave and free, often connected by kinship in the decades on either side of the Civil War. Visit my website for more information about my other books at https://www.sabrawaldfogel.com/books/.

The Low Country Series

The first book in the series is *Charleston's Daughter*. A Charleston belle with slavery on her conscience. A slave with rebellion in her heart. In South Carolina in 1858, no friendship could be more dangerous. As South Carolina hurtles toward secession, will their bond destroy their lives—or set them both free? Find out at mybook.to/CharlestonsDaughter.

The second book in the series is *Union's Daughter*. A renegade planter's daughter who abhors her past. A fugitive slave who fights for freedom. Will their battle for emancipation leave them casualties of war? Find out at mybook.to/UnionsDaughter.

The Georgia Series

The first book in the series is *Sister of Mine*. Slavery made them kin. Can the Civil War make them sisters? Find out at mybook.to/SisterofMine.

The second book in the series is *Let Me Fly*. The Civil War is over, but it isn't. For two women, one Black, one white, a new fight is just beginning. Find out more at mybook.to/LetMeFly.

Join the Inner Circle of Readers

Want to stay in touch? Get the first look at new books: covers, backstories, and prepublication sneak peeks. And as a thank-you, I'll send you a copy of my story, *Yemaya*. When a slaving ship meets an avenging African mermaid, what happens? Find out at https://www.sabrawaldfogel.com/sign-up/!

Leave a Review

Please let other readers know about this book by leaving a brief review at Amazon, Amazon UK, or Goodreads. Just a few lines will help other readers find the book and make an informed decision about it. It's the electronic version of telling your friends or your book club (although that's great too). Thank you so much!

Author Biography

 Sabra Waldfogel grew up far from the South in Minneapolis, Minnesota. She studied history at Harvard University and got a PhD in American history from the University of Minnesota. Since then, she has been fascinated by the drama of slavery and freedom in the decades before and after the Civil War.

Her first novel, *Sister of Mine*, published by Lake Union, was named the winner of the 2017 Audio Publishers Association Audie Award for fiction. The sequel, *Let Me Fly*, was published in 2018.

CPSIA information can be obtained
at www.ICGtesting.com
Printed in the USA
BVHW071922080223
658146BV00023B/345